THE DARK SORCERER'S INTERN

THE DARK SORCERER'S INTERN

GAVIN BROWN

Podium

This is a work of fiction. Names, characters, places, and incidents are either products of the author's imagination or used fictitiously. Any resemblance to actual events, locales, or persons, living, dead, or undead, is entirely coincidental.

Copyright © 2025 by Gavin Brown

Cover design by Mike F. Miller

ISBN: 978-1-0394-7555-7

Published in 2025 by Podium Publishing
www.podiumentertainment.com

Podium

For Chris, and for all who remember him

THE DARK SORCERER'S INTERN

MAGICAL SECURITY AGENCY

WEEKLY THREAT ASSESSMENT BRIEFING—TOP SECRET

TO: MSA DIRECTORS AND ABOVE

FROM: SPECIAL AGENT ANGELICA CRANE

Both intelligence analytics and arcanometer readings have confirmed the reports from our colleagues in the British and Canadian intelligence agencies. It appears that the dark sorcerer has once again relocated his base of operations, leaving his castle in Mycenae, Greece, due to sustained pressure from the European Supernatural Agency. He, as well as his collection of priceless artifacts, have moved to the United States within the past month. The strongest readings and several eyewitness sightings place him in either the Brooklyn or Queens boroughs of New York City.

Despite reports on social media, there is no hard evidence of any demonic presence either at home or abroad. The MSA Threat Analysis Department continues to believe that there are no demons of significant power currently active. The unregulated and unsupervised activities of the dark sorcerer remain the most severe supernatural danger to the United States and the world.

We believe that avoiding direct confrontation is still the safest approach. We continue to coordinate with other intelligence and law enforcement agencies to contain the threat.

CHAPTER 1

I slip my phone out of my pocket, holding it below the counter and breathing a sigh of relief. Moments like this, when the Samba Smoothies is totally free from customers, are a rare treat—no confused moms asking me which Flavor Blaster is healthiest, no teenagers loudly slurping their neon drinks, and no manager looking pointedly at the big industrial smoothie blender and then the sponge by the sink. *It's a smoothie blender, Carla! It's okay for it to have juice on it!* I've been working here for a year and a half, and not once has someone gone into anaphylactic shock because a tiny drop of Lemongrass Perk accidentally landed in their Boysenberry Bump.

It's crazy how, when your nerves are totally shot, a little thing like thirty seconds on your phone feels like a day at a spa. I pull up the WizardWatch server on Discord, and for a moment I'm immersed in breathless coverage and speculation of how a mage in Taiwan had somehow used illegal translocation magic to steal a hard drive full of Bitcoin wallet keys. Pretty badass, right?

Okay, to be honest, the posts on this server are like 95 percent speculation and 5 percent an article from a Taipei news report, automatically translated into English. But still, even hearing about flashy legal magic is pretty rare, and you only hear about the exciting banned stuff every few months.

And then an email notification pops up.

The preview at the top of the screen is enough to make my heart wither. I kind of knew it was coming, but still. That moment when hope ends, when your last, desperate half-court shot goes wide and it's all over—it's brutal.

I tap the email, but before I can read it, suddenly there's an older woman standing in front of me, hunched over a bit but smiling kindly from behind thick glasses.

"Hello, dear, can I get a Triple Protein Stimulus and an Appleberry Amp?"

"Hi, Susan," I say, writing her name on the cup. Susan is a wiry, white-haired lady who must be well past retirement age. She's come here twice a week for the past year, and she's never called me by my name, even though "Bryce" is embroidered in big bold letters on the front of my bright red Apple Apron. I got upgraded from a name tag pin to embroidery for my first anniversary working here at Samba. Please, kill me now.

"This should help you build those huge muscles," I say, handing Susan the smoothie and trying to give her the usual smile and put the email out of my mind.

"Oh, my dear, you know I just like the taste of it," she says, completing our usual banter. "Plus, sometimes things at the retirement home get a bit spicy, and I need to replenish my electrolytes."

She usually says something mildly inappropriate like that, but I've gotten used to it. Honestly, she's a sweetheart, and I'd much rather chat with her than the yoga moms and bodybuilders who don't even acknowledge my existence. With the number of calories in one of those things, Susan should have gained thirty pounds, but it doesn't seem to have affected her. Some lucky folks just have that supercharged metabolism, I guess. Or they have "spicy" times at the retirement home very frequently. Hey, I'm not here to judge!

Susan is happily on her way with her smoothie, but it's almost the end of my shift, which means that everyone who looked up our closing time on Google and *just barely* made it through the door before seven o'clock is lining up. I rev up the blender and grab a fistful of apple slices—the email on my phone will have to wait.

Two hundred and forty fluid ounces of Samba Smoothie later, company policy allows me to flip the sign on the door to CLOSED, and I finally pull up my email. I already saw the first two sentences, but I force myself to read the whole thing anyway. Just in case.

Dear, Bryce. Thank you so much for your application, it reads. *Unfortunately, we had an extraordinarily high volume of applications this year, full of qualified candidates, and we will not be able to offer you a spot in this year's class for our graduate arcane arts program at the Kotodama Institute.*

It goes on to say some nice-sounding BS about how hard it is to get in and then ends with a final dagger.

We also regret to inform you that, since you have now applied to our program the maximum of three times, we will no longer be able to accept applications from you in the future. Best regards, Professor Sakura Okamoto, Graduate Admissions Committee Chair, Kotodama Institute, Tokyo, Japan.

I take a slow, deep breath, holding in the scream that wants to claw out of my gut and cause a commotion right here in the Jersey City Galleria.

Two years ago, while I was still in school, the first rejection that I got was from the Kotodama Institute, and it hurt a lot. The ones that came in the following weeks, from places like the Harry Houdini School at Columbia, just added what felt like blow after blow, all while my friends were making plans to start their lives. By the end, I wasn't too surprised that the Merlin College at Oxford, the Sorcerbonne in Paris, and the Magicians Institute of Technomancy didn't take me. But I really, somehow, thought that with another full year of preparation, applications, interviews, and practical exams, one of them would have taken me. I just can't figure it out. My grades were pretty good, but something in either my interviews or the practical exams meant I kept getting heartrending rejections one after another. This was the last letter, for this year. And several of them had added on something like that last line—basically, *Dear, Bryce Alexander. You Suck. Goodbye.*

As I'm mulling over my abject failure, I'm on food service employee autopilot, robotically going through the closing routine. I just need to be done. I just need to be out of here.

"Bryce?" a woman's voice says, and I suddenly realize that I'm cleaning the industrial blender almost hard enough to peel the bright chrome coating off it. "You're really giving it to that blender, huh?"

I pull my sponge away from the blender and spin around. Carla, my manager, is standing there, wearing her neon green

Granny Smith Apple Apron and a matching bright headband to hold back her wavy hair. You get that green apron for five years of smoothie service to our juice-blasting corporate overlords. The color-coordinated headband came, on the other hand, from Carla's own personal buying decision. "No, no," she adds. "It's good. I'm glad to see you taking cleaning so seriously!"

"Oh, uh, thanks," I say. Carla's not so bad, honestly. She's covered last-minute shifts for me plenty of times and juggled the schedule around every year when I had to fly all over the world for grad school interviews.

"But when you're done cleaning up, can you come into the office?" she says. "I need to talk to you about something."

I stare at her for a moment. Am I really in trouble, on today of all days? Has someone put a tracker on the Wi-Fi to see my search history? Am I about to be fired? I only searched "how to cast a disintegration hex big enough for a mall" one day when I was in a bad mood! It's not like I can actually cast any sort of hex—my bachelor's degree in arcane theory from NYU only covered theory, history, and the modern regulatory environment.

"No, no!" she says, seeing my face. "Don't worry, it's a good thing!"

"Okay, sure," I answer, smiling weakly.

Ten minutes later, I finally pull off my apron and check myself in the mirrored wall. My brown hair is kind of a mess and should have been cut two months ago, but running through it three times with my fingers is all the energy I can put into my appearance at this point. I have a vague hope that maybe it comes across as a bed-head thirst trap, but we all know that only works for lifestyle influencers who take half an hour to gel their hair into just the right amount of tousle. Nope, I'm just another skinny white guy who's too disorganized to get a haircut on time.

I head back and take a seat in the only other chair in the tiny office at the back of Samba Smoothies, where Carla is finishing up with tallying the receipts, cash, and inventory from the day.

"So I've got some really good news," Carla says, beaming at me over the paperwork. "I've been promoted to associate regional manager!"

"Oh, congrats!" I say, though this doesn't sound like good news to me. A new manager could be a nightmare—Carla is really not that bad of a supervisor, just annoyingly chipper and definitely too bought in to the Samba Smoothies corporate credo. We blend fruit juice and turmeric, not energy and joy.

"Oh, thanks!" she says, beaming. "But this isn't about me. They'll need a new manager, and I put your name in for the manager trainee program. In ninety days, you could be running this whole shop!" She gestures around, like she's Mufasa in *The Lion King*, offering Simba future dominion over everything the light touches.

She can see my lack of excitement and smiles kindly at me.

"Look, Bryce," she says, "I know it's not as exciting as going to school to learn magic. But who even does that these days? It's soooo old-fashioned. Do a good job as store manager, and you could get a job at the regional office, like me! I won't even be paid hourly anymore; I'm going to be on salary!" Her enthusiasm is infectious, but not in a good way, more like pinkeye or strep throat. "You'll get a ten percent pay increase now and another ten percent when you finish the training program."

I sigh. This isn't where I'm supposed to be. I'm supposed to be learning real magic, from real mages and maybe even a wizard, in one of the few grad schools that actually still teach the arcane arts.

All the energy drains from my body, in a way that no smoothie could ever replenish. I slump down in the chair. What's the point? Good posture is for people who have something to look forward to in their lives.

"No more cleaning the smoothie machine!" Carla continues. "Unless somebody doesn't show up." Which happens pretty often, though she doesn't mention that. "Well, what do you think? Not everyone has the talent to become a mage, you know."

I grit my teeth, but I don't bother to correct her. That's the worst part of it. People used to think that you had to have a special talent to learn magic. But in the early 2000s, researchers at Merlin College proved that anyone could learn magic. It just took the right instruction, and hard work—like learning to do differential equations in calculus or how to bake a soufflé. But it's super illegal to teach magic anywhere but an accredited university. And it's been made extremely clear that I'm not welcome at any of those.

My friends from NYU have all gone into hip jobs at tech start-ups, trendy NGOs, or social media companies. Magic is an antique art, like horseback riding or sewing by hand. What's the point of a crystal ball when everyone has a smartphone in their pocket? Who needs to spend years learning to throw a fireball when any army recruit can pull the trigger on a rocket launcher? Magic is powerful, sure, but the modern world just doesn't have the patience for it. But I've always preferred dusty old magic to owning a Tesla or achieving Instagram fame . . . See where that got me?

Three years of applications. Three rounds of running around the world, doing stressful interviews and weird practical tests that I don't understand. And now most of the schools have told me to delete their contact info.

I sigh. It's over. And so is this soul-sucking limbo that I've been in all this time. I guess that's just my life.

"Okay," I say. "I'm in."

"Really?! That's so exciting!" Carla is beaming. "I was worried I wouldn't get to see you anymore, but I'll be checking in with you every week!"

"Sounds great," I say. She probably put in a lot of work to get me this spot, since I haven't exactly been a stellar employee. I can feel my soul melting, like every marshmallow that my little sister tries to roast into a s'more. But I activate the muscles to turn the outer edges of my mouth up. I figured that's close enough to an actual smile.

"Let me call my new boss really quickly and share the news!" Carla says. "He's going to be so excited, I told him you have real long-term management potential!"

She pops up and is on the phone immediately. I step outside the office and can hear through the thin walls as a quick update on my new manager-in-training status veers into an update on inventory levels and how some employees are putting a little too much Flavor Blaster in the drinks. Frankly, Susan deserves that extra blaster and I'm not going to stop.

I pull out my phone, instinctively opening up WizardWatch to check the latest updates, though today part of me just wants to delete the whole thing and forget it ever existed. I'm a Smoothie Man, now, right? Carla said I had *long-term management potential* here at Samba Smoothies. I mean, what more could a guy want?

I scroll to the newest messages, and my jaw drops. I mean, literally drops.

There's a new thread—there've been multiple sightings of Zambrano reported on social media. And he's just a few miles over, across the river in New York City. I start scrolling, unable to believe it.

"Um, Bryce?"

Startled, I yank my attention from my phone screen. I look up, suddenly realizing that Carla is back and has said several sentences, none of which I heard.

"What's the big deal?" Carla asks. "Did something bad happen?"

"No, no, it's just that some people I know saw someone," I say, though I've never actually met any of them in person. It's just a Discord server that I spend *way* too much time chatting in. "Zambrano. Apparently, he's been hiding out in an old industrial building deep in Queens."

"Oh, isn't he that evil wizard? The dangerous one?" Carla asks.

"Dark sorcerer," I say, automatically correcting her. "And most of the dangerous acts that he's accused of are alleged, not proven."

"Uh-huh," she says, raising an eyebrow at me.

It sounded cool when someone said it on WizardWatch, but I feel stupid immediately after saying it. It's amazing how things that sound smart in an online message group sound dumb when you say them in a smoothie shop at the mall food court.

"Isn't he still an evil wizard though?" Carla asks.

"Not exactly," I say. "There are three types of humans who can use magic. Magicians know how to cast spells. Wizards can actually change and adjust them. Sorcerers use magic forbidden by the Prague Convention." That I learned at the university, so hopefully I'm on firmer ground here.

"Ooh, naughty forbidden magic! Is that how the sorcerer guy has stayed alive for hundreds of years?" Carla says, shaking her head. "I'll never get your magic obsession, Bryce. Everyone needs a hobby, but couldn't yours be something useful, like my cousin who made an outdoor barbeque pit at his place in Hoboken?"

I glower at her. "Magic is awesome. Just because these days it's only really a hobby for rich people and academics doesn't mean it isn't useful. Hannibal used it to keep his elephants warm as he crossed the Alps! They built the Taj Mahal with it! British and French wizards used weather magic to turn the tide at the battle of the Somme! There's even evidence that they used magic to get extra thrust from the rockets in the original Apollo missions!" I get a little carried away, but historical magic is pretty awesome. Back before the internet and airplanes and machine guns ruined everything.

"Sure, that's all cool," Carla admits. "I mean, I learned how to light a candle with magic in eighth grade along with everyone else. It was so annoying and fiddly and hard. You had to get those hand gestures just right, and the pronunciation was impossible . . . Honestly, even algebra made more sense to me. Magic is just, like, random movements and words. It doesn't make any sense!"

"Yeah," I say with a sigh. I'm not going to admit it, but try as I might I could never get the damn candle to light up, no matter how many times I practiced the motions and words they said in the videos. But the latest studies all say that magic is about the proper study and understanding and practice, not some sort of innate talent or genetics. I'm sure it all would have made sense to me if I could just have had a chance to study it with the experts at one of the universities. But I guess I'm just part of the "extraordinary volume of qualified applicants" who will never get the chance to see how good they can be.

"Sorry," Carla says. "Magic always seemed like a hassle to me . . ." I'm giving her a glare, and she trails off. "Anyway, you're all set to go. I'll have the management trainee paperwork for you to sign tomorrow. I'm excited for you!"

I don't wait to be told twice. Three minutes later, I've grabbed my backpack and I'm out the door, walking quickly to try to get out of this concrete and glass hellhole and on my way home. I pass by the intensely sweet smell that I swear they pipe out of the Apple Pie Workshop on purpose, and I'm out of the mall. The gig at Samba Smoothies is crappy, but it does have the side benefit that it's within walking distance to my tiny apartment.

I hustle toward home, my mind careening back and forth between utter despair and obsessive wondering about why Zambrano is in the US. It's pretty crazy—they've got photos of him walking into the building, and someone even brought an arcanometer there, and the readings were off the charts. Everything about magic feels dull and distant to me right now, but this is a big moment. I'm looking forward to alternating crying and checking WizardWatch and refreshing news sites.

I'm only a few blocks from home when I pass the PATH train. Without really planning to, I stop and stare into the gaping maw of the entrance, a gloomy opening leading down to the station.

A crazy, stupid thought crosses my mind. A really boneheaded idea.

I could go home and cry and scroll through my phone, speculating and guessing. Or . . .

I grip the straps of my backpack and head down into the darkness.

CHAPTER 2

The adrenaline wears off around the second of three train transfers that are required to get me across the river into Manhattan, to another train in Manhattan, and to a final train that goes into the right part of Queens. By the time I'm climbing the steps out into the open air again, over an hour has passed and I'm not at all sure what I'm doing here. Deciding to do something risky is a lot more nerve-racking when you've spent ninety minutes sitting in fluorescent-lit subway cars thinking about it.

At first, I was just thinking that maybe I could snap some pictures or videos of the area where Zambrano was supposed to be. Maybe I could even meet him.

But then, an even dumber idea came to me. No one else would teach me magic. None of the legitimate universities wanted me. But surely that wasn't the only possible way to learn magic, was it? It might be stupid and dangerous, but maybe he would have an opening for an apprentice. Dark sorcerers often had apprentices, didn't they? Not much was known about them, but the stories often mentioned that.

On the train, I texted my friend Parth, who's also a WizardWatch nut like me, and I told him what I was doing. Someone needs to know where you are, right?

Glancing down, I see a response has come in. *Dude! That's super dangerous. Definitely don't do it. Too risky.* And then ten seconds later, another message from him: *Also, take pictures and videos; and if you meet him, ask if he really caused that earthquake near Lake Ilopango like the news said. But also be careful!*

There are several more texts of other questions about magic and current events that he wants answered, but I just shake my head and put the phone away. If by some chance I can find my way to the dark sorcerer, my priority is seeing if he'll teach me magic, not answering nitpicky questions about arcane theory.

I set out, quickly walking from the gentrified shops and apartments near the train to the farther-out aging warehouses and factory buildings that are too far from the subway to be worth renovating. The summer sun is setting, and the grim industrial area that I'm in is kind of beautiful, a mosaic of brick, concrete, and those old warehouse windows made of tons of small squares.

"Hot dog?" a street vendor with a small cart asks as I walk by.

"No, thanks," I say instinctively, before doing a double take. Why would there be a hot dog seller out here? There's no one around to buy them! And by now the sun has set, and it's getting dark.

I look around and notice something odd. There are more people here than there should be. Each of them makes some sense on their own—a telephone repair crew with a cherry picker, a private security guard hanging by a door, a sharp-looking woman walking her dog very slowly, a street cleaner sweeping up what appears to be nothing at all.

But the vibe is completely off. My first thought is that they're here to watch the big warehouse building that I'm approaching. But I notice that they all seem to be eyeing one another, like none of them knows who the others are.

I turn back to the hot dog guy. "Sure, I'll take one," I say and hand him the cash.

"Uh, great," he says. He then proceeds to open up the compartments in his cart like he's trying to disarm a bomb. He still somehow burns his hand with the hot water, gets the tongs twisted on themselves, and finally serves me up a hot dog on a bun. No condiments, but I don't even bother asking. I don't want him to cut himself on the ketchup packets.

You'd think you couldn't mess up boiling a hot dog, but somehow this guy has. It tastes like cat food mixed with that feeling you get when your aunt asks if you've gotten a girlfriend yet.

I eye the hotdog and raise an eyebrow at the man.

"So, who are you with?" I ask. I used to employ the same trick to get backstage at concerts and arcane expos. Just pretend you belong, and other people will let you roll on by.

The guy shrugs, clearly embarrassed that his cover is blown. "I'm just here with UBC News. I didn't know this street would be so deserted! Watch out for the telephone repair crew over there—I'm pretty sure they're CIA. Oh, and the woman with the dog is from a Chinese state intelligence agency. I'm not sure about the rest."

I gulp, and very carefully don't look their way. That's pretty scary. But I can see, up ahead, a chain-link fence surrounding the parking lot and loading dock of the big warehouse building. This is a public street—I have every right to be here. And I'm not going to leave until someone actually stops me.

"So who are *you* with?" asks the reporter with a side business in inedible hot dogs. "Do you think there's really a dark sorcerer in there?"

"WizardWatch," I say, because I can't think of anything else, and walk away as he tries to ask follow-up questions. And I'm too embarrassed to say that I somehow got the crazy idea that maybe a dark sorcerer will teach me about magic. But the rest of the world has said no, so it's really their fault, isn't it?

I walk toward the entrance, which is a chain-link gate closed with a normal-looking chain and padlock. The fence itself is only five feet tall with no barbed wire or anything. It's not at all secure. Would Zambrano really leave himself so unprotected? Or is there actually nothing here?

As I'm about half a block away, the street sweeper sidles over to me. Up close, I can see that he's way too buff to be a street sweeper and he's wearing those wraparound sunglasses that went out of style before I was born and, unlike every other fashion trend, were so dumb that they never got cool again. The kind that only cops and soldiers can wear, because they carry guns around and no one wants to make fun of them to their faces.

"You shouldn't get any closer," the guy says.

I stop. I try to look him in the eyes, but the damn sunglasses are so shiny that I can't get a read on him. I pause for a moment. He nods at me, like he's satisfied that I'm following his commands. And that just doesn't sit right with me.

I take a step forward.

He flinches a tiny bit, and I can see from his face that he's pissed at me. But he doesn't do anything.

"You should head home," he says, his voice low and gravelly in a threatening way that just comes across as fake.

I cock my head at him. "You don't . . . you don't legally have the authority to stop me, do you?" I say. "Whatever agency you work for." I feel like a crazy idiot, but it's this or spend two hours making the trip home just to reread the rejection letter over and over, hating myself more and more. This guy can't do anything worse to me than what I'm already feeling.

The man in the wraparound sunglasses glares at me. "I'm just saying, for your own protection, you should leave."

I take another step forward. He leans toward me menacingly.

I take another step. He glares, but . . . doesn't do anything.

More confidently, I walk forward. He says something quite insulting under his breath but melts away and is soon sweeping the clean gutters with his broom again.

Once I'm at the fence, I realize that I have no idea what to do next. Of course, since this is the modern world, I snap a few photos and post them to WizardWatch, which get some immediate likes and comments. You can never have too much meaningless validation from online strangers, right?

Should I yell? Shake the fence? If I try to really do anything, one of the multiple government and intelligence agencies may decide to actually do something about me.

A screech pierces the air, and I spin around in surprise. Two big black SUVs have pulled up, and people with FBI emblazoned on their jackets are piling out. Immediately, the guy with sunglasses and the telephone repair crew are running over and yelling at them, and they start yelling back.

They're throwing around fancy legal phrases like "recognized jurisdiction," "lawful order," "no authority in this matter," and "just go call your boss, asshole, you're in a metric ton of trouble."

I take a deep breath. For this one moment, they're all yelling at one another, and from the way their hands are drifting to their hips, it almost looks like they're about to pull weapons out and make things even less friendly.

As quickly and quietly as I can, I climb up the fence and hop over. Just as I swing over the top, I hear a buzzing sound in my ears and feel a sudden bit of nausea, like when you're flying on a plane and it hits a surprise patch of turbulence. But the sound and feeling are gone by the time my feet land, so I jog forward. There aren't any streetlights on this side of the fence, so I'm hoping that the farther I go, the more I'll disappear into the evening gloom. I head for the only door I see, right next to the loading dock.

As I arrive, I see that the door has a sign on it. Above the doorframe, there's a weird sort of gem affixed, held in place by a setting of bronze. I snap a quick photo of the setup, grinning. This is the first evidence that there really is something happening here. I look down, straining a bit to see the sign in the dim light.

For a moment, the sign looks dark, fuzzy, and written in symbols that I don't understand. And then suddenly, even in the twilight, I can read it perfectly.

Okay, idiots. This sign used to say "turn back now," but none of you bozos ever seemed to do that. So I'll lay it out in a way your tiny little intellects can comprehend: if you pass this sign, you will die. You may think you're clever for making it past the fence, but that was child's play.

Beyond this point I have mystical defenses set up to destroy demons, government agents, meddling "good" wizards, and all other people who annoy me. If you try to come in, you will get squashed like the little bug that you are. And that will be on YOU, not me. Don't come complaining to me when you wind up dead. Oh, right— you won't be able to, BECAUSE YOU'LL BE DEAD.

Love,

Zambrano

It's really quite a long sign. I'm not even sure how it all fits on the small piece of paper in that large font, but it somehow happened.

I try to take a close-up photo of the sign text, but the light seems to be too dim here for it to work. Or, and my heart starts beating faster as I realize it, this is *real, actual* magic. And while everyone has seen real magic before, this means that WizardWatch is at least onto something here.

Now comes the real moment of truth. I'm not any of those things that he listed. Maybe I'll be fine? And I know what's waiting for me back on the other side of that fence. The FBI most definitely can and will arrest me if they feel like it.

I knock on the door, nice and loud. I've wanted this for so long, I'm not going to be deterred by a stupid sign. I can't believe that Zambrano would actually just kill me on sight like that. Not after all the times I've defended his reputation on social media. There's really no solid proof that he did all those terrible things they say he did.

No one replies to my knock.

"Hello?" I say, somewhat loudly, but hopefully not so loudly that the FBI, who I can hear running around setting up positions around the building, come for me.

Thirty seconds more pass, and nothing.

"Hi, I'm Bryce Alexander, and I'm here to learn from you. To be your apprentice, I guess," I say, hoping that someone inside can hear. I look up at the gem above the door. Maybe it acts like a camera? It does feel vaguely like it's watching me. "I've been studying your history since undergrad, and I think the Intergovernmental Council on Banned Magics is wrong about you. I don't think you did the things they say you did—the numbers just don't add up. Can I come in?"

There's no response. I wait for another minute, nervously looking over my shoulder and seeing more headlights arriving in the gathering darkness.

Well, there's one more thing left to try. There's no way it will work, of course. I'm very shortly going to have to go back and face a horde of cranky FBI agents.

I reach down and turn the doorknob.

I pull it, and the door swings open.

CHAPTER 3

Oh, shit.

I have to be honest—I didn't really expect this to work. I was just frustrated and angry and hopeless, and . . . I think some part of me kind of hoped that the guy with the sunglasses would beat me up and arrest me. Or maybe that Zambrano would just fry me and end it. At least that would be a badass way to go, blasted to bits by magic.

And then the gem above the door suddenly starts glowing, and I realize that it's definitely not too late to be blasted to bits by magic, and I really, really don't actually want to die.

But the gem just glows, and I hear the same kind of buzzing noise that I did when I jumped over the fence, and I feel the same twist in my stomach. But nothing happens. No fireballs, bolts of lightning, or spinning astral blades. The gem goes dark.

That's about as clear an invitation as I could hope for. I step forward and close the door behind me. I breathe a sigh of relief as the sounds of the voices and vehicles outside grow quieter. But after a few seconds, I realize that they haven't just faded. They're gone entirely. I'm standing in pitch darkness and total silence.

I instinctively pull out my phone and turn the flashlight on.

I draw in a slow, deep breath. I have somehow ended up in the inner sanctum of one of the greatest dark sorcerers in history. The only remaining dark sorcerer still alive.

The room is vast, far beyond the scale that it appeared to be from the outside. But that's not what impresses me. What's incredible is the wealth of artifacts that my phone illuminates.

Just within the few feet around me there's a glass sword, a golden telescope pointed at a blank spot on the exposed brick wall, a small black pebble with swirling white glyphs sitting on top of a cactus with a dimpled top, another wall covered in paintings and clocks, and shelves of books. Many, many shelves of books, going back endlessly into the darkness. Old leather tomes, modern hardcovers, and paperbacks—it's all here. Normally I'd complain that it's a waste of space to collect these books when you can just download them all to your phone or Kindle, but I'd guess that a lot of these books aren't exactly listed on Amazon.

"Hello?" I say into the darkness. Shining the light around, I see a spiral staircase in what looks to be roughly the middle of the room.

I really want to peek through that telescope, or flip through the books. And I especially want to pick up that sword. But as awesome as that might be, I figure that would be pretty impolite. And I don't dare imagine what happens to impolite houseguests in the home of a dark sorcerer. So I head across the floor, past a pile of something like fabric that is so dark it absorbs every bit of light from my phone, leaving only a blank black spot on the ground.

I jump a bit as I hear a quiet pattering sound to my right. I spin to face it and stare down in shock as a small duck pads out from behind a stack of books.

"Quack," says the duck. Not the sound "quack." It actually says "quack" in a human voice. And not just any voice. A regal voice, with rich overtones. The voice of a queen.

"Um. Quack yourself?" I answer awkwardly.

We stare at each other for several long seconds. She stares back, somehow having the bearing of a haughty lady, despite being about a foot tall.

Then she starts preening, using her bill to do something to her feathers as she shakes her wings. It's over almost as soon as it began, and she seems to give whatever the duck equivalent of a shrug is. She turns and starts waddling back into the bookshelves.

"Nice . . . to meet you," I say to her rapidly retreating tail feathers.

Part of me wants to follow along to figure out what the heck that was, but visitors who cause trouble and possibly break things probably don't get made into apprentices. So I turn, take a breath, and head toward the stairs. And I start to hear, faintly, the sound of singing coming from the top of the stairs.

I pause for a moment and snap a pic of the room full of artifacts to post to WizardWatch in case I somehow make it out of here alive. As I head up the stairs, the sound of singing grows louder.

It's a folksy-sounding tune, sung in a melodious baritone. As I get closer, I realize it sounds good. I mean, really good, like on those TikTok videos where someone starts singing a song and someone else just wanders into the room and happens to know the exact song and harmony and sings along with them. Definitely not rehearsed over and over again to get it to sound just right and look like a lucky coincidence.

It sounds like an old tune, the kind of thing you would hear at a Renaissance Fair or from your funny uncle who plays guitar. Something about a traveler and a farmer's daughter, way outdated to modern ears.

This floor is less of a laboratory and more of a living space. The ceilings are high and vaulted, and the lighting and furniture are a weird mix between furniture you'd fine in Crate & Barrel and a medieval castle, right down to some literal crates and barrels.

I advance nervously and walk through the door where I hear the singing coming from. A large cast-iron tub stands on clawed feet, and in it a man is soaking, leaning back and relaxing with his eyes closed as he belts his tune. Beyond the tub, a large ornate mirror is hung on the brick wall.

"Hello?" I say again as I enter the room, but the back half of the man's head is underwater and the front part is belting out the climax of the song, where the mischievous traveler finds out, much to his chagrin, that while he thought he had been kissing the farmer's daughter, it was actually a cow.

"And so that night I got the surprise of my life," the man sings. "But that's how I found myself a mighty fine wife!"

I groan. I want to say that humor has advanced tremendously since whatever century this song was written in, but I've seen what they turned *The Simpsons* into in recent years. But what's really upsetting me is that there's this young guy here. Is Zambrano going to want an apprentice if he's already got one?

As I'm standing there, the man jolts upright in the tub, his blazing green eyes staring right at me. And yes, they're truly a brilliant green, just like the eyes described in every bad fantasy novel or self-insert Mary Sue fanfic. And he's handsome to boot, with a perfectly squared jaw, flawlessly smooth brown skin, and long hair thicker than a dog's fur. The one odd thing is that his hair and eyebrows are completely bone white, not even a hint of gray or any other color. Otherwise, he looks like the kind of guy you would cast in commercials to try to convince men that yes, they actually do need to use conditioner, and it's a totally tough and hardcore way to wash yourself.

"What?! How?!" the man yelps. He jumps up to his feet, splashing water wildly. He half steps, half falls out of the tub, slips and falls on his butt, and scrambles to his feet.

I hold up my hands. "It's okay, I'm—"

"Fizzlewumps!" the man shouts. He swings his arms, and bright violet light explodes from his hands. My jaw drops, and I step back as the light hits me. But it has no effect, other than making a loud buzzing noise.

"How did you . . ." the man sputters, standing there completely naked, with water still pouring off him. And yes, I can tell he's a shower, not a grower, even as I desperately try to keep my eyes on his face. "That should've ripped your magical defenses to shreds. How did you counter it? No living wizard knows the secret of that spell!"

I try not to look at his dangling bits, but that just means I look in the mirror behind him, where I can see his butt. Which is, like the rest of him, almost too perfect, like he used whatever the equivalent of Facetune is for butts. You could bounce a quarter off those buns, and it would probably spring back and hit you harder than you threw it.

"I . . . my name's Bryce," I stammer. "I'm here to apply to be Zambrano's apprentice. But . . . you're already his apprentice, aren't you?"

"*Vestimi!*" The man snaps his fingers, and an embroidered red silk robe flies from the wall and wraps itself around him. There really is something about him that seems a bit uncanny, but it's hard to put my finger on anything particular that's wrong.

The man's nostrils flare, and he bares his teeth. "Eye of Jupiter! " He makes a subtle motion with his hands, then pushes them forward as if throwing an invisible ball at me.

This time, I'm flung back violently, crashing against the wall with a painful crunch. Rather than falling to the ground, I stay pinned, feeling a massive weight pressing down on every inch of my body.

"I am no apprentice!" the man roars. "I am Zambrano, the last living sorcerer! Defeater of Demons, and Bane of the Fiery Depths! They call me the Devastator, the Lord of Havoc, or 'a dangerous terrorist.' But without me, this world would be a smoldering pile of ashes. I trapped the Leviathan of the Pacific Rim *and* the demon queen. You are trespassing in my domain, and your life is forfeit. Now, who sent you to infiltrate my warehouse? MIT? Merlin College? Those meddling nitwits at the MSA?!"

He's puffing himself up and holding his arms as if he's a puppeteer controlling strings, but he looks a bit comical with his fine silken robe half soaked and clinging to his body in spots. But it's him. It's Zambrano. I gulp.

I try to speak, but my entire face feels as if a pile of sandbags has been dropped on top of it. All that comes out is a slight mumble.

"Whatever trick you just pulled was clever, but I guess you didn't prepare to have the gravity of Jupiter thrown at you, did you?" Zambrano makes a slight gesture, and the pressure on my face lessens. "Now tell me, how did you evade my mystical defenses? How did you pass my portal guardian?"

I try to shrug, though my shoulders barely move against the gravity. "I don't know," I squeak out. "I just . . . walked in." My heart is pounding, and while most of me is afraid for my life, some tiny part of my brain is saying *Holy shit, the world's one remaining dark sorcerer is doing magic on me. This is incredible. I really hope I get a chance to tell Parth and everyone on WizardWatch before he kills me.*

Zambrano leans forward, growling at me. "That's impossible. My defenses were created to detect and challenge even the most powerful wizards. A regular mortal simply would have been roasted to a crisp. And I didn't even get a warning signal! Are you one of the Wardens of the Wild, with some sort of druidic magic? Is that it?"

There's a sudden peal of laughter from my left. It's that same rich femme voice, the one that came from the duck on the first floor. I try to move my head over to look, but it's still pinned down by the gravity of Jupiter.

"Do you really not get it?" the voice says.

"Stay out of this, duck!" Zambrano shoots back.

"You speak English?" I blurt out as the duck waddles into view. The duck looks at me like I'm a particularly annoying child. "When you don't have arms or hands, information is the only currency available. It seemed early to give that tidbit away."

I just blink, not sure what to make of her. The duck takes a regal hop and turns to face Zambrano.

"You really can't believe that a dumb kid could defeat your sophisticated defenses, can you?" the duck says. "He doesn't know magic, and he still smells faintly of New Jersey."

"Hey," I protest. "It may not be one of the five boroughs, but it's got a rapidly developing arts scene and the rents are lower than—"

Zambrano holds his hand up, palm out, and the full weight of the gravity of the gas giant is on me again, pressing me down like a bug on a windshield and cutting off my defense of the trendy and bustling metropolis of Jersey City.

"Okay, if he's just some kid—who I'm about to kill for trespassing, by the way—then how did he make it through? Someone powerful must have helped him!"

"Why are you here?" the duck asks, rounding back on me.

Still pinned to the wall, I try to marshal my thoughts as the handsome man lowers his hand a bit and the gravity decreases slightly. "To be his apprentice!" I start. "Look, I was rejected from all the great schools of magic, even though I had a 4.0 GPA in all my pre-mag classes. I wrote a senior thesis on charm objects that won two awards! And right now . . . I'm stuck working at a Samba Smoothies. In a mall."

"That is a grim fate, indeed," the sorcerer says. "But not at all my problem. And you don't get to make it my problem, just by barging into my home."

The duck clucks, shaking her head sadly. "Measure his mystic potential."

"Seraphex," Zambrano says, addressing the duck, "if you are playing a prank again . . . Is he some sort of wunderkind? More powerful than any other in his generation, using magic with instinct rather than training? Maybe there's a mysterious prophecy with wording so vague that it could mean anything?"

The duck laughs for several long seconds. "No. But I'm pretty sure you're going to want to see the results of this divination."

"Good. It would have really bummed me out to have to kill another 'chosen one.' That never turns out well." He rolls his eyes. "Well, young man, I guess we'll try the divination. I have to trust her judgment that it will be worth my time, since she's incapable of lying," Zambrano says with a resigned sigh, as if that fact is some sort of longstanding annoyance.

"That's right!" The duck bobs her head happily.

Zambrano gives the duck a dirty look but strides to a cabinet, yanks it open, and pulls out a small basin of water, into which he sprinkles what looks like small filings of some metal. He speaks a few soft words and then holds the basin up. The water ripples in the pan unnaturally. I remember the wizards at the Sorcerbonne doing a similar divination on me during my practical exams when I applied there, though with a much fancier apparatus and several minutes of measuring and balancing.

The sorcerer shakes his head, then holds the pan up to my heart. And then my head. He keeps it there, staring at it like it's a surprise text from his ex saying she's suing for alimony.

"Really?" he says, shaking his head. He tosses the contents of the basin out, then refills it with fresh shavings and water.

"Yup," Seraphex says. "That's how he did it." She's smirking at him. How exactly a duck's bill can smirk, I cannot explain. But I know a self-satisfied smirk when I see one.

"What?" I ask. "What is it telling you?"

"Well, kid," Zambrano says, suddenly looking at me with pity, rather than rage. "I have some bad news for you. You aren't just bad at magic. You have the least potential for magic of anyone I have met, heard of, or read about. If this divination reading is correct . . . statistically speaking, you are almost certainly the least magically sensitive person who is alive today, has ever lived, or will ever live. Honestly, it shouldn't really even be possible, but I never understood how the mental magic side of magic really works. One of my old colleagues always said it was theoretically possible."

"What?" I say, my jaw dropping open. It hurts, and I have to force my mouth closed, fighting through the gravity that's still pinning me to the wall. "Everyone is magically sensitive. You don't need a special talent. Anyone can learn at least some amount of magic! That was proven by—"

"Yes, I read the paper by those doddering old fools at Merlin College," Zambrano interrupts, "demonstrating what any competent wizard has known for centuries. Anyone in the world can learn magic. Except, well . . . *you*. But, some become mages, some continue into wizardry, and certain very rare and talented individuals—like me—become sorcerers."

The gravity on my whole body is starting to feel a lot less like a fun carnival ride and more like all my blood is being drained by vampires with teeth locked onto every inch of my backside.

"What? Really? That bad?" I'm heartbroken. Now I kind of just want him to crush me and get it over with. Years of dreaming and fighting for this, and it was never even possible in the first place. "Not just bad, but the worst ever?"

"Even the dumbest of you sad humans," Seraphex says, "those assholes who never use their turn signals and think you should get money from Free Parking in Monopoly, have that vital life force. When a spell is cast, their hairs stand on end. When a crystal sphere is observing them, they feel like they're being watched. There is a strong magical essence in every conscious being. Except you. You're special!" she adds cheerfully.

I want to grab her and wring her little duck neck, but the gravity is unrelenting. And . . . it explains everything. Why I never got into the programs even though my grades were good and I totally vibed with most of the interviewers. They think I can't do magic because of some silly basin full of water. But I know better—maybe it'll be hard for me, but it must be possible.

"I suppose this little trespasser is special, isn't he? A true genetic aberration," Zambrano says, staring at me and shaking his head as if he's pulled out his fishing line to find a particularly ugly fish wriggling on the hook. "I was going to kill him, but maybe I should freeze him in a slow-time case or something. For later study."

I grimace. I mean, it's certainly nice that I've been upgraded from being killed to being frozen in time. But as upgrades go, it's kind of a shitty one.

The dark sorcerer taps a finger against his chin thoughtfully. "What an interesting specimen you are, little intruder. Perhaps I could get some value for you at auction?"

CHAPTER 4

As we've been speaking, small creatures made of wood have appeared from an open door and started cleaning up the soapy water on the floor, draining the tub, and scrubbing it clean with tiny sponges. They look like old-timey kids' toys, but are about a foot tall and carved of a light-colored wood to look like tiny butlers with wooden suits and tiny wooden bow ties. I would think it was adorable and charming if a sorcerer and a talking duck weren't currently debating whether to kill me.

The wooden butlers suddenly freeze as the image of Zambrano's (now thankfully clothed) backside in the mirror begins to swirl and fade into red and black streaks. The dark sorcerer spins to face the mirror.

"It's not a good time, Vulkatherak!" Zambrano says, practically spitting at the mirror.

"It's always a good time," a powerful voice says from the mirror, which continues to swirl. "A good time for threats. A good time for blood. A good time for you to accept that you cannot defeat me." The voice reminds me of the duck's powerful tones, only pitched in a low bass with a faint rasp to it. "This is my final offer. If you allow me to invade this country's agricultural land, then I, in the spirit of generosity, won't send my demonic servants to tear you limb from limb."

"Hah!" Zambrano stands up straight and makes a rude gesture. "You think I'm going to just give up the Midwest? I teleport in a Tater Tots casserole from Michigan at least once a week! Have you ever been to the Minnesota State Fair? They will deep-fry *anything*.

Pickles, Twinkies, candy bars, entire sticks of butter . . . anything! Come on! There's no way I'm letting you burn it up! Though I don't approve of Chicago's deep-dish pizza BS—if I want a lasagna, I'll just get an amazing one straight from Florence."

"Amusing," the deep voice says. "But pointless. I have broken open the arcane seals around the chamber that foolishly tried to hide in the Ilopango Crater, and I have claimed the arcane conduit and the power that it brings. You should take my deal now—my terms will grow less favorable with each step closer to my victory. Once I trigger a massive earthquake, the weak human government will fall apart and I will be able to seize a vast portion of this land."

Zambrano glares at the mirror. "If you use the arcane conduit to disrupt the seismic balance of this world, I promise that you will pay a terrible price." Zambrano makes a chopping gesture, and the swirls disappear and the mirror returns to reflecting the room.

As soon as the magical swirling is gone, Zambrano slumps and shakes his head.

"I hope you don't think you can fight the demon duke and his forces on your own," Seraphex says quietly with just a hint of mockery in her voice. "You wouldn't be able to stand against just him alone; Vulkatherak is far too powerful."

"I know, I know!" Zambrano answers. "Especially not while Vulkatherak has the arcane conduit from Ilopango. Once he figures out how to work it, he could trigger a natural disaster at any moment. And there's no way into his penthouse—between the mystic defenses, the demonic magic, and the security magicians, I'd be utterly screwed."

"Maybe there's another way?" the duck says, seeming to have a sly smile on her face.

"Maybe," Zambrano says. "But first I have to deal with this trespassing asshole." He looks at me with renewed rage in his eyes.

"You could kill him, or freeze him," the duck says. "But is that really the best way to use him?"

"What do you mean?" Zambrano says. He grabs a towel from the rack and starts drying his thick mane of white hair, which is still an odd contrast to his Instagram-model face. But I have to admit it's certainly a striking look.

The duck waddles over to one of the small wooden butlers cleaning the room and pecks at it. It topples over but jumps up without complaint and resumes its work. It's starting to get hard to breathe, my lungs struggling to overcome the gravity on them.

"Why must you mess with the birch butlers all the time? They don't feel anything," Zambrano says. "Now, out with it. What are you thinking about the trespasser?"

"My dear demonic cousin in Chicago," the duck says. "The inner sanctum of his penthouse in Willis Tower is protected by powerful demonic magic. Ultimately, it works on the same principle—detecting magical life force and incinerating it. This kid could walk right through it."

"I don't need a helper." Zambrano growls as he uses the towel to dry out his ears. "And I'm not taking care of this idiot. I do what I do alone, for reasons of life and death. And also because having idiots around is infuriating."

The duck hops toward the sorcerer and stares up at him. "What, you don't think you could keep him alive for the mission?"

Zambrano scoffs. "Of course I could if I wanted to. But I'm not babysitting this idiot. That never ends well."

"Um, that sounds pretty good to me," I croak out.

"Your opinion is irrelevant," Zambrano says. "You are an uninvited intruder in the home of the greatest magic user alive, who, quite frankly, just had his bath interrupted and is not in a good mood. So no, kid, you don't get a say." Zambrano waves a hand at me, and the extreme gravity comes back. Once again, I can't do anything more than mumble.

"I'll bet you're wrong about that," Seraphex says, hopping over to examine me like I'm a piece of meat at the supermarket. "I'll bet you get him killed."

"I will not! But do you really think I'll fall for this game?" Zambrano shoots back. "I'm just going to put him in a slow-time case and get it over with. Why are you so focused on him, anyway?"

"I kind of like him," Seraphex says. "He's so cute, in an incompetent sort of way."

I try to object, but all that comes out is a grunt.

"You're an odd duck, Seraphex," Zambrano says.

The duck seems to smile. "If you win, I'll tell you the secret passphrase to Merlin's Vault in the Challenger Deep. If I win, you let me read the books in the sub-basement."

The moment he hears the words "Merlin's Vault," Zambrano freezes. "How do you know that?" he hisses at the duck. Then he turns and stares at me for a long moment. "Exact terms," he says, a hard edge in his voice.

Merlin's Vault? I've never heard of that before. Of course, everyone knows about Merlin, the mythical ancient sorcerer, but mostly from movies and TV shows. I didn't think anyone actually knew anything real that he left behind, if he even really existed.

Seraphex says, "You must keep our young Bryce here alive long enough to sneak into the Duke's penthouse and steal the artifact that he found at the Ilopango Crater. I will not sabotage you in any way, and I will probably even help."

Zambrano sighs. "All right, you crafty demon duck." Zambrano turns back to me. He waves his hand again, and the pressure on my body lessens. "Okay, kid, here's the deal: you help me, and I won't kill you or freeze you in time. Unless you really annoy me. Fair enough?"

I take a deep breath, drawing in air that has been crushed out of my lungs. Now's my chance to do something, to change this situation. I have leverage, and I'm going to use it.

"I came here to be your apprentice," I say. "And that's what I want. No more or less."

"You can't learn magic," the duck says. "I explained that whole thing, didn't I? Every person alive has a spark that you don't have, and all that?"

"Not even if I try really, really hard?" I ask. "I wasn't good at calculus when I started either, but I worked my ass off and eventually got an A-minus."

"Nope," the duck says. "Your magic potential is so low, it's practically undetectable."

"And who are you to tell me that?" I'm angry now, even still pinned to the wall. "What gives you the right to decide that for me?"

The duck preens. "I am Seraphex, the demon queen, empress of the Red Wastes, and high priestess of the Unending Torment. I am old beyond reckoning. And I am a demon, which means that I cannot lie."

"That's true?" I ask. "My undergrad arcane theory professor wrote a paper on that—he thought it was made up by demons to get gullible people to believe them."

"Well, who are you going to believe," Seraphex says, "some foolish professor or me, an actual demon? Because that's what I am."

"You're also a duck," Zambrano points out, suddenly in a good mood again.

"That, as you well know, is a temporary situation." She stands up to her full duck height. "Despite how infuriatingly long this duck form has continued, I remain Seraphex, the demon queen."

"I still want to be your apprentice," I say stubbornly. "Learning magic is all I've ever wanted. Teach me, and then we'll see whether I can do it or not." I'm not going to let some duck, demon queen or not, tell me that something's impossible that I've never even tried.

Zambrano shrugs. "I really can't actually teach you magic. So you can't be my apprentice. But I guess you can be my . . . intern?" He grins. "Yeah, that seems about right. How about I explain how some magic things work, and you help me with my problems?"

I glare at him. I want to learn magic, not be some pawn in his battle with a demon. Or do coffee runs or whatever an intern for a sorcerer does.

"I can also give you a nice hat that has the word 'intern' stitched on it. How about that? That's the best I can do. Final offer."

At this point, I feel like my ribs are starting to buckle under the gravity, and my vision is starting to narrow, making it look like Zambrano and Seraphex are at the end of a long tunnel.

"We have a deal?" Zambrano asks, raising an eyebrow.

"Okay, okay," I gasp. "It's a deal." A few minutes ago, I was going to be frozen in time and left to rot. Well, to rot very, very slowly, assuming that's what the name "slow-time case" implies. This is at least something!

Zambrano grasps the air and pulls his hand backward, and the weight on my body finally lifts. I collapse to the floor in a heap. Every part of my body aches like a hippopotamus sat on top of me for her entire lunch break.

CHAPTER 5

Okay, so it's a bargain. You can stay. If you break any of my stuff, I'll turn you inside out. The incantations and gestures of that spell are very fun, so don't tempt me," Zambrano says and walks away.

"Oh yeah, that one is very dramatic," Seraphex says and waddles after him, chattering something about how excited she is to win the bet and read his books. I can't follow her words with the rushing blood pounding in my ears.

I was kind of expecting them to tell me what to do, or where to go, or something. Anything, really. Instead, I'm just lying on the floor with a pounding headache, noticing that my clothes are starting to get wet from the spilled bathwater. The little butlers seem to be ignoring me, carefully cleaning around me with little brushes and towels.

I lie there for a few minutes as my body recovers, staring up at the bathtub, the mirror on the wall, and the little wooden butlers continuing their tasks. This isn't exactly how I had hoped to start my apprenticeship. Well, technically it's an internship, I guess. Whatever. But despite all that, here I am, in the inner sanctum of the infamous dark sorcerer Zambrano!

Slowly, I gather myself and stand up, wiping bathwater—and, to be honest, a little bit of drool—off my face. I glance around. The sorcerer and the duck are long gone. Should I continue exploring the rest of this floor? Go back down to the first floor? But there was so much stuff to break there, and I like having my insides, well, inside of me.

It feels worth the risk, just to be here, with all these artifacts and the most powerful magic user in the modern world. But still, this is not what I was hoping for.

I stare at my face in the mirror. That guy, right there, that face I've seen every day for my entire life, as I hoped to one day do magic. Understand the true nature of reality. Unlock the secrets of the universe. Shoot awesome fireballs.

But no, I think as I grab a towel in an attempt to dry my wet clothes. I'm supposedly incapable of magic. Uniquely, specially, individually unable to do even the simplest of spells.

I jump as I feel something tugging at my pant leg. But as I spin away and glance down, I see that it's only one of the little birch butlers.

"Careful there, little fellow," I say. "I almost kicked you across the room!"

The butler doesn't react to what I say; he just gestures for me to follow him. Shrugging, I follow along. He takes me down a few halls, away from the fine carpets and sconces to a relatively unfurnished part of the warehouse. It leads me to an open door, where a small army of the little birch butlers is hastily assembling a low bed. I can see from the small tools and wood shavings lying on the floor that they only hammered it together moments ago, and they're somehow pulling the mattress onto the bed platform and putting the sheets on at the same time.

I stand there, taking in the show for about thirty seconds, which is all it takes for them to finish their preparations. And then I'm forced to step out of the way as they run past me in a flood of clattering bodies, and I'm left standing alone in the room. It's now spotlessly clean, and there's the bed, a crude table with a carafe of water on it, a mirror on the wall, and I can see through a side door that there's a small bathroom. There's no window, which means it's not legally a bedroom. But somehow, I don't think the New York City Housing Authority has much sway in a dark sorcerer's warehouse. It'll do.

Not knowing what else to do, I close the door, brush my teeth with the toothbrush that the butlers have thoughtfully provided, and collapse into bed. It's not that late, but my body is exhausted from a long workday, and trip into the city, oh, and also being crushed by the gravity of Jupiter for a fairly lengthy conversation in which I was only allowed to participate tangentially.

I'd like to fall asleep and wake up refreshed, ready for my next adventure. But, of course, I pull out my phone and spend the next hour scrolling through it aimlessly. It's disconcerting. Something so insane, so unexpected, so huge, has happened to me. But the outside world is all exactly the same. The same news stories, posts about pets and meals and an engagement. (Really, Becky and Ishmael are still together? And getting married?!) Nothing has changed. I open up WizardWatch, but it's fairly quiet. I try to start typing, to tell them what has happened, but it's too big. It would take all night to try to explain it.

So I just open a private message to Parth, my best friend from WizardWatch, and type *I made it in. I met him. I'm still here. This is wild.*

I suddenly shake my head and pull up the camera app to take a pic and show him . . . but it's just a room. A cool abandoned industrial warehouse room that looks like where a comic book villain would be discovered hiding, that would make a great spot for an Instagram photo shoot. But still, it's just a room. Parth lives in India, where it's the middle of the night, so I don't expect a response anytime soon.

I finally put the phone down and see that the birch butlers have helpfully put a phone charger on the table by the bed. Those little guys are impressively thorough. I plug my phone in, lie back, and close my eyes.

And then open them and stare at the ceiling.

Am I really here? Is this real? Am I going to actually be working for a sorcerer?

What happens to my old job at the smoothie shop? Do I have to do both now?

I think I won't be able to fall asleep, but my body has been pretty wrecked by Zambrano's gravity spell, and at some point I drift off to sleep.

I wake up the next morning to a sudden thump on my chest and groggily try to bat whatever it is away as I open my eyes.

But the duck on top of me smoothly dodges beneath my waving arm and stands there preening in the morning light.

"It's here!" Seraphex says, brightly.

"Huh?" I say, groaning. "What? What's here?"

It takes me a moment to remember, but when it all hits me, I sit bolt upright, sending Seraphex scrambling off me. She leaps, flaps her wings, and lands on the footboard. I stare at her.

"What's going on?" I ask, fully conscious far more quickly than I usually am. To be honest, I usually take like three or four snoozes before I can even sit up, so I have to give the duck some credit. I'm definitely awake.

"The hat!" she says, pointing her beak at the bedpost by my feet. And there it is, a pointy blue hat with a broad brim and a thick black band around the center. The word "INTERN" is emblazoned onto the band in large block letters in some sort of sparkly material.

"Oh," I say. The lettering reminds me of the hats that say "BOSS BITCH" or "BOY TOY" that you'd find at tourist shops in Chinatown, in between New York City T-shirts and snow globes of the Empire State Building.

"Try it on!" she says, hopping up and down with excitement. "The birch butlers sewed it for you overnight."

"That's . . . nice of them," I say with the same complete lack of enthusiasm that I feel.

I push the covers aside, stand up, and pick the hat up. I'm suddenly aware that I'm standing here in front of her with nothing on but my boxers. But then, I think, she's just a duck. It's not a big deal to be naked in front of animals. On the other hand, she can talk and claims to be an ancient and powerful demon queen. I'm not sure quite what to do with that one. So I just try to suck my belly in and stand up straight.

I stare at the hat. It's gaudy and unstylish, even in the bizarre fashions that academic magicians and wizards tend to adopt, like art school kids but older, rattier, and often paunchier. Very aware of the duck's gaze on me, I put the hat on and turn to look in the mirror. I look about as impressive and appropriate as an ostrich on the red carpet at the Oscars. The hat does fit perfectly though.

"Come on," I say. "This looks silly. Do I need to wear the hat?"

Zambrano is clearly messing with me. I pull the hat off, toss it on the bed, and turn back to Seraphex.

"I really need to call work and—" I start to say and then catch a glimpse back in the mirror.

The hat is back on my head.

I move to pull it off, then stop my hand.

"So, this one of those deals where the hat will keep reappearing on my head no matter what I do, huh?" I ask.

"I don't think Zambrano is super happy about this whole situation. When he gets like that, he acts out," Seraphex says with a little ruffling shrug of her wings. "You're lucky it's just a hat. Want some breakfast?"

I take a deep breath. I want to pull the damn hat off, but I know that trying again will only make me look dumber.

"Okay, sure," I say. Then I look at the mirror again. "Um," I ask, "can that demon duke guy call me through this mirror? Like what happened yesterday?"

She looks at me like I'm crazy, shaking her head. "I don't think you have to worry about Vulkatherak calling you directly."

"Oh, good," I say. "That's a relief. So it's just that one mirror?"

"No," she says, "he can speak through any mirror. I just can't imagine why a demon would ever want to talk to you."

I raise an eyebrow at her. "You are, right now, aren't you?"

She gives an exasperated sigh and jumps off the bed, starting to waddle for the door. "I said 'want' to talk to you. At the moment, I am 'tolerating' talking to you."

"Okay, fair enough. What, um, what do we eat around here?" I ask, quickly pulling on my jeans and T-shirt and following after her. I notice that they seem to have been fully cleaned overnight. The birch butlers must have snuck in during the night and done it, which is both awesome and kind of creepy. Also, I slept in my underwear, so they kind of missed the most important part. Next time I should leave my boxers out for them . . . which I would be happy to do if I wasn't then also thinking about them sneaking in while I'm sleeping naked. I should probably figure out how to get some more clothes here if I'm going to be spending the night frequently.

Luckily, with her short legs, Seraphex hasn't made it that far down the hall by the time I catch up. "Do I have to fetch it—is that one of my intern tasks? Do the birch butlers cook too? Is there, like, a banquet hall or something?"

Seraphex laughs, her voice ringing like a bell. "Oh dear, no. The butlers tried to cook once, but they don't have a sense of taste, so it was a total disaster. Sometimes Zambrano teleports in his favorites from around the world, but mostly we just order delivery online. There's a tablet down the hall that Zambrano set up for me. I'm sure you can use it too."

I stare at her with curiosity. "What does a duck order from a restaurant in Queens?"

Seraphex shrugs. "Honestly, most anything. This body really likes Japanese food—sushi, seaweed salad, lots of seafood. I do miss biting into entrails and quenching my thirst with the blood of the innocent, but they don't really taste the same with a duck tongue."

". . . blood of the innocent?" I ask.

"Oh yes, the really morally upright people have a special umami flavor that only demonic taste buds can perceive." Her eyes roll back slightly, like when my mom tells stories about that pasta she had in Tuscany that one time.

I stare at her.

"And what are *you* going to order for breakfast?" she demands.

"Bacon, egg, and cheese on a bagel," I say, automatically. It's the one thing you can consistently get in any neighborhood in New York City—and I ordered an awful lot of them when I was in college here.

"Well, there you go. The pigs that your bacon is made out of are the most perfect, innocent creatures in the world. So don't get all up on your high horse, Intern." We've arrived at the tablet, which is just sitting on a low pedestal, the right height for a duck to peck at it. "The food will come through that door," she says, pointing at a door that definitely shouldn't connect to the outside based on where it is in the building. "Come downstairs when you're ready to get started."

I'm too confused and hungry to argue, so I awkwardly sit on the floor to reach the tablet and just order my bagel. Not knowing what else to do, I also text Carla to say I'm sick. She's super nice about it and is still excited I'm going to be in management training. I play along, because somehow this whole "intern" thing doesn't exactly seem to be going so great.

In just a few minutes, a buzzer does go off and a delivery guy brings the sandwich to the random door in the hallway that, as far as

I know, is on the second floor but appears to connect to the street. This is much better than the normal space-enhancing magic, which just makes rooms feel bigger than they are.

I eat and hop into the shower. I try to take the hat off several times, but in the end I just kind of shampoo up under and around it. It does seem to dry about as quickly as my hair does, which is pretty cool. Somehow, by the time I get out of the shower, the cheese stain that I got on my shirt has been cleaned by the birch butlers. Not too shabby.

Finally, not wanting to keep them waiting, I wander around until I find the stairs that lead down to the first floor. I'm worried that the corridors will be constantly shifting, but it's just the normal amount of confusion of being in a large new building. Which, honestly, is still pretty confusing. But I am able to find my way down.

On the first floor, Zambrano is sitting at a workbench that's covered in lenses and mirrors of all different types, something between an optometrist's office and the people who make steampunk goggles for music festivals.

"You look good in the hat," Zambrano says, glancing up at me and eyeing the hat that's still stubbornly sitting on my head.

"No I don't," I say, glowering at him.

He shrugs as if to say *You win this argument.* But I know I have won nothing. I look dumb. But I'm not going to give him the satisfaction of being embarrassed. I stand tall. I'm going to rock this hat.

"Okay, well, if I've got the hat, then I guess I'm your intern," I say. "So what do I do? Grab complicated coffee orders? Answer the phones? Make copies? Fax things to the legal department?"

"Make copies? Faxes? What is this, the 1990s?" Zambrano eyes me like I'm a pimple he just noticed on his chin.

I shrug. "Everything I know about interns I learned from old episodes of *The Office*, so I really don't know how this stuff works. You could always just . . . teach me some magic?"

"Sure, later," he says. "But before that, it's time for your first job. We need an artifact that will help us find what we need when we break into the Duke's penthouse in Willis Tower, and I need to see if you're competent at something other than interrupting my bath. Plus, I can't wait to see the reaction when it goes missing . . ." He grins like he's just found one last M&M in a seemingly empty bag.

"And then you'll teach me magic?" I ask.

"Sure," he says with a shrug. "As far as that's possible, given your fascinating limitations."

When he says that, I'm already kind of sold even though this whole thing sounds pretty sketchy.

"And, um, what exactly are we doing?"

"You don't have a spark of magic inside you," Zambrano says. "Not like I do, not like wizards do, not like normal people do. Less than your average housefly, to be honest. So I can't even teach you the basic magical skills needed to detect a powerful artifact. We need an enchanted spyglass," he continues, seeming not to notice my glare, "to be able to find the arcane conduit in the Duke's penthouse. I could make one"—he gestures at the table of lenses and mirrors—"but honestly, that would take all day, and I have dinner plans."

"So," I say, "we're going to steal it? Hopefully from a demon? A mass murderer? I don't know, someone who says gross things to kids on Xbox Live?"

Zambrano shrugs. "Nah. Just someone who constantly annoys me and gets in my way. And now, with you, I can finally do something about it."

"Zambrano's goal here is to stop a demon from triggering a giant earthquake in the Midwest," Seraphex chimes in from the steps. "Maybe from your perspective that makes petty larceny not such a major sin? Not to mention, Zambrano doesn't actually have the ingredients or particular skills to make an artifact of the precision of the Spyglass of Spinoza."

I sigh. "I guess that's a decent argument," I admit.

"Look," Zambrano says, standing up and putting away the lens that he was working on. "I don't want or need this thing. My little toe is more sensitive to magic than the best spyglass in the world. When we're done with it, you can keep it or return it, I don't really care."

"Okay," I say. "That seems reasonable."

"Great!" he says, grabbing me by the shoulder and leading me across the warehouse floor to the wall covered in paintings and clocks. "Then let's do this!"

As we get closer, I can see that the wall is covered with small oil paintings of landscapes and cityscapes, each with a tiny brass label plate and a clock below.

"Okay," I say, suddenly feeling rushed and a bit stubborn. "I'm ready, but while we go, you have to at least explain what we're doing as we do it."

"Really?" Zambrano says with an exasperated sigh.

I raise an eyebrow and tap the band of the blue hat on my head. "You put the hat on me and made sure I can't take it off. Learning on the job is what interns are supposed to do."

"Fine," he says, gesturing at the wall in front of us. "What do you think this is?"

I take a look at the paintings and clocks. They seem to be different landscapes, mostly cities around the world but some rural areas as well.

"The places we're going. Wait a second. Are we *teleporting* somewhere?" I tense up. "Isn't that super dangerous? It's really only done under extremely careful research conditions—you're not supposed to use it just to travel!"

Zambrano shrugs. "Using teleportraits is only dangerous because modern wizards are so bad at it. And they don't understand it. The teleportraits have to really reflect the locations." He points at them with pride. "I have to repaint them roughly once a year, or the pattern correspondence breaks down. It's a matter of feel that's hard to exactly explain or reproduce, like a lot of magic."

I take a deep breath, then a closer look. "These are really impressive. You really painted them yourself? You're good." They truly are excellent—and fairly stylized, not super precise like the attempts I've seen in videos of research that is still being done on teleportation. As I remember it, the paintings had to be so precise and could so easily fail to match the destination that the teleportation failed more often than not.

He shrugs. "I got decent at painting, but I gave up trying to get people to appreciate them as art more than a hundred years ago. There was this asshole from my home country who kept beating me out at all the good shows in Paris. So I cast a spell that made him only able to paint in one color, just to mess with him. And he turned around and made it some of his most famous work! He was a rare lucky genius, to actually be appreciated in his own time. I didn't see the point in trying to get the public to like me after that. In painting or in magic."

I glance over at Seraphex, who's watching with a glimmer in her eye.

"I can't tell if he's telling the truth or not either," she says. "He's not bound by the Demonic Code like I am. And I wasn't in this realm at the turn of the century."

"The Demonic Code?" I ask.

"Yes," she answers. "It has three elements. Element one: a demon cannot lie. Element two: a demon is bound by the terms of any pact that they enter."

I wait expectantly, but she doesn't continue.

"And the third element?" I ask.

"Oh, that's a secret," she says. "We don't tell that one to humans. Which is sort of an unofficial fourth element, but it's not magically enforced. I could tell you, but I am choosing not to."

"My guess is that it's 'Element three: a demon at all times must be unspeakably arrogant and irritating,'" Zambrano says.

"I can neither confirm nor deny your guess," Seraphex says, and the two stare at each other in silence. I genuinely can't tell if they're angry at each other or just having fun.

"Okay," I say, breaking the silence and returning my attention to the artwork on the wall in front of me. "So the paintings—the teleportraits—need to be kept closely matching their destinations. But then why are they so impressionistic? I mean, I know that's been tried before. They even tried cubism."

"Yeah, I don't envy whoever had to clean up the bloody mess after that fiasco." Zambrano smiles, somehow happy about the fact that a guy got turned more or less inside out and promptly died. We studied it in my arcanology classes at NYU; it was gruesome. "Precision isn't everything. Mine work for about a year because they capture the real spirit of the place. And, as with all magic, there are a thousand other little details that you have to get just right. These modern wizards are trying to quantify and codify everything. Or they want to try to get all artsy and spiritual. Neither works. Magic isn't science. Magic isn't art. Magic isn't religion. Magic is *magic*."

I stare at the teleportraits, noticing how permanent details like buildings and hills are etched in more detail, while others are blurry and indistinct, sort of like time-lapse photographs.

"You're really good," I begin. "Maybe you should try sharing these—"

"No," Zambrano says, suddenly shutting down. "End of lesson. Here we go."

He steps up to the painting that says *Yanaka Cemetery, Tokyo, Japan* with a clock reading just a bit after one o'clock in the morning.

"Here, give me your hand," he says.

I put my hand out. I guess he must do this all the time, so . . . it's probably safe?

He looks like he's about to grab my hand, then stops. "Yeah, that feels weird. I usually do this with people I want to get with. It's super romantic. And, no offense," he says, looking at me, "but you're not the kind of guy that I'm into."

I glare at him. "What a relief," I say sarcastically. "Thanks for saving me the trouble of letting you down easy."

He shakes his head, grabs the back of my neck, and looks into the painting, face contorting into intense concentration, the kind of funny look you see on a metal guitarist while playing a blistering solo.

"Good luck, boys," Seraphex says. "I'd promise not to get into trouble while you're gone, but, you know, the Demonic Code makes that a hassle."

"Because then you'd be required to actually not get into trouble?" I guess.

"Precisely," Seraphex says. "We demons have to be very careful about what promises we make. Once a promise is made, we're forced to do our very best to deliver. Which can be a real hassle at times."

"I want to go to there," Zambrano says, still staring at the painting, and suddenly the world feels like I'm looking at it through binoculars turned the wrong way around. And I feel pleasantly warm. That kind of warm when you're in the swimming pool as a kid, and you really, really have to pee, and you just . . . let it go.

And with surprisingly little fuss, there we are, standing in a cemetery in Tokyo in the middle of the night, a light breeze wafting over us. I'm glad I'm not easily creeped out, because the gravestones outlined by the more distant lights of the city look pretty spooky.

"Come on," Zambrano says, starting down the path.

"The cemetery," I say, following along. "Is that to keep the teleportation a secret? Or is it because the landscape doesn't change that much?"

The sorcerer nods as if impressed as he brings out his phone and pulls up what looks like a taxi app. "Good guesses. It's a bit of each. All the bigwigs in every country know that I teleport around, but it keeps the random bystanders from putting videos of me everywhere. Just fewer hassles overall. And it changes a lot less than a general street corner. One extra grave here or there doesn't make too big of a difference."

Before long we're out of the cemetery, and a car is waiting for us. After the teleportation, I was kind of expecting a magic carpet or a flying horse or something, but the car cuts quickly through the streets. I want to ask more questions, but Zambrano is staring out the window and thinking intently about something, so I don't bother him. It's only a few minutes more, and the car deposits us on an empty street in a quiet residential district lined with expensive-looking apartment buildings.

Zambrano chats with the driver in what sounds to me like fluent Japanese, even making the guy laugh at a joke. I catch the driver taking a glance at my hat and smiling and resist the urge to slump down—the moon is out tonight and bright, so there's no hiding. Instead I try to sit up straight, like I belong here.

Zambrano stares up at one of the buildings and then leads the way to an alley. A moment later, he's pulled a large cardboard box out of the recycling bin and lays it on the ground face down. He pulls a Sharpie out of his perfectly-tailored jeans and draws a quick series of mystic runes on the bottom of the box, flowing airy symbols surrounded by a strong square. I've got to admit, the guy has an artistic eye. Why did no one tell me that I should have done a minor in fine arts to be able to do magic?

He flips the box, places one hand on either side, and murmurs a series of words in what sounds like maybe Russian or Yiddish. The box floats off the ground a few inches.

"I could fly us up, but magic with that level of power would probably set off alarms," he whispers. "Plus, I'm sure as hell not carrying you. Come on, get in!" I follow his lead. A moment later, the two of us are standing inside the cardboard box.

"*Voskhodyashchaya bumaga,*" he says with an upward floating gesture of his hand, and my stomach lurches as the box rises into the air.

Holy shit. What have I gotten myself into?

CHAPTER 6

A moment later, I'm feeling dizzy as the box carries us higher and higher until we're maybe twelve or thirteen stories in the air. It's beautiful though, as I'm suddenly able to see the nighttime cityscape of Tokyo, quiet dim streets and the glittering skyscrapers of the city center. Which is great until I look down. I know, you're not supposed to do that, but I can't help myself.

I also suddenly realize that the only thing between me and falling a dozen stories and making a bright red Rorschach blot on the pavement is the thin piece of cardboard that is somehow holding two fully grown adults in the air.

Forcing myself to look back up, I see the apartment window we've arrived at. Outlined by the moonlight, it looks like a pretty nice living room. The design is classic and opulent with expensive-looking furniture, a big TV, and a mixture of art and family photos on the walls. There's also a corner that looks like a home office with a desk, bookshelf, and several filing cabinets. There are a bunch of books on the desk, and on the shelf that I recognize are standard texts from my arcane theory classes in college.

It's easy to see into the apartment because there are also a couple glass statues that have shifting and pulsing blue lights inside them. They're called SpellStatues™ even though they're enchanted objects, which aren't really related to spells. Oh well, I guess that's just how marketing goes.

A long time ago, like in the '70s and '80s, they used to be a big deal, a mass-produced enchanted item that anyone could own. But that was back when magic was cooler; nowadays they're kind of an old person thing to have, like fine china or wall-to-wall carpeting. It looks like this apartment has the wolf and the dolphin designs. In addition to the light, the glass sculpting appears to move slightly so that the wolf's fur waves in the wind and the dolphin's tail gently sways back and forth. I always thought it was a cool effect and not one that you could effectively achieve with traditional materials.

I was actually able to get my mom to buy me one used, which I had in my room for all of middle school and most of high school. It was real magic that I could have in my room! But then I had a date over for the first time, and she made fun of it, and so it disappeared into a box in the basement.

"Okay, open the window," Zambrano whispers, pressing something into my hand.

I look down at the small blade that I'm now holding. It looks like a tiny saw, thin and delicate.

"What am I supposed to do with this?" I ask. "You want me to . . . cut through the glass?"

Zambrano gives an exasperated sigh. "Really? You don't know how to break into a house? What sort of intern are you?"

"Can't you do it?" I ask. "I've never been much for criminal activity—I can't think of anything I've done that's worse than taking extra ketchup packets at Wendy's or staying at a movie theater for an unauthorized double feature."

"No," Zambrano answers. "If I get within about an inch of the apartment, it'll sense me and trigger the magical defenses, and they'll know we're here. That'll cause me all sorts of headaches. Look, these windows are easy," he continues, as if explaining to a child. "You just have to cut this bit of the rubber away from the molding, then you can use the saw to trip the latch. It's not like the windows on the fourteenth floor are built to be secure."

I take a closer look at the spot he's pointing at. I do see what he's talking about; I can see the latch on the other side of the window that connects here. Swallowing hard, I lean in and start sawing away at the rubber. I try really, really hard not to glance down, and I'm grateful that the cardboard box is somehow not just holding us up but also compensating for my unbalanced weight as I hack and prod at the window. Still, my pulse seems to be going ever faster, like a middle school drummer who's a little too excited to be performing in their first recital and is kind of ruining it for everyone.

Still, I'm somehow able to trim the rubber away and use the razor-thin saw blade to get the latch to unlock. And with a lot of effort and a fairly painful bent fingernail, I'm able to slide the window open. I haven't learned any magic yet, but I guess I've started Breaking and Entering 101.

"Okay, go in!" Zambrano says, practically pushing me through the open window.

I clamber in and stand up and look around at . . . someone's apartment in Tokyo.

"Uh, what do I do now?" I ask.

"What you need is in the bottom left drawer of the desk," Zambrano whispers. "But it's got a trap enchantment on the lock."

"Wait, what?" I ask.

"Yeah, if you trigger it, the blood in your hand will turn to hydrochloric acid."

"WHAT?!" I whisper-shout.

"Don't worry, it's fine," Zambrano says. "I know how to disable it. You just use your finger to trace a square around the lock clockwise three times."

I quietly step across the couch, carefully navigating around the SpellStatues™ and a few cat toys scattered around the floor.

"Do it!" Zambrano whispers from the window.

Leaning down to stare at the wooden drawer in the dim light, I shake my head. "That's easy for you to say; you're not about to have your hand turned to acid."

"Just your blood. The rest of your hand will be fine," he shoots back. "Apart from the acid damage, of course."

I turn and glare at him. But for all my complaining, I'm going to do my best to succeed at this. Opening a magic trap to steal an artifact . . . Holy shit, that's awesome.

"Is this right?" I ask, tracing squares in the air. In my nervousness, I'm suddenly not sure which one is clockwise and which is counter-clockwise? Righty tighty, lefty loosey? I shake it off and concentrate. This is simple, I can do it.

"Yes, yes, you've got it," Zambrano says urgently. "Now do it!"

Ignoring his impatience, I make him go over the instructions three more times. Finally, I feel ready. I crouch down and slowly trace out a square on the wooden panel clockwise three times. As soon as I'm done, I pull my hand back. I stare down at it and flex my fingers.

It's still there. It's not melting off in a pile of acid and liquified flesh. That's nice. I gasp in some air, realizing that I've been holding my breath for the last thirty seconds.

"Great. Did you feel the magic shift off?" Zambrano whispers from the window.

I squint at the desk drawer. "Um, not really? Is it supposed to glow or something? I do think I heard a click though."

"Oh right, right, you can't sense magic; you don't have a soul. It's fine, you can open it now."

"No *soul?*" I hiss back. "I thought I just wasn't very magic sensitive!"

"It's not as big a deal as you'd think," Zambrano says. "It's not like there's an afterlife you're going to miss out on or something. At least . . . Well, no one really knows for sure, I guess. We can talk later—get the spyglass!"

I gingerly reach out and pull the drawer open. It opens easily—I guess when I heard the click, it must have unlocked. Inside, gleaming brightly in the moonlight, is a silver spyglass. I pick it up, holding it delicately in both hands. It's telescoping, but currently collapsed into its smallest size. I close the drawer and stand, still holding the spyglass like it's a baby that might try to wriggle out of my grip at any moment.

In the open window, I can see Zambrano gesturing. "Okay, enough dawdling. Get over here and let's go!"

I nod and step toward the window, but suddenly a black shape darts across the dark room. Startled, I jump away from it, stumble, try to grip the spyglass, and catch myself. I stay upright, but I feel my elbow hit something hard and cold. I spin and see the dolphin SpellStatue™ teetering. I grasp at it with my free hand, but it's too late. The glowing statue rocks back and falls to the floor, shattering on the dark wood. The blue glow inside flickers off.

I freeze and look up in horror. On the other side of the room, the black cat that caused this disaster is sitting in the corner, staring at me with its judgy little cat eyes as if this is somehow *my* fault.

Before I can make a move, the bedroom door flies open. An older Japanese woman is standing there in a kimono and with messy hair.

"*Te wo kuttsuku*," she says, pointing a spread pair of fingers at me and then snapping them together.

Suddenly, my hands are snapped together by a glowing figure eight of blue energy. I try to pull my hands apart, but it feels like I'm trying to push against impossibly strong magnets. I awkwardly hold my hands downward, cradling the small collapsed spyglass behind one of them so that she can't see.

"What is this?!" she says, indignant. "Why are you in my apartment?"

I realize with a sinking feeling that I actually *recognize* her. I can't quite remember her name, but she was one of the professors who gave me the practical exams when I applied to the Kotodama Institute here in Tokyo. I stare at her, not sure what to do.

Then I glance over at the window. Zambrano is *gone*. And, to add insult to injury, the window is closed. I guess he left me high and dry.

"Wait, I recognize you," the woman says. And then it hits me—this is Professor Okamoto, who just yesterday sent me that final rejection letter that sealed my fate as a student of magic and sent me off in search of Zambrano. "Even though you're wearing that very ugly hat, you're the young man who has no magic potential. No life essence. It was a shame that we had to reject you. Is that why you're here? For revenge? I'm sorry if you're angry, but you never would have been able to learn magic. And I certainly won't let you hurt me."

She starts to trace something in the air with her finger, the tip of which is gently glowing blue. The hairs on the back of my neck should probably start standing on end, but they don't. Because apparently I'm not sensitive to magic, which means that I don't have "life essence," whatever that is?

"Wait, I'm not here to hurt you!" I say. I don't need a second wizard in as many days blasting me for trespassing. My ribs are still sore from the whole gas-giant gravity thing.

Professor Okamoto stares at me, her eyes blazing angrily. "You've broken into my house, interrupted my sleep, and broken one of my possessions. Why shouldn't I cast Widow's Venom to paralyze you and call the police?"

I already feel almost as paralyzed as I would if she had cast the spell. It's really starting to hit home just how outmatched I am in a world of wizards and sorcerers. I'm just as helpless as Seraphex is in her little duck body, even with all my limbs and five feet, eleven and a half inches—yes, I round up to six feet on dating apps; shove off.

What was it that Seraphex said? Something about how, as small as she was, *information is the only currency available.* Maybe she had the right idea. I try to think quickly. What do I have to offer? I could give away what I know about Zambrano, but that seems really foolish. He did totally bail on me, but he also can squash me like a bug if I cross him. So I go with something that seems a bit safer.

"I'm sorry I woke you up. And I'm so sorry about the SpellStatue™." Though I don't mention it, most people would say the apartment is much classier without them. And two was definitely excessive. "But I came to warn you."

"Warn me of what?" Professor Okamoto demands, hand still raised and ready to hit me with her spell.

"Th-there's a demon in Chicago," I start. "He lives in a penthouse there. He's planning to use an ancient artifact to trigger earthquakes that disrupt the government and allow him to take control of the whole Midwest. For its farmland." I take a deep breath. It really sounds like a lot all laid out like that. But it's true. And, I hope for a moment, maybe she can actually help do something about it. Maybe Zambrano and I won't have to handle it alone.

Professor Okamoto smiles sadly, shaking her head. "You poor dear. I can see that you're the real victim here."

"What?" I ask, not expecting that response at all.

"Did you see some videos on the internet? Wild theories on dark web message boards? They told you that our world is in danger? Earth is perfectly safe. The United Nations Arcane Threat Committee has determined that there is no evidence of rumored demonic activity. I should know, I am Japan's delegate to the committee."

"No," I protest, "I'm not one of those conspiracy theory crazies! I actually heard his voice!" Even though I can't tell her, I did really hear this demon guy threatening the world's one living sorcerer. But how much can I really trust Zambrano? I barely know him. And he did just send me into a dangerous situation and then dip at the first sign of trouble. Maybe I need to get a little more information.

She shakes her head sadly. "The age of sorcerers, demons, leviathans, and all the rest is over. If you want to help save the world, go carbon neutral."

I want to yell at her. I mean, I'm not an idiot. I don't trust the crazy stories I read on the internet. But I also can't say I really trust when I hear politicians say everything's fine either. Or when they want to start yet another war. It's a fine line, trusting facts and science and expertise but not falling for self-serving authority figures. And I've met a sorcerer, a real demon, and heard the voice of another through a magic mirror, threatening to destroy half the United States. Including, I suddenly realize, my grandma, who lives in Milwaukee.

But none of that would help right now. She's clearly made up her mind already.

I let myself slump a little. "Really?" I ask, trying to act brokenhearted. "It's all a lie? There aren't any demons?"

"I'm sorry, young man, I think you've been fooled by someone who doesn't have your best interests at heart. They prey on people like you, who have failed in their lives."

"Okay," I say, pretending to be contrite and ignoring my rage at her dismissiveness. "I'm really sorry I woke you up. And broke in. Can I . . . can I buy you a new one?"

Professor Okamoto sighs. "Just stay here, I'm going to make a quick phone call to someone who can help you."

I nod as if defeated. She disappears into her bedroom, dialing the phone and speaking to someone in Japanese. From the clipped and authoritative sound of the voice on the other end, it sure sounds like the cops.

I look at the cat, which is still staring at me sullenly from the corner.

"Yeah, screw you too," I say to the cat.

And then, when the professor has her back turned to me, I quietly open the apartment door, step out into the hall, and shut it as gently as I can. I look for the fire-exit sign, yank open the corresponding door with both of my magically cuffed hands, and charge down the stairs. It's hard to run with your hands tied together by a magical force, but I'm feeling highly motivated to make it work.

I hear the professor yell something angrily just before the door slams shut, but I scamper down the stairs. Can she turn me into a salamander or make my head explode from a distance? In my arcane theory classes, they said that most spells need line of sight to be cast, but who knows what's really possible?

But, luckily for me, Professor Okamoto either can't or doesn't want to murder me from a distance. That's probably more Zambrano's kind of thing anyway. Which kind of makes me wonder why I seem to be on his team, but it's too late now. I've got to get out of here and hope he can help me. I'd guess that Japanese prison isn't as terrible as the ones they have in the United States, but I bet it's not a fun experience.

By the time I've run down more than a dozen flights of stairs and out the door, I'm short of breath. I hug close to the outside wall, hoping that she won't be able to spot me from so high up. As I dash past the alley, I hear a voice.

"Over here!" Zambrano hisses from the shadows, standing next to a flattened cardboard box that looks like it's been run through a trash compactor. I guess when the strengthening and lifting magic runs out, it doesn't go so well for that poor little box even though it tried its hardest. Something to keep in mind. Both literally and metaphorically.

I duck into the alley, staying close to the wall and looking up. Thankfully, I don't see Professor Okamoto poking her head out the window. But the night is starting to be disturbed by the sound of police sirens coming from two different directions.

"What took you so long? Did you sit down for a cup of tea with her or something?" He waves a hand and mutters some unintelligible word, and the glowing handcuffs wink out of existence.

I stare at him angrily. "What took me so long?" I hiss back. "You bailed on me!"

He shrugs. "Strategic withdrawal. If she gets hard evidence that I was here, I'll have those pompous hyenas from the United Nations all over my ass. I'd probably have to move to a new city or something."

I shake my head. "Can you get us out of here?"

"Oh, yeah," he says. From his pocket, he pulls out a small tele-portrait of the inside of the warehouse and grabs my neck. "I want to go to there," he says, and the world suddenly looks oddly distant and distorted, and my body feels nicely warm.

We're plucked from the Tokyo night and are back in the ware-house with afternoon sunlight streaming through the windows. I stand there blinking for a moment, letting my eyes adjust and still breathing heavily from my sprint down the stairs.

Seraphex clucks with satisfaction from a sunny spot on a large wooden table that she's settled onto. "Everything went perfectly smoothly, I assume?"

"Yeah, it was all fine," Zambrano says with a shrug.

I glare at him. "We stole from a famous professor who's on the United Nations Arcane Threat Committee! And I almost got caught! Is this what you do, just rob people when you need something?"

"We do need it to, you know, save the world from demons. But if you're feeling bad and want to give it back, that's fine, I can easily drop you off back in Tokyo with the spyglass so you can explain what happened to the Japanese police. Did you know they have a nine-ty-nine percent conviction rate? It's true, look it up," Zambrano says. "Or if you want, you can stay here with me. And I'll show you how the fabled Spyglass of Spinoza actually works."

I look down at the silver spyglass, which is still held in the death grip I had on it for my entire escape. It gleams at me in the sunlight, practically sparkling with potential.

"She was kind of a jerk," I admit. "And she insulted my hat."

"Great," Zambrano says. "Come up to the roof, I'll show you what it can do."

CHAPTER 7

Getting to the roof is less magical than I expect it to be. It involves climbing through a large window and walking up a fire escape. It's a hassle, but a few minutes later Zambrano and I are standing on the rooftop, taking in the sights and sounds of a gritty industrial part of Queens. But it's not all warehouses and factories—a few blocks over, there's some green space . . . a graveyard! But it's a gorgeous day with a clear blue sky, and the early June weather is very pleasant—we haven't yet hit the first summer heat wave.

The crowd of different observers is still outside the warehouse, but the fake hotdog guy and repair crew seem to have retreated down the street, leaving the FBI taking up all the closest positions.

"Don't worry about them," Zambrano says, noticing me shrink back against the wall. "I've got an illusion barrier set up over the whole building." He gestures at a crystal pyramid that's right next to the air conditioning vent. Its surface reflects the sky and horizon but with a slight swirling appearance. "It's an illusion prism, which I've set to create a continuous illusion. It can maintain one particular illusion, even if I'm not directly connected to it. Outsiders just see an empty warehouse with no one in the windows, on the roof, or anywhere else. No matter what we do in here, from the outside it just looks completely uneventful. Which I find amusing, given how many people out there are carefully monitoring us.

Emboldened, I peer over the low wall at the edge of the roof. "They're just waiting out there, watching us?"

Zambrano shrugs. "It took them a couple years to figure out that this was my new hideout. They've learned from previous mistakes to keep their distance—they let me do my thing, I let them do theirs. But eventually, they'll probably start making pests of themselves and I'll have to move again—it's just such a headache."

I have to sympathize a bit. Moving sucks enough when you have to deal with a couch, a bed, and choosing which of the five different almost-empty shampoo bottles you actually want to bring with you. Doing it with a giant arcane library, a laboratory full of artifacts, and space-bending doors for receiving pizza deliveries sounds like a true nightmare.

"Oh, and check this out," he says, reaching down and touching the illusion prism. I can see colors swirling in it, and he stands up and begins twisting his hands as if conducting a chaotic symphony. A shadowy blob appears above us, and as he continues it solidifies into a pterodactyl. He casts his hands toward the street, and the illusory flying lizard swoops down, dive-bombing a couple of the government guys loitering on the street wearing subway worker outfits, despite there being no subway stations near here. As soon as it passes outside the magically hidden part of the roof, the guys go into a panic, diving to the ground and shouting. Then Zambrano throws his hands up and the pterodactyl disappears. They leap up, seeking cover farther back down the street and yelling to one another.

"Suckers!" Zambrano crows. "Illusion prisms can be set to hide things on their own or project one steady illusion, like an empty warehouse. But with a sorcerer actively connected to them, they can create illusions that look sort of real, at least from a distance or when moving fast. Illusions that look real upon closer inspection take a lot more time to craft, but it's a great party trick. Cool, huh?"

"Yeah," I say. "Yeah, that is pretty awesome. Magic is awesome. I think one of the professors at the Magicians Institute of Technomancy used something like that during my tour there, but it was nowhere near as impressive as that."

He looks at me for a long second, his face starting to form a smile. But then he shakes his head, returning to his usual gruff, annoyed look.

"Okay, enough showing off. Let's do what we came up here to do."

"Sure, so how do I do this?" I ask, holding up the silver Spyglass of Spinoza.

Zambrano takes the spyglass from me and shows me how to extend and compress it by simply pulling. As it telescopes longer and shorter, I hear a faint whirring sound, like the gears inside are spinning madly. "First, you can use it as a basic monocular. The longer you extend it, the higher the magnification. Here, use it to look at the top of the Empire State Building. Start with it short, then extend it to zoom in."

I take the spyglass, and sure enough, I can see the building closer and closer. It's way better than the zoom on my phone camera, and with a little practice adjusting it, pretty soon I can actually see the tiny figures of tourists on the upper observatory deck.

"Whoa, all right, that's pretty cool." I look around, checking out the whole scene. "What's with the dude with the glowing head?" I ask, peering closer. "Is that some kind of demon or something?"

"A demon? Let me take a look at it," he says, yanking the spyglass from me and pointing it toward the distant building. He laughs. "No, no, that's just a guy with an enchanted toupee. Looks pretty expensive, probably from that new artifactory in Monaco. Those assholes will enchant anything for cash."

"A magic wig?" I say. "Really?" The stupid things people will use magic for baffles me sometimes. It's basically just rich people trying to be fancy and impressive rather than anything actually useful.

"Going bald sucks." Zambrano shrugs and hands the spyglass back to me.

I glance at his perfectly coiffed white hair, and he glares at me and unconsciously lifts a hand to touch it. "This is all real, thank you very much. A wig with an illusion enchantment to make it look natural is bush league. I paid to look this good the hard way, with hundreds of hours of intricate biological spellcasting."

"Okay, okay," I say, backing off from his pique. "But the wig glows? What's the point of that?"

"Oh, no," Zambrano replies, chuckling. "That's the spyglass. When you look through it, it outlines any enchanted item or artifact with a glow."

I immediately turn the spyglass toward Zambrano and point it directly at his hair. Unfortunately, his entire body is covered in a sort of hazy, cloudy glowing.

"Easy there," he says. "I'm warded against that sort of thing. But try pointing it at the illusion prism."

I dutifully point it at the pyramid by the AC vent and can see that it's outlined in a strong blue glow along with motes of glowing light floating inside of it. The lights seem to illuminate the edges of mystic symbols etched into the sides of the pyramid. Next, I look across the rest of the roof. I can see a glow at the edge of the building walls and on several pipes poking out from the roof of the building. It also draws my attention to a handful of objects along the roof wall that I hadn't noticed before—gems that look similar to the one I saw at the front door when I arrived the day before.

"You're probably seeing the perimeter defenses," Zambrano says. "And those pipes are protected against chemical or biological attacks. I really wish whoever figured out I was here had shut up about it. Setting this up again somewhere else is going to suck."

I stay quiet, knowing that it was Parth and the other folks on WizardWatch who first put together all the clues that they'd been gathering for weeks. But there's no need to get them in trouble or let Zambrano know that I told Parth I'm here.

"How much danger are we in from that kind of attack?" I ask him, hoping to get him on a different topic.

Zambrano shrugs. "Most of the planet's power players, both magical and not, have learned not to provoke me. But the governments slowly cause inconveniences and annoy me for years until it becomes easier to just move to a new place rather than deal with them. Don't worry, you're not in too much danger, unless Vulkatherak decides to start triggering volcanoes and earthquakes, or sends his small force of demons here."

"How often does this happen?" I ask. "Big threats to the world?"

"Major-scale threats, like the Leviathan, or Seraphex, or the demon duke? Apocalpyse-level events?" Zambrano shrugs. "I don't know, once a century or so?"

"How is none of this in the history books?"

Zambrano sighs. "When someone discovers a threat to the whole world, and unites a small group of heroic sorcerers to stop it, why would anyone know that it happened? How can you prove an apocalypse that you prevented was ever actually a threat? Especially if you do it before it can kill millions of people?"

"Huh," I say. "So, saving the world is kind of a thankless job?"

"The better job you do, the less thanks you get," Zambrano answers with a humorless laugh.

"Anyway, I've got to get ready," he says. "I've got a date with this cute guy in Buenos Aires. If you want to, you can practice using the spyglass downstairs. You're going to need it to find the arcane conduit in Vulkatherak's penthouse. So get comfortable looking at things with it. Just, like, DON'T TOUCH ANYTHING. If it doesn't kill you, then I will."

I follow him downstairs, and he heads back to the room where I first met him. Before he disappears, he pokes his head back out. "And let's not have another idiotic bath-interrupting incident again, m'kay? There's a good intern."

I shake my head. "Don't worry, you and your bubble bath can play in private." I guess I'm willing to let him trap me in an apartment with an angry Japanese wizard, but I'm not going to let him call me an idiot without a little pushback.

He glares at me but shuts the door and disappears.

Smiling, I head to my room and take a minute to flop down on the bed and catch my breath. We've been going nonstop for hours. I take a minute to check my phone and see that Parth has replied to my message.

We blast a series of messages back and forth, with me trying to explain what's happening and him asking a thousand questions that I have no answers to. Finally, I realize we're being dumb and just press the video call button, and his face pops up on my phone.

"Dude, this is unbelievable!" he says. "Like, I wouldn't believe it if I hadn't heard rumors about Japanese government magicians doing a full sweep of several neighborhoods in the past hour."

"You have to keep this quiet," I say. "Just between the two of us."

"Ugh. Really? Seriously?" He rolls his eyes. "Fine. Of course."

"This is serious. Zambrano is not quite right. I think he's starting to like me a bit, but I don't know what he'll do if he thinks I'm spreading his secrets. Plus, I want to keep working for him. Interning for him, whatever. I want him to like me, so I have to treat him well."

"I get it, dude, don't worry about it." He purses his lips. "Are you safe there? Are you sure you shouldn't just get out of there? What if you get hurt?"

I sigh. "I'm fine. It seems like I've lost my chance to learn magic. Well, I never had it in the first place. But with Zambrano, I'm able to see and learn about it at the highest level. That's worth a little risk."

I can see him looking off-screen, thinking it over. "Have I tried hard enough to get you to be safe?" he asks. "Should I say it a couple more times? Or are we good? Because honestly it's getting tiring, and I have *so many* questions to ask you."

I laugh. That's Parth. He knows what he's supposed to say to be a good person, but he just can't help himself.

I try to explain everything that's happened so far and all the magic and artifacts that I've seen. We talk it back and forth for a while until he clearly can't keep his eyes open.

"I have to get some sleep," he says, "I've got class in just a few hours. Don't worry, all your secrets are safe with me."

After ending the call, I go downstairs and spend the next couple hours using the silver spyglass to examine various items on the ground floor. Through its lens, most of the objects glow in complex ways that I don't understand. But hey, pretty colors! And it feels like I'm learning something about magic even though I haven't the faintest idea what the glass sword, the golden telescope, the black pebble with white painting on it, or any of the rest of the items do.

Well, that's not exactly true. I suppose the sword probably cuts things. The telescope looks at something. I'm guessing it can't do what the spyglass does though, since otherwise we wouldn't have needed to steal it.

The pebble . . . just kind of sits on a cactus? But there's got to be more to it than that. Some artifacts are responsive to touching organic or inorganic matter, so my best guess is that the cactus is keeping the pebble in touch with something that's alive either to power it or hold it in place.

Pointing the spyglass at the bookshelves, I can see that most of them are normal books, but quite a few have a magical glow to them. I'll admit that I'm sorely tempted to pull those ones down and just give them a quick skim. Most of them don't even have titles that I can read on the spines, just glyphs or characters in Greek, Chinese, and other languages that I don't even recognize.

Eventually it starts to feel too much like hanging out at a candy shop without enough money to buy anything, and I head upstairs and order dinner through the tablet and door that shouldn't open onto the street. After the delivery guy hands over the bag of tacos, I step just outside the door and pull out my phone, leaving one foot on the other side to keep the door from shutting. The GPS in the maps app takes a few seconds to get its bearings, and when it does, it tells me that I'm a few blocks away. Peering down the block in the dusk, I think I can even make out the warehouse building that my other foot is theoretically inside.

Somehow, that hits harder than all the unknown magical objects downstairs or the illusion prism on the roof. Real, powerful magic that can bend space! Maybe it's mostly used to get food deliveries, but it's still a whole lot cooler than glowing animal statues or enchanted toupees.

I head back down to the first floor laboratory again and take a walk through the books, reading their titles and trying to guess what's in them. I don't know how to turn the lights on, but luckily the moon is full and casting bright light through the large warehouse windows, and I supplement it with my phone's flashlight to read the pages themselves.

I'm just about to call it a night and head to bed when I hear a quiet whooshing sound from the other side of the room by the artifacts and teleportraits.

I peer through the stacks and see Zambrano outlined in the moonlight. He doesn't have his usual perfect posture; instead, his shoulders are slumped. With a sigh, he walks over and puts two teleportraits back on the wall. He takes a few slow steps, then heavily drops into a chair at one of the tables covered in magical artifacts and gadgets that I can't pretend to understand.

He sits there for a long moment, slowly shaking his head. Then he looks up, scanning the moonlit room.

"I know you're there, Intern," he says. "Might as well come out."

Sheepishly, I walk out of the stacks and give him a smile.

"Date no good?"

Zambrano shrugs. "Nah, it was fine. Honestly, he was a great guy. Smart, attractive, funny."

"Going to see him again?" I can't resist prying a bit, and I get the sense he might need someone to talk to.

"Him? Oh, no," the sorcerer says, staring down at his shoes. I can tell from his voice and body language that he's been drinking, but he's not plastered or anything.

"What, you only like the dumb, ugly, boring kind?"

"No, I had a great time. It's just . . . he was too good. I can't see him again. He doesn't deserve to deal with my bullshit and my baggage. None of them do. I went out with this woman last month in London; it was the same thing. As soon as I start liking someone, I realize they shouldn't be involved with me."

This is a completely different Zambrano than I've seen so far, suddenly no longer perfectly poised and arrogant.

"Shouldn't they be the ones to make that choice?" I say, parroting what I feel like is the nice thing you're supposed to say. I want to say *That sounds like typical narcissistic avoidant behavior* or *Are you protecting them or protecting yourself?* but everything I know about psychology I learned from watching fifteen-second viral videos on my phone, so I don't really feel qualified to diagnose a sorcerer who's hundreds of years old.

He shrugs. "Better to just get out early before they get too attached," he says. "Easier for everyone that way."

He looks at me almost as if he just realized I'm there, though we've been talking for the past minute. "Why are you here?" he asks.

"Oh, I was just about to go to bed," I answer. "I was just looking at the books and artifacts. Without touching, I promise!"

He smiles slightly at that. "No, I don't mean why are you in this room. I mean why are you here with me, being my intern. What made you come here, really?"

"I . . . I don't really know," I say. I sit down at the table across from him, trying to think about it. "I ran out of options applying to magic grad schools, and this was the last and best— and only—option."

"Certainly, I understand that," Zambrano says. "But why magic? Why waste your life in a smoothie shop trying to apply to magic schools? Why venture uninvited into a place full of magical traps? It was only your peculiar . . . condition . . . that let you make it in."

"Why magic?" I sit silently for a minute, pondering that. It's been such a constant ambition in my life for so long, it's hard to remember how it all started. "I'm not sure," I say. "I've just always been fascinated by it. It's the most mysterious part of life. We may not have a perfect understanding of physics or chemistry or biology, but we can trace the past and future of the universe, and we understand so much of it. There's more to go, but it's all details. But magic? Spells? Demons? It's the last great mystery. I don't know, I've just always been drawn to it. I kind of never saw the point in learning about anything else, in learning how to do anything else. But I realize now, I somehow didn't notice that I was never able to do any of it. I just figured I needed real professional training to get started."

Zambrano nods in recognition. "It's a tough break, Intern. Honestly, I wish I could teach you a little magic."

"But you can't," I finish for him. I feel frustration rising in me. "And so here I am. I spent my whole life pursuing something I can't have. I just couldn't ever imagine doing anything else once I got the fascination of magic."

Zambrano smiles sadly. "I was the same way, you know. Back in the sixteenth century, running away from home and the family farm, desperate to learn magic and mostly finding fakes and charlatans. I had to have it."

"And you got it," I say with a mix of sympathy and regret.

"I did," he says. "For everything else that's happened, I've gotten to play with magic, with its power and joy."

He looks around the warehouse laboratory, with the moonlight streaming through the windows. "*Sidera noctis aestatis,*" he says with an elegant open-palmed gesture at the ceiling, and the room is bathed in soft starlight as little spots of light float through the air and galaxies twist and spin on the walls.

"What's that spell?" I ask, looking around in wonder at the elaborate twinkling lights turning the room into a better show than any planetarium I've ever seen.

"It's the oldest known spell that was created purely for artistic reasons," he says. "It doesn't blast anything or move anything or grow anything. And there are much easier ways to create light. No one even knows who created it—some sorcerer of ancient Rome. These days, any wizard can use an illusion prism to create effects close to this, so no one really learns it. But it's not quite as good, and I really enjoy the simplicity of a spell that serves one simple purpose, just the beauty of magic and light."

We both take a moment to revel in the feeling as the motes of light twist through the air in blues, whites, oranges, and reds, blending into a symphony of starlight.

Finally, the spell comes to its conclusion and the lights fade out. Zambrano stands up. "You know, I actually wish I could teach you magic," he says. "That could be fun. Sorry you can't learn it, Bryce. I really am." He gives my shoulder a pat and crosses the room and heads up the stairs, leaving me alone in the moonlight.

I sit for a few minutes, sad and happy at the same time. Then I stand up and catch a glimpse of myself in a mirror hanging on the end of one of the bookshelves, with that stupid intern hat on.

We may have had a touching moment, but Zambrano is still an arrogant jerk.

CHAPTER 8

The next morning, I wake up early, shower, and look around the warehouse for Zambrano. He's nowhere to be found in the parts of the warehouse I know, and I figure snooping around his room or the locked doors isn't such a good idea. I do, however, find Seraphex sitting primly in a square of morning light coming from one of the big windows on the first floor.

"I, uh, guess I have to go to work," I say to her. It feels weird to be telling a duck that I have to go to my job at a smoothie shop. I mean, it feels weird to talk to a duck, period, but somehow talking about normal life feels even weirder than talking to her about enchantments or magic delivery doors.

"Have fun, or whatever it is that happens at 'work,'" she answers. "Can't say I'm very familiar with it."

Shrugging, I grab my things. "I guess I should grab some clothes and other things. Um, should I come back tonight? Tomorrow? Does a sorcerer's intern have, like, set hours?"

Seraphex cocks her head to the side. "I'm a demon queen, Bryce, I'm not human resources." She turns and waddles away.

Not knowing what else to do, I head out through the delivery door. I'm not sure what I expected being the intern of a dark sorcerer to be like, but it certainly isn't . . . whatever this is.

As I take the various buses, subways, and trains back to New Jersey, I glumly ponder what to do when I arrive. Should I give my notice? Quit on the spot? Just keep working? This internship thing doesn't feel that secure. And while it does come with free room and delivery food, I haven't quite got up the nerve to ask for a stipend. I wonder what else I can order with that tablet . . . You can get anything delivered these days. Could I order some clothes from Target? The newest iPhone with the scent identifier? A couch from IKEA?

Also, how am I going to go to work with this stupid intern hat magically stuck on my head? I don't remember the specifics, but I'm pretty certain that it does not live up to the Samba Smoothies corporate dress code.

I'm not getting any closer to a plan by the time I arrive at the mall, and I get a sudden sense of dread. That's not a surprise. Every day showing up to work at Samba Smoothies causes that feeling. But this time, it's accompanied by seeing something odd at the shop. There's a couple there who just look out of place.

Well, if you ask me, anyone is out of place in a Samba Smoothies because it's a terrible corporate hellhole that no one should ever be in. But these two aren't talking. They're just holding empty smoothie bottles, standing by the glass wall, and scanning the area. I drop my head, hoping that my hat will hide my identity.

My phone buzzes, and I pull it out as I turn around, awkwardly bumping into a tall, skinny white woman with a craggy face.

"Uh, sorry," I say. I slink to the side and around the corner, and unlock my phone.

The message is from Carla. *Hi Bryce!! Some friends of yours are here asking for you!* it says. *I told them you'd be in soon! Don't be late, it's going to be a fun day!!!*

Oh, shit. For once her generous serving of exclamation points isn't the worst thing about the message. How did I not realize that my incident in Japan would cause trouble back here? Professor Okamoto had identified me.

Was I about to be arrested and extradited to Japan? Would Zambrano help me if I was? That seemed . . . like a long shot.

I shake my head and start walking back the way I came. I need to get somewhere safe and think this through.

But as I'm striding along, I notice that someone is next to me.

"Where are we headed, Bryce?" the craggy tall woman who I bumped into earlier asks, calmly matching pace with me. "Somewhere with coffee? Maybe a slice of pie? I could use some pie."

I stare ahead and keep walking, as if ignoring her will make her disappear. Out of the corner of my eye, I can see that she's wearing a suit with no tie. I glance down again and notice as her jacket flaps that there's something on a strap holstered there. I gulp.

"I suppose this slice of pie isn't exactly optional, is it?" I ask. We're near the exit to the mall now, getting close to the Apple Pie Workshop that's the last store before the doors.

"In a sense, it is," the woman says, as if mulling the idea over for the first time. "If you keep walking through those doors, the FBI agents outside will arrest you. You could also run back to Samba Smoothies, but you already saw the poorly disguised agents there. Or, I suppose you could duck into Sofa, Shower, and So Much More and hide under one of the beds or something and hope the FBI are really bad at hide-and-seek. Though that's a pretty major part of their jobs." I glance over again and see her smiling tightly. "Or you could step into this lovely Apple Pie Workshop and have a slice with me. Personally, I'm particularly fond of the caramel. Don't worry, the United States government is paying for it."

I pause for a moment, and we both stand there. Is there another option? I seem to have really walked into a trap here. I shrug and turn into the restaurant.

"Booth for two," the woman tells the host, and a moment later I'm sitting across from her, staring at her sharp face.

"Bryce Alexander," the woman says with an admonishing tone. "What have you gotten yourself into here?"

The server approaches, and the woman turns to her before she can even introduce herself.

"Two coffees, black, and two slices of caramel apple pie," she says. "You'll love it, believe me," she adds, to me.

I guess she's trying to show her power and dominance by ordering for me, like some kind of bizarre business or mating ritual. But the joke's on her—I'm perfectly happy to absolutely murder this slice of pie. I mean, I'm totally terrified and I ate before I came. But screw you, government woman, I'm going to eat this whole damn thing.

"So are you FBI too?" I ask. "Am I under arrest? Am I being detained?"

She sighs, shaking her head sadly. "Ah, so is that how it's going to be?"

Look, I've watched those videos on YouTube. I know the deal. You don't talk to the cops. It's just never a good idea. They don't have to tell you that you're a suspect, and they're allowed to lie to you. Just clam up, wait it out, and call your lawyer if you have to.

I don't actually have a lawyer. Who has a lawyer? I mean, my parents have a guy who did their wills and a woman who drew up my adoption papers and all that. But somehow I don't think that guy could help with this being arrested for stealing valuable magic artifacts.

I shrug. The server brings our coffee, and I turn to her, glancing at her name tag. "Hi, Julia," I say. "Thanks. Could I actually have some sugar and milk for mine?"

"Of course," she says and grabs them for me as we sit in silence.

The craggy woman scowls, and I calmly make my coffee the way I like it and take a nice long sip.

"Okay, Bryce," the woman finally says. "You don't want to talk to me. That's fine. How about I just tell you what I have to say, and you just listen? And then you can decide what you want to do."

"Sure," I say, trying to sound nonchalant. Of course, internally I'm completely freaking out. I am definitely going to jail. And I still won't be able to get this hat off my head. That's going to be . . . awkward during prisoner intake.

"To start, I'm not one of those meatheads with the FBI. They can posture all they want, but this case involves a known user of banned magic, so ultimately it's in my jurisdiction. If I tell them to, the FBI will back off. I'm Agent Angelica Crane, Magical Security Agency."

I take a deep breath. The MSA is serious business. They are not known for messing around. Or for being particularly careful around pesky "constitutional rights." My understanding is that, given that they sometimes have to deal with very odd magical crimes, they are given a bit more leeway in what methods they are allowed to use.

"So here's what we know. You were seen entering what we believe to be the home of an individual known as Zambrano, a well-known 'dark sorcerer' who is a frequent and flagrant repeat user of internationally banned magic. And then, last night, you broke into the home of a high-ranking United Nations official and stole a priceless magical artifact. The driver of a rideshare service gave my colleagues in the Japan National Police Agency a positive ID for both you and Mr. Zambrano as riding directly to the apartment building where the theft was committed."

I try to keep my face neutral while absolute panic explodes in my brain. How did I think I would get away with this? Of course Zambrano will be fine; he's a powerful dark sorcerer. But me? They can lock me away, and I doubt my "dark sorcerer" sponsor will even lift a finger to help.

But I shove all those thoughts away. I'm going to fight this.

"Hold on," I say, not able to help myself. "You're saying that I committed a crime in Japan last night and somehow flew back to the US in time to show up for my job at a Samba Smoothies?"

Agent Crane gives a tight smile. "I know that your university education may have said that teleportation is almost impossible, but the MSA understands that Zambrano has some means of rapid global transit." She holds her phone out, showing what appears to be security camera footage of me and Zambrano getting out of the car at Professor Okamoto's apartment building. "That sure looks like you, doesn't it?"

I sit back, silently fuming. I'm not sure if I'm mad at Zambrano for exposing me or myself for coming in to work, but either way it seems like I am royally screwed. I guess it's back to Plan Don't Talk to the Cops.

She notes my reticence and shrugs.

"You are the"—she glances at the hat on my head—"new 'intern' of a dark sorcerer. In the forty-eight hours since you began that dubious occupation, you've already stolen a precious magical artifact and, I assume, transported it across national borders. Your actions violate the laws of Japan, the United States, and numerous international treaties."

I sit quietly. The pie arrives. Shrugging, I take another sip of coffee and grab my fork. At this point, every moment that I'm not in handcuffs seems like a gift. I can barely taste it with the adrenaline racing through my veins, but if I'm headed to jail, I'm going to try to enjoy this goddamn apple pie first.

Agent Crane takes a few bites of hers, taking her time and enjoying it.

"Look, Bryce," she says. "The FBI figures they have you dead to rights. They want to toss you in jail and be done with it. In past decades, experience has shown that Zambrano will not make a move if you are incarcerated in a high-security magical prison. He's a criminal who only attacks targets of opportunity and runs away from direct confrontation."

Typical Zambrano, it seems like. Or is it? I have a gut feeling that there's more to him than this. More than some heartless opportunist. And some part of me thinks that he might actually be enjoying having an intern, someone to explain things to.

I take another bite, desperately trying to focus on enjoying what may be my last meal before I'm locked away.

"I imagine that you're wondering," she says, "why we don't just bust into that warehouse and arrest Mr. Zambrano himself. Unfortunately, the United States government has determined that attempting to detain Mr. Zambrano in a populated city could result in significant collateral damage. While he is wanted in every industrialized nation for repeated violations of the Prague Convention and a laundry list of crimes of death and destruction, currently we believe that direct confrontation could lead to unacceptable casualties. No one wants to be the agent who ordered a raid that resulted in half of Queens getting blown up."

I'm already running out of apple pie, which suddenly feels like a major tragedy.

"So here's my thinking. We've done our research on you. We understand that you have been attempting to learn magic, and you're probably getting to do that right now. Honestly, I'm happy for you."

I guess she doesn't know that I'm some sort of non-magical freak without a soul, but I'm certainly not going to break my silence to enlighten her.

"It's vital for national security for the MSA to know what Mr. Zambrano is doing," Agent Crane says. "You seem to have gotten access to him that our undercover agents have utterly failed to achieve. Any insights you can provide would be received by a grateful government. In exchange for your cooperation, we are willing to provide legal immunity, and, if necessary, protection and relocation."

I breathe a slow sigh. No jail sounds great. Being a double agent against a legendary sorcerer seems . . . stressful. Okay, terrifying. Stupid. A death wish.

Agent Crane shows me a small metal orb with intricate runes inscribed on it. "You've probably felt that buzzing in the air. This artifact has ensured that our conversation is private."

I haven't felt any such buzzing, but I guess that's just due to my 'condition.'

I nod. I'm not sure what to do right now, but it seems like the path of least resistance.

"I'm not expecting you to make a decision or commitment right now," Agent Crane says. "But here's what I can do for you. First, I'll call off the FBI and make sure they leave you alone. They're way too excited to get their hands on you, and I won't mind asserting my jurisdiction so those meatheads have to go home empty-handed. Next, I'll speak to your employer and make sure that they continue to pay you on, let's say, indefinite workers' compensation. For someone as terminally foolhardy as you seem to be, that's not so surprising," she says with a chuckle that I don't share. "In any event, if you believe that you have information about Zambrano that is important for me to know, buy a round-trip ticket on a New Jersey Transit train to visit your parents. I'll meet you on the way back and provide what assistance I can."

I look her in the eyes and give a slight nod. I'm not willing to really commit, not in some verbal way. She may say that Zambrano isn't watching, but how do I know what that dark sorcerer can and can't do?

Agent Crane smiles, her deep-set eyes gleaming with grim satisfaction. "You're a good kid, Bryce. I know you want to learn magic, but I trust that you won't let that get in the way of doing your duty to your country and the world. And Zambrano has the power to be a threat not just to this city or the United States, but to the whole world. I'm depending on you—if he's doing something that endangers this nation, you have to let me know."

My plate and cup are both empty. I take a deep breath. I don't like Agent Crane and her dramatic posturing, but she does seem like she's at least trying to be one of the good guys.

"Zambrano says that the real threat right now is a demon," I say. "I heard the demon's voice. He's actually . . . trying to stop it."

Agent Crane shrugs. "Demon this, demon that. It's always his excuse. He shows up somewhere, blasts a hole in the earth or sinks a museum into a swamp, and claims 'demons did it.' The MSA has not found evidence of any confirmed demonic activity since the 1980s. And never forget that Zambrano can manipulate light and sound. If he wants you to hear a voice, you'll hear a voice."

I nod. I'm not sure what to believe. But at least I'm not going to jail. And I get to keep learning about magic.

"Very good," Agent Crane says. "I'll be in touch. And, Bryce . . . don't screw me. Don't screw your country. Don't screw humanity. Don't screw yourself." She smiles, suddenly pleasant. "Have a good day. That was a good slice of apple pie, huh?"

I stand up and walk like a zombie out of the mall.

I'm totally on the edge of panic but still, despite everything, excited. I get to learn about magic! I won't be going to jail or a secret government detention facility! Both pretty solid wins, I'd say.

On my way out, I don't see a single FBI agent—they've all melted away without a trace. As I walk out into the mall parking lot, I take a moment to look back. Alive or dead, rotting in jail or incinerated by a magical fireball, hopefully I never have to set foot in Samba Smoothies or the Jersey City Galleria ever again.

It's the little wins that keep me going, you know?

CHAPTER 9

With work out of the picture, I spend the rest of the day back at my apartment, emptying out my fridge and packing up a bag of things to take to Zambrano's warehouse. I'm not sure how long I'll be staying there, but I don't want to be making the trip back out here just because I need my spare glasses or fresh socks.

I'll admit I also spend some time lying in bed, scrolling through arcanology threads on social media and catching up on WizardWatch. After that I head to the more traditional news sites, where I check for any mentions of my misadventures in Japan, but the news is crowded with all that junk about the colony ship that Lukas Volker is sending to Mars. Apparently, he quickly built his space company from scratch, and in the course of a few years passed all the other rich guys trying to do it. But who cares about space stuff when there's magic to learn about? I skip past all the tech articles, looking for the latest in magic.

In the magic news section deeper in the news app, they're all talking about some new study from South African researchers that claims some popular magic spells are becoming more powerful while old ones are weaker than they were decades ago. Fascinating stuff, but I'm mostly relieved that no one is talking about me, and the Zambrano fervor seems to have cooled off to bored speculation.

I also take some time to update Parth on what's happening. I figure there's a good chance the MSA is watching the messages, so I leave them out of it for now. Luckily, he's actually awake and available at the same time I am, and he gives me a call. It's comforting to see his face pop up on my phone, even though he's on the other side of the world.

"Dude, this is crazy!" he says. "I have to go to dinner in a second, but I am so proud of you! Intern for a real sorcerer! That is amazing, my friend! That's a . . . pretty dope hat you got too."

"Yeah," I say, angling the phone down so that most of the hat is cropped out of the picture. "I have to admit, I'm feeling a bit less of the unbridled enthusiasm and a bit more of the mortal danger over here."

Parth nods, and I can tell he's trying to contain his smile, but he's still grinning like a maniac. "Still, the access that you have! The history Zambrano must know! Even if you can't learn magic, maybe you can figure out how to move magic forward. If you can't be a magician or a wizard, maybe you can be the greatest arcanologist of all time. Bring the mysteries of the sorcerers to the rest of us."

"Like, why are there no other sorcerers left?" I ask.

"Yeah, sure," he says. "Though I guess ultimately we know that they all died in various ways. But I mean, the big ones. I'm more interested in how to discover new spells! They say Merlin and Abe no Seimei each discovered hundreds, and even Rasputin figured out over a dozen novel spells. Now, the researchers finding a new one every decade or so win a Nobel Prize in arcanology."

"Yeah, definitely," I agree. Parth has always been more the lore and history guy; I mostly just wanted to learn how to levitate and shoot lightning. But he's right, if I could figure out some of Zambrano's tricks, I could advance magic for everyone else. I frown though. Because I still won't be able to actually do any magic myself.

"Like, why are so many spellcasting words Latin, or Greek, or ancient Korean or Sanskrit? Why those languages? No one has a good answer for that. I've got to go or I'll miss the train," Parth says. "But stay safe, and let me know what you learn!"

I head back to Zambrano's warehouse ready to ask some pointed questions, but when I walk in he's sitting at a table covered in open books, looking through several at once. His fingers are flying, and his eyes are flitting across pages at what looks like a rate that even people who take those speed-reading courses couldn't approach.

Zambrano looks up at me. "Oh, you're here. I'm not ready for our trip yet. What do you want?"

"Trip? Where are we going?"

"Peru," he says with no further elaboration.

Shrugging aside his rudeness, I just blurt out the question. "How does magic work?"

He shrugs. "You say the right words, make the right motions, and it happens. Or create the item you're enchanting into the exact right shape and with the correct materials. There are also potions, but frankly, I try to avoid messing with those. That's witch stuff."

I sigh. "I'm not a total idiot. I mean, *why* does it work? Why those words? Why those shapes?"

"Ah," he says, nodding. "It's complicated."

"Okay," I say, tapping the hat that is still magically stuck to my head. "Explain it to me."

"Ugggghh." He shakes his head. "Tell you what, come on this little trip with me, do me a solid and help me get somewhere I can't, and I'll try to explain hundreds of years of knowledge in a simple enough way that you can handle," he says, but it's with a friendly smirk.

"Okay, you've got a deal," I say.

"Give me a couple hours and then we'll head out."

"Sure," I answer.

I spend the time unpacking my things and setting up my room. For someone who's spent the last six years in tiny New York City and Jersey City apartments, it's honestly pretty nice. And the little birch butlers clean things up every day, which makes it basically like living in a hotel. I dig it.

"The time for our journey has arrived," Seraphex says from the door in her regal tones. "Prepare to venture into the unknown!" Her tone makes it sound like she's mocking me, but I decide not to pick a fight with a demon over that, no matter what shape she's in.

She leads me downstairs where Zambrano is waiting in front of the landscape wall. He's dressed in what looks like a parody of a rich-guy safari outfit, complete with gloves, boots, and hat. Of course, he still kind of looks like a movie star.

Meanwhile, I wore jeans and a sweatshirt because I had no idea where we were going or what we were doing. I did at least wear sneakers because, based on how things have gone so far, it seems like I'll have to run away from something.

"Where are we going?" I ask, walking up and looking at the landscape painting on the wall.

"We have another job to do. Well, let's call it a quest—does that make it seem more fun? It's time for another quest. It's in Peru, like I said!" he says, pointing at a teleportrait that looks like your coworker's vacation photos from Machu Picchu that he's forcing everyone in the whole place to look at.

Without asking permission, Seraphex hops over and plops onto my foot.

"You did *not* say," I begin objecting, but he grabs the back of my neck, and I start to feel that weird distortion and distance. A moment later we're standing there, a few levels up on an ancient ruin in Peru. Seraphex hops off my foot and starts pecking at something on the ground.

The view from up here is gorgeous. The ruins that we're on are fairly modest, nothing like the grand citadels of Tikal or Chichén Itzá. But we're on a hill with ancient terraces evening out the height of the hills, and lush Amazon rainforest stretches out around us, a living green organism draped over the landscape. But there's a big difference from what I saw in the painting—in the valley to our right, a big swath of the rainforest has been clear-cut, leaving nothing but a large patch of brown desolation.

"Wow," Zambrano says, eyeing the destruction. "I guess I'm going to have to redo that teleportrait soon. If they cut down too much more of the forest, the teleportrait image will be too inaccurate and will stop working."

I take a moment to take in the view, then look down at the crumbling stone ruins below us.

"Hold on," I say. "We're not going to steal stuff from the ruins, are we? I really don't want to rob some Incan person's grave or take historical artifacts that belong in Peru. That's not cool."

"Well," Zambrano says, "the good news is that, no, we're not going to desecrate these ancient Incan ruins. I'm not totally insensitive. We're actually going to steal from Vulkatherak, the demon duke. One of his cronies owns a series of shell companies that control the logging conglomerate that's illegally cutting down all those trees you see there. Or rather, don't see." He gestures at the clear-cut area down in the valley. "Think of it as helping save the rainforest!"

"Oh, okay," I say, pleasantly surprised. "Great!"

"The bad news is, his headquarters is a three-hour hike from here, and we can't use magic to go faster. Even at this distance, his hire-a-magicians could detect magic as powerful as teleportation or any sort of flight. And then they'll try to kill us, and I'll have to kill them, and then more of them will come, and it will be a whole thing." He swings down off this section of the ruins and starts walking.

"You couldn't have told me to bring hiking boots, or a water bottle, or anything?" I ask, following along.

Zambrano just ignores me and instead pulls out a map, checks a few things, then puts it back and keeps going.

"Is this what we're going to be doing? Just robbing people?" I ask, hustling to keep up.

"Isn't it fun?" Zambrano says with a grin. "I've been wanting to mess with this dickwad for *years*, but he's obsessive about security."

We take a few minutes to get down off the ruins and start into the rainforest.

After we reach the trees, Seraphex flutters down and then lands on my shoulder, balancing herself comfortably there. I ignore her, and before long my sneakers are soaked and my sweatshirt is torn and stained from the mud and branches, but I'm gamely hiking on.

"Okay," I say, catching up to Zambrano after having taken some time to think about what I want to ask. Parth asked some really good questions that I had never thought of before. To be honest, I'd always just wanted to be able to do magic. "Like, a baseball pitcher can learn how to throw a curveball without ever thinking about gravity or air resistance or parabolas or any of that. It looks impossible, but I took high school physics, so I have a general sense of how it works. Or at least, I can look up a video on YouTube and see how spin affects the air or whatever. It makes sense."

"Sure, the human ability to perform very tricky actions is very impressive," Zambrano says.

"It's amazing what you humans can do without understanding at all what you're doing, just on instinct," Seraphex adds. "You're clever little beasts, able to learn how to sail ships and carve statues and juggle, all without really knowing how anything works on a deeper level.

Ignoring her, I plow on. "But the things you do to make magical spells don't make sense. Magic is just, like, random words and motions. Sometimes they make sense and seem connected with what the spell or item does. It's super, super cool. But overall, it just doesn't make any *sense*. Why that specific motion or words for a spell? Or why that particular object to be that type of enchanted item?"

"Whoa there, okay," Zambrano says. "Asking the big questions, are we? Okay, let's start with the basics. There are four main types of human magic users, right?"

"Uh, I know the three types, I guess," I answer, ignoring my squishy shoes and the mosquitos that are starting to find and follow us. "Magicians can cast spells and enchant objects. Wizards are more powerful and can also modify spells and enchantments to improve or change them. And dark sorcerers use forbidden magic banned by the Prague Convention."

"Hah! They've really sold that 'forbidden magic' line, huh?" Zambrano says with a laugh, pushing a branch out of the way and thoughtlessly letting it swing back and almost hit me. Typical. "The 'dark' part is something they just made up to make us sound bad. Or to describe those who've lost their sanity to the magic. But I'm . . . let's just say I'm still rational, and let's not think too hard about it. Sorcerers are the most powerful magic users—we know how to properly create brand-new spells and enchantments. The teleportation one I use these days is a new and improved one I created only a few years ago. No one else can get even close to matching it."

"You never pass up a chance to marvel at your own incredible skills, do you?" Seraphex says with what I can only assume is an eye roll.

"Wait. *Create* spells?" I ask. "I thought all the spells existed, and we were just discovering them and modifying them. Hold on. Is that why they're all in different languages?"

Zambrano shrugs. "That's pretty much it. The spell is usually in the language of the person who creates it. Some people use a sort of fakey Latin-like made-up nonsense, but those spells annoy me. I did create this one in Swedish just because it's such a goofy language. *Hoppa högt!*" he says in a silly voice and leaps through the air, hopping up a steep bit of a hill in one easy jump. Don't worry, a little spell like this won't set off any alarms."

"Nice," I say as I trudge my way up the incline in the old-fashioned way.

"Over the centuries, we've lost the names and stories of many early sorcerers, as records have been destroyed. It didn't help when Julius Caesar torched the Library of Alexandria with fireballs. But their spells live on, passed down through generations of wizards and mages. For instance—*Merisis*!" He gestures in a flowery motion with his right hand and touches the leaf of a tree. The leaf suddenly starts growing, and a fan of other leaves blossoms out from the branch. "That's an ancient Greek spell, probably created by one of the Pythagoreans."

"Awesome," I whisper. Any demonstrations of biological magic that I've ever seen require intense concentration and have fairly slow results. Zambrano does it so effortlessly. I do notice, glancing back as we walk on, that the leaves start wilting and falling off as if they've grown so far they popped right off.

"Here's another fun one," he says. "It's a Sanskrit word that means 'binding.' *Bandha*," he says and claps his hands a single time, then taps my right hand.

"Right," I say. "One of my classes had a whole section on how the earliest evidence of magic use comes from the Indus Valley."

I don't feel anything from the spell, but that's normal now, I guess. I see him glancing back at me, looking at my forehead like there's something on it. I instinctively put my hand to my head to check that it doesn't have a jungle spider or bird poop or something on it . . . and my palm sticks to my forehead. Without thinking, I try to grab my arm with my other hand and pull it back, but the other hand sticks to the arm.

Zambrano, laughing, keeps walking. I follow along, arms stuck up in the air and pulling at my forehead in a really annoying way. "Um, very impressive," I say. Because it is. Why can't I do that sort of thing? What a dumb, unfair world. "Shouldn't I be immune to this? Because magic doesn't detect me, or whatever?"

Zambrano shrugs. "It's a spell that makes whatever I touch stick to the next thing it comes into contact with; it's not keyed in on a human soul or body pattern or something. To magic, you're just a skinny collection of atoms, and it's more than happy to stick you to yourself. It's a pretty cool spell once you get the hang of the Sanskrit pronunciation."

"Oh, I'm so very impressed," I say, rolling my eyes. "I . . . bet you're not powerful enough to undo it, are you?"

"Nice try," he says with a hint of a chuckle. "Very cute. But okay, okay," he adds, and claps his hands a second time with a sort of opening gesture, and my limbs are freed. "We do have a job to complete here."

I follow along for a few minutes in annoyed silence. Finally, my curiosity gets the best of me.

"Okay, okay," I say, swatting away bugs even as I glance back to admire a beautiful view of the mountain we're leaving behind. "But you said there are four types of magic users. Is there an even more powerful one than sorcerers?"

"More powerful? Of course not!" Zambrano scoffs. "The other one is witches. They're just . . . frustrating and dangerous."

"What about demons?" Seraphex asks indignantly. "Don't we count? Aren't we also frustrating and dangerous too?"

"I said *human* magic users. And demonic magic is . . . a whole other thing, different, with more fixed rules. Your power comes from your magical nature not from your skillful manipulation of the rules magic."

"Yeah, better rules that make sense," Seraphex says, pouting from my shoulder. "It doesn't have any of these random spells that were named by ancient Greeks who would drown a guy for revealing the dark secret of the square root of two. Demon magic is way better. Just let me out of this duck body, and I can give a quick demonstration . . ."

"Hah!" Zambrano shoots back. "Fat chance. And the Pythagoreans advanced math, music, and magic tremendously . . ."

Zambrano and Seraphex proceed to argue about whether the Pythagoreans were cool, most of which is in shorthand historical references that I can't really follow. All I really take away is that the ancient Greeks took numbers way too seriously, the way British soccer hooligans will start a riot over a bad call by the refs.

I'm almost relieved when we come to the edge of the rainforest, where the clear-cut devastation begins.

"Okay, enough chatter," Zambrano says. He reaches into his safari vest and pulls out a small object covered in black felt. He pulls the cover off, and a small prism glints in the light.

"An illusion prism?" I ask. It looks like a miniature version of the one on the roof of the warehouse.

"This will hide us as we approach. But we'll have to avoid using active magic spells, move slowly, and speak softly."

I shrug. "You're the one who was just yelling about a Greek guy who was drowned over a thousand years ago."

"I could literally turn you into a squirrel," Zambrano says. "I learned that trick from traditional Scottish druids."

"That transmogrification never lasts more than an hour," Seraphex says. "We'd be stuck with him again before long."

"If I don't have a soul, why would hurting me even matter?" I say, glaring at him. "Without a soul, how could you even take satisfaction in my suffering? Am I even conscious?" I certainly feel conscious. I can't prove it to anyone else, but I think I have a pretty real internal monologue, and isn't that the only real proof a person can have?

"Touché," Zambrano answers, giving a rare chuckle and clapping me on the shoulder. He holds the prism out and starts leading the way through the desolate landscape. "Okay, Mr. Intern, I'll explain just how we're going to use your lack of a soul to steal from the asshole who cut down all these trees."

"All part of our quest to save millions of lives," I add.

"Yes, of course, but also to really piss off the arrogant demon duke, and it is so satisfying to see Vulkatherak angry. So everybody wins, really."

CHAPTER 10

Two hours later, I'm hiding in the brush next to the river, watching Seraphex happily float in the water nearby.

My nice new sneakers are ruined by hours of trudging through mud and over rocks, but that's not such a big deal because I'm going to be leaving them behind to swim out to the building downstream, which isn't next to the river like I thought but actually floating on it.

Despite the important mission and mortal danger ahead, my mind is choosing to focus on how wrong it feels to ditch my sneakers here, which feels like littering. Probably because it is, in fact, littering. I guess that's keeping my mind from focusing on the plan, which involves stealing from a houseboat guarded by Peruvian security magicians.

We've been waiting for an hour and a half after Zambrano used an illusion prism to escort us here. The sun is nearly down, which means it's almost time for us to start. He's gone off to create the tempting magical distraction that will hopefully draw the security mages away from their boat.

"You have to always tell the truth, right?" I whisper to Seraphex.

"Correct," Seraphex answers, paddling around in a little circle in our shielded area at the edge of the river. "We've gone over this already. I can't lie, and I can't break an agreement that I've made."

"So, like, is there a god?" I ask. I mean, if you're going to ask questions of an ancient demon, you might as well go for the big ones, right?

"Everyone I've met who's claimed to be god has been lying or hallucinating," Seraphex says, with what I've come to recognize as a duck's shrugging motion. "But it doesn't work like that—you can't use me as some sort of oracle of truth. I just can't say anything that I know to be false, but I can be mistaken or misinformed. Not, mind you, that I am mistaken very often."

"Oh," I say, disappointed. "I guess that makes sense."

"Zambrano, on the other hand, is wrong quite frequently," she adds smugly. "And also a rather habitual liar."

"I'll consider myself warned," I say. It's a weird position to be in, to know that I can believe everything she says, but I still definitely can't *trust* her since she's a demon.

A few minutes later, I can see that the sun has disappeared below the mountains, and I check my phone and the pocketknife Zambrano gave me. It's go time.

I put the phone in my pocket and quietly slip into the water. I sure hope my phone is as "water resistant" as the ads said it would be. Swimming in jeans sucks, but at least nothing is going to slip out of the clingy soaked denim pockets. I start with a sidestroke through the water, and the goofy hat on my head is immediately soaked and flopping down over my eyes. And yet every time I toss it off, as soon as I stop paying attention, start swimming, and dipping my head through the water, it somehow reappears.

I try holding one hand on my head as I swim, and this time, the hat doesn't come back. But the moment I take my hand away, start moving, and stop paying attention, it reappears. Eventually, I just accept a soggy mess in the way of my vision.

But despite that, I'm able to navigate my way, quietly swimming up to what I can only describe as a giant wooden houseboat floating on what Zambrano told me was the Urubamba River. While I'm struggling in the water, Seraphex easily floats along next to me as happy as . . . well, as happy as a duck in water.

The current is running fairly rapidly, so from my starting position upstream of the houseboat, it's largely a matter of waiting for the current to pull me close to the boat and then swimming hard to get out of the current and grabbing on to it as I pass by. Seraphex peels off, keeping her distance from the boat and watching, ready to create an additional diversion if needed.

Soon the houseboat looms large above me—it's two stories tall and reminds me of a ramshackle seafood restaurant I went to in some seaside town on the north shore of Long Island. Before long I'm up against it, awkwardly pulling myself along the slippery wooden hull to reach the rear of the boat, where I can see in the dim starlight the outline of the mooring ropes and gangplank that attach the boat to a tree on the shore. On the deck of the boat, I can see a small lantern and hear bored-sounding voices speaking Spanish in soft tones.

This is stupid. This is just plain dumb. What the hell am I doing here?! Those voices up there are security magicians, trained experts in the kind of magic that tears you limb from limb or fries you with electricity or . . . It doesn't matter. Even without their magic, they could probably murder me and toss my body in the river to be eaten by the piranhas.

Wait, are there piranhas in this water? I really wish I'd had a chance to look that up before I came. This is really, really idiotic. But here I am. Part of me wants to just let go of the boat and take my chances hoping that someone will find me and take pity on me. But then, I guess, the piranhas would get me if I'm remembering correctly and not freaking out. What the hell are you doing here, Bryce? Float off into the night. Maybe you'll be taken in by a nice family in a small fishing village and start a new, simpler life.

But instead, I push off the boat, try to swim as quietly as I can, and hide in the water under the gangplank. I want this, whatever the magical goody is inside. I can't do magic, but maybe with these tools I can do something like it. Or learn enough to figure out how, even in my strange state, I can do magic. Plus, I kind of promised the United States federal government that I would keep an eye on Zambrano. Which I'm feeling a bit conflicted about, as we seem to be starting to become friendlier, even if the sorcerer is a total jerk to me.

Here I'm supposed to wait until the appointed time. I awkwardly check my phone, which I've set on the lowest possible brightness. Only eight minutes until the next stage. And the water doesn't seem to have busted it—that's a win.

Zambrano's plan is relatively simple: he fakes a falling meteor out in the field. The two mages, who are the greedy kind of people who work for a company that illegally cuts down the rainforest and raids ruins and captures magical animals as a side business, will go after it. For reasons I don't quite understand yet, meteoric metal is super valuable for creating artifacts. Then I cut the mooring rope, climb aboard, and take my time ransacking the boat as it drifts farther and farther away from the security magicians.

At their level of skill, they shouldn't have any sort of teleportation or flying abilities, so in the dark with jungle brush on either side of the river, they won't be able to successfully pursue us. That's the theory, anyway. It seems like an awful lot could go wrong, but at least Zambrano is also putting himself in danger on this one—he plays the bait in our little scheme.

Suddenly, the night is lit from above. I stare up in awe as a brilliant light streaks across the sky and crashes down in the nearby field, maybe a quarter mile off. It looks incredible, and I can't help but marvel at the majesty of it—even if I know that it's just an illusion that Zambrano created using an illusion prism. And it's not even a new spell. As he told me, *Greedy magicians have been chasing my meteor illusions for over a century.*

Which is great, but it means that he gets to hide out in the woods, and I'm the one who gets to try to get onto the boat, which is protected by magical wards that would set off alarms if a human steps on board. But since I don't have any magical spark or soul or whatever, I won't register as human. Or so the sorcerer told me, anyway.

I can hear the astonished gasps from the boat and see the silhouettes of two shapes at the railing, pointing and arguing. A large thin man is yelling excitedly, while a heavyset short woman is replying with what sounds like condescending sarcasm. I took some Spanish in high school and college but can only catch a word here or there. Variations of the word "*confío*," which means "trust," do seem to be repeated a lot, so I'm guessing they don't trust each other.

I almost hope that at least one of them stays. In that case, the plan is for me to just slip away into the water, and we scrap the whole plan for tonight. It would be nice to just let the strong current carry me away and get picked up somewhere downstream. But the two of them can't seem to agree, and so they both walk down the gangplank together.

"*Handlicht*," the woman says in what sounds to me like German, rather than Spanish. She raises her hand, flexes her fingers in a waving pattern, and a bright glow comes from her hand, illuminating the area. I guess it just underscores how different cultures use the same words to trigger spells.

I slide deeper into the water, doing my best to not make any splashing sounds. Luckily, they're not focused on the water at all, and they push their way through the brush at the edges of the water, the only remaining vegetation in this area. Cutting down the soggy small trees and bushes along the water must not be worth it for loggers in a hurry to clear-cut and get out.

As soon as the two security magicians and their magic light have moved up onto the banks and out of earshot, I pull out the pocket-knife, open the saw, and start on the rope. It's harder than I expected. In movies, chopping a rope takes only a few seconds, but from my angle in the water, reaching up and sawing the rope is a struggle.

With the security magicians gone, Seraphex can approach, and she swims up to me. She appears to be an animal, so the security wards on the boat won't detect her, apparently.

"This better work," I say, gritting my teeth as I hack away at the rope. It might be easier to get out or try to untie it, but I'm committed now, maybe halfway through the rope. "If they realize they forgot to bring a shovel and come back, they'll probably fireball us first and ask questions later."

"Us? Sorry, just you. I'll be fine," Seraphex says, preening happily in the moonlight.

"Why?!" I demand. "Are ducks fireproof now?"

"Oh. Yeah, I'm essentially immortal," she says, sounding far too self-satisfied for my taste. "Did I forget to mention that? I'm a demon queen. Certainly, there's nothing these low-level magicians can do to hurt me. If blasting me with a fireball or lightning worked, Zambrano probably would have done it many years ago."

"Why do you get to be immortal and I get roasted like a rack of lamb?" I complain.

"Well, I can't lie and have to honor my agreements. So there are downsides."

"The downsides don't seem like that big a deal when I'm about to be a smear on the hull of a houseboat!" I protest.

"I can't lie to you, so I'll have to admit that you're right, this body is frustrating, but it's a lot more durable than that flimsy thing you've got," Seraphex answers primly, waddling up the gangplank onto the ship.

I, of course, have a much harder task. I finish sawing through the rope, hold on to it with one hand, and drift down the river behind the boat as I close the pocketknife with my other hand. Finally, I climb up the rope, scrambling against the sides of the boat, and flop over the rail onto the deck.

Seraphex peers down at me the whole time and doesn't lift a feather to help. I suppose that, in her duck body, there's really nothing she can do to help me. But it still feels rude.

"You could have just gotten onto the boat and then cut it from this end," Seraphex notes.

That's even ruder, and I glare at her as I lie on the deck and catch my breath.

"Hey, don't get mad just because you don't want to hear the truth. I'm not allowed to say anything else," she says defensively.

"It's the timing that's the problem," I say through gritted teeth. "Besides, Zambrano said to . . ."

"Cut the rope and get on the boat," Seraphex says, but her voice is a perfect impersonation of Zambrano. More perfect than an impersonation, it sounds like a recording of what he said. In her own voice, she adds, "That's all he said. It was fun to watch you struggle. And I *am* a demon queen. Now, should we get down there and finish the job?"

Shaking my head, I stand up and glance around. We are already drifting down the river, picking up speed and moving into the center as the current takes hold of us. This should buy us some time, but the security magicians could come back at any moment. If it weren't for the imminent threat of getting hit with a lightning bolt from a security magician, it would be a relaxing sight, gliding down the river with the stars above us.

I open the door to the houseboat and use my phone flashlight to look around. It's a worn wooden boat, and the first floor is just a galley and work area. There's a ladder leading up to the second story where the living space is and stairs leading down to the hold. Seraphex and I head downstairs, our footsteps echoing in the wooden boat.

Below, I run my flashlight over the hold. There are ropes, shovels, pickaxes, tarps, and various crates. It looks less like logging gear and more like everything one would need for an archeological dig. And there, in the corner, I see what I'm looking for. A steel box, a shiny cube around eight inches tall with a large padlock on the side of it.

But before I can walk over to grab it, I hear footsteps thudding on the stairs behind me. I spin, expecting to see one of the security magicians there to blast me away.

Instead, it's a different person, a short man with a shaved head and a bristly moustache, yelling at me in Spanish. He's holding something in his hand, but it's not a magical artifact. The metal gleams in the light from my phone.

He doesn't cast a fireball at me or turn me into a toad. He's just holding a plain old gun, black metal that gleams from the illumination of my flashlight. It's pointed right at my chest, and I can see his finger curling around the trigger.

CHAPTER 11

I can't understand what the man is saying, but I get the idea enough to raise my hands above my head in surrender.

He flicks the boat's lights on, takes my phone, and motions with his gun for me to back into the far corner by a wooden beam. He tosses me a pair of handcuffs, and with a series of angry gestures, gets me to understand that I'm supposed to cuff myself to the beam. Reluctantly, I do so, trying to leave them loose enough that I could slip out if I really tried.

Unfortunately, he's not an idiot, and he walks up and cinches them tight, yelling more and waving the gun in my face. Once I'm secured, he pulls out a handheld radio and barks something into it as he climbs back up the stairs.

I glance around for help, but Seraphex is gone again. I guess she's no better than Zambrano. A few minutes later, I can feel the gentle rocking of the boat stop with a jerk, and I can only assume that it's moored to the shore again. And then I hear the voices of the two security magicians.

The woman comes stomping down the stairs and points a finger at me.

"Did you really think Vulkatherak would let us leave his property totally undefended? And who the hell are you?" she demands.

I notice that the pointed finger is swirling with tiny bits of glowing magical energy. I take this as a bad sign. I can't sense the magic, of course, but the lights coming off her finger make me very nervous.

"I'm just . . ." I panic. "I'm just a tourist. I got lost in the ruins! Can you help me contact the American consulate so that I can go home? It's such a relief that you speak English!"

I like to think I'm a decent liar. After all, I did three and a half semesters with an improv troupe in college. I'm not sure if that makes me a practiced fibber or just someone who you don't want to be friends with in case I decide to take it up again in my thirties and pressure you into coming to my shows.

I try to focus on what the woman is saying, realizing that my mind is racing. Probably due to, you know, the mortal peril.

She glares at me. "You are a thief. And you are lying to me. Who made the fake meteor? Is there someone else out there?"

I gulp. "I don't know what you're talking about!" I protest. "Please don't hurt me. I can pay you!"

I'm not lying about that. I would totally Venmo her whatever she wanted to not find out what destructive spell is pulsing in her outstretched finger.

Someone upstairs yells something that I can't quite catch, and she glares at me. She steps over and double-checks the handcuffs, which are quite secure and starting to cut into my wrists in a rather painful way.

"I have to go make a report to my boss," she whispers. "I'm sure you already know who he is. The lava demon, who can melt your skin with a touch. He's not the sort of person who takes disappointment well. When I get back . . . you are going to tell me the truth. Or I will toss you overboard just so that I can hit you with a fireball that will melt your bones."

Well, that answers the question of what spell she's holding at the ready. Not that it's any comfort to me.

She stomps her way back upstairs, and I slump against the wooden beam, trying to get my hands into a more comfortable position. Seraphex quietly steps out from behind one of the crates.

"Well this is a bit of a pickle," she says. "In a metaphorical sense, of course."

"What do we do?!" I hiss. "Zambrano will come get me, right?"

"Him? Help you?" She laughs quietly. "They've called Vulkatherak, and his agents will be here in a few hours. Zambrano is the most powerful magic user alive, but he's just one guy. He's survived as long as he has by avoiding stand-up fights. He's the only one who has the teleportrait ability, which he relies on quite a lot. And if Vulkatherak is in the area, Zambrano won't last long—sorcerers can do more interesting things, but high-ranking demons have much more raw power."

I groan. "Really? Well, this sucks. Okay, then you need to help get me out of here! Do some demon magic!"

"I can't do any demonic magic," she says. "Activating demonic powers requires movement from a demon body to activate. That's why they trapped me in the body of a duck—it's enough to hold my nature but not something I can use to activate my powers." She glances at the cuffs on my wrists. "I do think I can help with those cuffs though. Can you get a splinter off the wood?"

Frantically, I rub the handcuffs against the beam. The metal takes, and before long . . . well, before long I end up with a long wood splinter in the base of my right thumb, and it hurts like hell. But Seraphex hops behind the beam and yanks the splinter out of my hand.

"Thanks," I mutter.

"Hold your hands still!" Seraphex demands, and I do my best to comply.

I crane my head around and am shocked to see her, splinter clutched in her beak, jamming it into the handcuff locks. Shockingly fast, she's picked one lock, then the other, and the cuffs fall to the floor.

Upstairs, I can hear the booming voice of Vulkatherak berating his security magicians and guards. It seems like he's on a roll, but I know it can't last forever.

"Okay, what now?" I whisper. "Is there another way out? Can you create a distraction so that I can escape?"

"I'm pretty distracting, sure, with these glorious feathers and curves. But even if you could get out of here," Seraphex points out, seemingly with some satisfaction, "they would just cast tracking spells. You wouldn't get very far."

"Huh," I say. "So, I can wait to get interrogated and possibly incinerated by an angry security magician, or I can try to run away and get tracked and hunted down. I mean, I'll choose running, I guess. But I really don't like those choices."

Seraphex shrugs. "It doesn't sound so good when you put it that way."

"There's got to be a way out of this," I say, adrenaline and will to live temporarily overpowering my fear.

"Technically," the duck points out, "dying is a way out of it. So you're not wrong."

I stare at her, suppressing the urge to grab her and wring her little duck neck. Which wouldn't help, because . . .

And then I get an idea.

"Sera," I say. "Hold on. You can do voices, right?"

"I am Groot!" she says, but it's perfectly in the voice of Vin Diesel's Groot from *Guardians of the Galaxy*—a role in which, and I looked this up once, he got paid fifty-four million dollars just for saying pretty much that one line.

"Did anyone see you come down here?" I ask.

"No, they were too busy arguing with one another to pay attention to a bird," the duck answers.

"Okay, great," I say, taking a deep breath and crawling behind the same boxes that Seraphex hid behind. "Here's my plan."

I've only just finished explaining it and curling myself in a tiny ball behind a crate, when I hear the same mage tromping her way back down the stairs, followed by the voice of the guy with the gun.

"What the hell?" she yells.

I can't see the security magician from my angle, but I can see Seraphex standing next to the handcuffs with a few feathers strewn around.

"What do you think? Bryce Alexander has escaped your handcuffs!" she declares in my voice. "A pair of silly metal cuffs can't hold someone who is able to transmogrify into other forms!"

"You think that will help you?" the woman demands. "You're still trapped here."

"What, do you think you can stop me?" Seraphex yells in my voice. "Bryce Alexander will escape this situation one way or another!"

I notice that, true to her demon nature, Seraphex hasn't actually told any direct lies. Though I really feel like her version of my voice is a bit screechier and whinier than mine actually is. Or maybe it's just that listening to your own voice always sounds weird.

"Oh, we will destroy you, Mr. Alexander," the woman says. "Whatever shape you are."

I lie behind the tiny crate, pulling my limbs in tightly while the hold of the ship is suddenly filled with squawks, feathers, curses, and two gunshots. But within thirty seconds, the flapping and squawking is proceeding upstairs, and both of my captors are following after it.

As soon as they're gone, I stand up and take a deep breath. I almost just make a run for it, but at the last second I turn and grab the ornately forged metal box. Then I creep up the stairs. Peering out the top, I see that Seraphex is in the air, missing a few feathers but flying and jeering at the two security magicians and the guy with the gun. Thankfully, they're all totally focused on her.

"Look at me! Bryce Alexander is about to escape!" she yells in my voice, taunting them without saying anything untrue.

One of the mages lets loose a lightning bolt, and the guy with the gun fires two more shots at the duck as I slip over the rail on the other side of the boat. I lower myself and drop into the water, trying to swim as quickly as I can while holding the box.

After my swimming and the current have pulled me fairly far away, I glance back. Near the boat, I see Seraphex dive toward the river, where she's finally hit, blasted by what looks like lightning and fireballs at the same time. She disappears into the water in an explosion of feathers and fire that boils the water and sears my eyes with its brightness. I kind of feel bad for her, but she assured me that she's almost invincible and will survive just fine.

I continue to swim downstream, trying to keep my head and limbs below the water as much as possible. As I swim, I notice that I feel something moving in the metal box, and that part of the decorations on top of the box are small air holes. As I float, I try to let its natural buoyancy keep it above the water in case something inside needs to breathe.

Before long, the current pulls me downriver, and the boat is disappearing around a bend. I alternately swim and drift for well over an hour, until finally it seems certain that no one is coming after me.

I'm grateful, relieved, scared . . . and *furious.*

CHAPTER 12

The morning light is glowing on the horizon, and I'm miles down the river when Seraphex catches up to me. Exhausted from swimming and floating, I've pulled into a little grotto on the side of the river.

"Thanks," I say with a sigh as the duck paddles up to me. She's scorched from her beak to what remains of her tail feathers but seems otherwise unharmed.

"Being almost invincible does have its little pleasures," Seraphex says, "but I'd rather not do that again. And you owe me one, Mr. Alexander."

"Fair enough. You look like Wile E. Coyote after getting blown up with his own TNT," I say, smiling slightly. There's a sinking feeling in my stomach though, as I realize that I now owe a demon queen an unspecified "one." That can't be a good thing.

"Seraphex, what happened to you?" Zambrano says. "You're a mess!"

I glance up to see him standing on the shore, looking perfectly spiffy and unperturbed in his safari chic outfit.

I pull myself up out of the water, knowing that I am a mess of mud, weeds, and sweat. My jeans are so soaked that they are several times heavier than usual, and I need to hold my belt with one hand to keep them up.

"You got it!" he says brightly, pointing at the box gripped in my other hand.

I shrug. "Can we go?"

"Yeah, yeah, sure," he says.

He pulls out a small teleportrait and grabs my neck while Seraphex hops up, flaps her crispy duck wings, and grabs on to my shoulder. Zambrano's touch suddenly feels invasive, but I grit my teeth and tolerate it. I need to get home.

An *I want to go to there* and a perspective-warping moment later, we're back on the roof of the warehouse. I step away from the sorcerer and the duck and breathe a sigh of relief, looking around at the familiar skylines of Brooklyn, Queens, and Manhattan.

"Let's go open the box! This will be fun," Zambrano says.

I just shake my head and glare at him.

"What in the ever-living shit was that?" I demand.

"What do you mean?" he asks. "You got the box, you pulled off some clever plan that got Seraphex toasted, you seem unharmed. What, do you want me to buy you a new pair of jeans or sneakers or something? Those weren't designer, were they? If you wore five-hundred-dollar sneakers on a quest, that's on you . . ."

"You left me to die," I say flatly. "There was another guy there, with a gun. They tied me up, and they were going to interrogate me. Probably torture me and then turn me over to Vulkatherak. And I can't imagine a demon duke would be any gentler. And you just bailed on me, *again*."

Dawn is just starting to break over the city, lighting up the rivers and bridges. I would stop to admire how beautiful it was, if I didn't want to punch everything I saw.

"Oh, yeah," he says. "Sorry about that. If Vulkatherak saw me there, he would consider it an act of war and come after me. At the moment, he's leaving me alone because he thinks we have a truce. Plus, a big battle down there would draw the attention of the UN and all their regulations, which would be a whole new hassle."

"So?" I say. "So you just give up and wash your hands of me?" I shake my head, clenching and unclenching my fists. "Bryce ran into some trouble, oh well, I guess he's on his own now? I hope the bad-guy mages don't torture him too bad."

"Hey, now," Zambrano protests. "I would have . . ." he starts, but he just trails off.

"Would have what? You don't even know, do you?!"

He looks away from me. "I would have figured out a way to come get you and the box. I wasn't about to just give up."

"Yeah, because you want that box, right? It's not about me, is it?" I can feel my jaw tightening and my brows clenching. "Why is my life worth so little to you?!"

"Look," Zambrano says. "I'm not some kind of loner who hates everyone. I'm not the monster all those academic wizards and magicians think I am. I go out, I do things, I try to help the world. But you wanted to be my apprentice. Even though you can't do magic. That comes with risks. You wanted to do good in the world. I do too. I've literally saved this world from destruction on multiple occasions." He glances at Seraphex, who is watching us with rapt attention like this is a scene from her favorite Netflix show. "There's one of them things I've saved the world from, sitting right there."

"Sure. That's great, thanks," I say, but I don't really mean it. "But that's no excuse to hang me out to dry. Or to toss me aside like a broken light bulb. Maybe try to do something good, huh? Maybe consider taking some risk yourself, when you got me into trouble in the first place? Why should you expect me to sacrifice when you don't? Do you even know what sacrifice is?"

"Sacrifice?" he says, practically growling the word at me. "Do you know why there aren't any more sorcerers?" he says quietly. "At your college, do they teach why there are no more?"

"There are . . . theories," I say. "Mostly that they never really existed, not in the way that they claimed. Or that magic is getting weaker over time. Or that the most talented thinkers are going into other fields."

"There are no more other sorcerers," he says, "because I killed them all."

"You what?! And that's supposed to make you a good person?"

"No, I don't think it does. Not most days." He shakes his head. "They were my mentors. My students. My friends. Some even lovers. We made magic together, created it spell by spell, over the centuries. And one by one, the power got to them. Communing with magic, mapping the patterns, building new ones, creating new spells . . . it's heady stuff. Those that didn't get lost in it, slowly lost their sanity.

Became unstable, or megalomaniacs. One by one, they gained power and became more distant from the world. They turned away from their humanity, lost in the patterns. They started to see everyone around them, the world, as just more resources."

I take a step back, not knowing what to think. His eyes are blazing with a passion I haven't seen from him before.

"They started to conquer and kill, casually using their powers. Some for more power, some for research, some for whims, some for ego, some for pure delight in suffering. At first I tried to imprison them, or take their powers, but they were only temporary solutions at best. Eventually they would escape. And so one by one, I watched them ascend into power and descend into madness. And so I had to stop them. Every one of my peers, everyone who understood what I understood—I had to kill them. At least the final one, the great Polish mentalist Zuzanna, took her own life in the early '80s when she realized she was too far gone. That was a great mercy. Since then, it's been just me."

I'm speechless. Still angry at him, but I have no idea what to say.

"So yes, I know what sacrifice is. I know what living with sacrifice is. So excuse me if some random twentysomething who snuck into my home and demanded that I teach him isn't particularly important to me."

"Is that all true?" I demand of Seraphex. I can't help but think he's trying to play for sympathy or just mess with me.

"It is," she says.

I sigh. "That's a very sad story," I say. "It really is. And I suppose you've done a lot of good. But it doesn't excuse you. It doesn't make this work for me."

He looks away, putting his hand on the railing and staring at the city, which is now brightly lit by the morning sun.

"Good luck with Vulkatherak," I say. "I hope whatever's in that box helps."

I pull the intern hat off and throw it on the ground. Without looking, Zambrano makes a series of chopping motions with his hand.

As I turn and walk away, I can feel the breeze continuing to ripple through my hair. For the first time in days, the hat doesn't reappear. I head down the stairs and keep going until I'm out of the warehouse and in the street. None of the stealthy observers waiting there bother me as I walk past.

CHAPTER 13

By the time I cross the city and get back to my apartment, the adrenaline is long gone, and I'm starting to wonder just how much I've screwed myself over. But no long-range magic spells fly through my window, and no MSA agents bust down my door. Which is nice, though I feel too numb to really care that much. I make myself a meal from frozen leftovers, try to watch a few shows, and mostly just let thoughts swirl around in my head.

Along the way, I stopped at the Apple Store and bought myself a new phone. I got one of the older models, but it's still not cheap. But you have to have a phone—and in Peru, the dude with the gun took my phone, and I doubt he'd be willing to mail it to me. So, before I can do anything else, I have to go through the whole annoying process of setting it up and downloading all my junk from the cloud.

Once it's set up, I check my messages, but the only messages are a photo Carla sent me of some minor celebrity who got a smoothie, a buzzing group chat from my old college friends about the Nets game they all went to, and Parth messaging to check in on me. I can't bring myself to tell him what happened, not yet. I realize that Zambrano definitely has a phone—but also never even bothered to exchange numbers with me. I kind of wish I could text Seraphex to check in, but . . . can a duck's beak or webbed feet work a touch screen? I honestly have no idea. I'm pretty sure that a duck's feathery wings wouldn't work.

I do enjoy sleeping in my old bed, and I'm exhausted enough from the previous night that I'm actually able to get some decent sleep. I wake up the next morning in a panic that I'm late for work, but then I realize that I don't need to go in, so I sleep in. But I do need to deal with that whole situation. Probably better to deal with it sooner rather than later.

So I text my parents to let them know I'm stopping by. When I get to New Brunswick, my parents are excited to see me, and it turns out Dad ran out to buy ingredients to make his chicken parm, which they know is my favorite.

They're surprised by the visit but take it in stride. I know they can tell I'm preoccupied by something, but when they ask how I'm doing, I just show them the picture Carla sent and say that everything is fine. They've never been the type to pry. But, finally, after dinner while my mom is driving me back to the train station, she goes for it.

"What's really going on, Bryce, honey?" she asks. When I don't immediately say anything, she waits a minute, then takes a stab at it. "Did you get more rejections?"

Oh yeah. It's crazy, so much has happened in the past few days that I almost completely forgot about the applications.

"Yeah," I say. "I . . . well, it seems I'm not going to be a magician. I guess I just don't have what it takes."

After past setbacks, she's tried to tell me that they're idiots for not taking me and other nice things like that, but I think she can tell by my voice that it's not the time for that.

"Do you know what you'll do next?" she asks. Of course she doesn't bother saying *You can't work at that smoothie shop forever,* but I can tell it's implied.

"I don't know, Mom," I say. "I really don't know." I'm not lying to her. Magic was the only thing I was ever interested in, but between the school rejections, quitting as Zambrano's intern, oh, and being the least-magically-inclined-human-ever, it's clear that it's not happening. Now that I'm out of the warehouse and away from Zambrano, Seraphex, and all the artifacts, that feels like even more of a loss. It's an emptiness just sitting in my stomach.

"I'm sure you'll figure something out, honey," she says. "You've always been very clever. Those schools are all idiots for not taking you."

Just kidding, there it is! Thanks, Mom.

She drops me at the station, and I find a seat on the train. Not many people are going in toward the city this late at night, so it's easy to find an empty window seat. I watch the scenery go by for one stop before Agent Crane slips into the seat beside me.

"Peanuts?" she says. "They don't give them out on airplanes anymore, so I figured maybe it could be a train thing now. They're the good kind, honey roasted."

I'm expecting a little travel-sized bag, but she's brought on a giant can of them. Shrugging, I take the can and shake a few out onto my hand. I try to hand it back to her, but she's already got a second can out and is happily munching from it. These are not your average Kirkland Signature brand fare—whatever expensive artisanal organic nut purveyor makes these, they're really quite good.

"So," Agent Crane says once she's chewed and swallowed what I'm sure the can lists in the ingredients as several servings, "I saw the video of you coming out of that warehouse. You looked pretty pissed. Are things not going so great in there? Worried about what will happen when you get back?"

I roll my eyes. "When I get back? I don't think I'm going to be going back, to be honest. I thought I was going to die several times. And he didn't seem to give a damn. I've never wanted to do anything but learn magic. I love magic, but it's not worth it. Not like that."

Agent Crane nods slowly. "So you're out, then?"

"Look," I say, "I'm sorry. I know I'll need to go back to work. Or are you going to arrest me or something? But I can't work with someone who leaves me hanging every time we go on one of his 'quests.'"

"Don't worry, I'm not going to let the FBI arrest you or anything like that. I just need you to tell me what you know."

"Thanks," I say. And, look, I fully recognize that she's playing classic 'good cop' here, trying to be my friend while totally threatening me with the FBI as proverbial 'bad cop.' But still, it's nice to have someone at least trying to be on my side.

"What about this demonic presence that Zambrano claims is in Chicago?" Agent Crane asks.

I shrug. "Still there. He had a whole plan to stop him, but it relied on my ability to not be detected by magic. I'm sure he'll figure something out."

"Interesting." Agent Crane raises an eyebrow. I guess she hadn't known that before. *Information is the only currency, like Seraphex said,* I think, mentally kicking myself.

It feels like a little betrayal, telling Zambrano's secrets to the government. But at the same time, I'm still really pissed at him. And . . . it's nice to feel like I actually know something of value. I've got to make sure to at least get something back from her.

"Does the demon even exist? Or is it just an illusion Zambrano made to get me to help him steal things?"

Agent Crane sighs. She's stopped eating and suddenly looks more troubled than I've seen her before.

"I don't think he's lying," she says. "Unofficially, at least, that's what I believe. Since our last chat, I've been looking into it. I've searched through documents, had arcane readings taken around various cities in the country. There is demonic magic of some sort at play. I've sent my findings up the chain. But I've heard nothing back. The problem is that MSA leadership and the UN Arcane Threat Committee don't think anything is happening. They refuse to believe there are real, existential dangers at play. They're focused on artifact trade agreements, magical stock market manipulation, and the ethics of transmogrification."

That doesn't totally surprise me, but it does suck.

"Well, shit," I say. "What does that mean? Is Chicago just boned?"

Agent Crane gives me a meaningful glance. "That's up to you, isn't it? I believe that the best chance to minimize casualties is for you to help Zambrano carry out his plan. He might figure out how to do it without you, but that would be more of a frontal assault, which would probably have massive collateral damage in the Chicago city center, even if it was ultimately successful and saved the broader Midwest."

"Oh," I say. And then I realize where this is going. "Oh, damn it."

"The MSA isn't going to do anything," Agent Crane continues. "I'm not allowed to do anything. But you're classified as an informant. That means you're allowed to go along with whatever Zambrano tells you to do, and legally I can give you immunity because it's part of a key investigation."

"So . . . you can't do anything, and now it's up to me? And I have to go back and make nice with that maniac?"

"Yes, that's pretty much how it is," Agent Crane says, nodding. "I'll help you as much as I can. But I have to keep my distance, so neither Zambrano nor my bosses suspect anything."

"I can't believe this," I protest. "I just wanted to learn some magic. And now I'm supposed to save Chicago from demons . . . and I don't even actually *get to learn any magic*."

Agent Crane shrugs, and I can see from the lines in her tight face that she's very tired.

"Look, I won't make you do this," she says. "I'm not going to force or threaten you. I need you actually on my side for it to work. If you'd prefer, I can debrief you, get you your job back at the smoothie shop, and leave you alone. This will all just be one weird week that happened to you in your twenties. If anything big happens in Chicago, you'll see it on the news one way or another . . . or in a demon's army showing up on your doorstep eventually. I doubt he'll be satisfied just to rule the Midwest once he's established a kingdom."

I sit still for a long moment, chewing it over and watching the New Jersey landscape slide by through the window.

"It's your choice," she says. "This is your story, Bryce. Do you want to take a shot at being a hero? To be part of the world of modern magic? Or do you want to sell smoothies? Apparently, there was a lovely older woman who was asking after you at Samba Smoothies, saying no one made them quite as well as 'that handsome young man.' I'm sure she'd be happy if you went back. Unless a demonic earthquake wrecks our economy—"

"Okay, okay, I get it," I interrupt. "I just don't know," I say. "I don't know what to do."

"Well, this is your stop," Agent Crane says and stands up to let me out. In a bit of a daze, I stand and step out into the aisle.

"I hope we'll be talking again soon," she tells me, placing a hand on my shoulder. "If you need to get in touch, just ask Google."

I stare at her. "What? I mean, I know how to search for information on the internet . . ."

She grins. "No, I mean, just type whatever you need into Google search. Don't worry, the message will get to me," she says, looking giddy, like she's just revealed a playful little secret.

"Really?!" I say. I want to lecture her about constitutional rights and invasion of privacy, but there's a group of kids behind me in the aisle waiting to get off the train, so I just shake my head at her and head toward the exit while Agent Crane retakes her seat.

An hour later, I'm back at my apartment, lying in bed and staring into my phone. Of course WizardWatch is the first thing I open up, quickly skimming past all the news articles about Lukas Volker, that Austrian billionaire launching a colony ship to Mars. I've got to admit, it's pretty impressive stuff.

The latest chatter on WizardWatch is about some rogue wizard who apparently broke into a quarry outside of Chicago late at night and cast a bunch of fire spells that melted some of the stone itself. There's security footage from a construction site across the street, though it just shows a big shadowy figure and a bright flash of light before the camera broke.

And then I open the latest message from Parth.

Did you see about the quarry in Chicago? his text says. *The news says it was a wizard, but we analyzed the security footage, and whoever did that was over seven feet tall. So, either there's an NBA player who knows magic . . . or what you said about demons is true. What are you and Zambrano doing about it?*

I put the phone down and stare at the ceiling.

Damn it.

I want to pretend that I'm going to consider the options. Maybe become a manager at Samba Smoothies. Or maybe move away, or go back to school and learn hotel management or something?

But no. I can't open up the possibility to learn about magic and then just walk away. And I'm not the type to bail when other people are in danger. Millions of them, in Chicago and across the Midwest.

Damn it. Just . . . damnitty damn it.

I'm definitely going to get myself killed. I'm going to wake up tomorrow, head back to Queens, and go to work for a maniac who's been driven insane by centuries of loss. And I'm going to try to stop a disaster and end up a smoking pile of ash or turned into a ferret or something.

I distract myself with some video games and Netflix and eventually drift off to sleep, wondering if I haven't already missed my chance to be part of it. But the next morning, I wake up to a duck's bill tapping on my window.

CHAPTER 14

Groggy and blinking my eyes open, I reach over and push the window up. Well, first I try to do it without getting out of the bed or leaving the covers, but the angle is all wrong, so I have to stand up and do it that way. With nothing on but my boxers, I'm once again nearly naked in front of Seraphex. But I imagine that, as a demon queen, she's probably seen it all before.

"I think you should come back," she says, hopping in through the window and onto my pillow. "We need you."

I've already decided that in order to save lives, I'm willing to go back and risk my neck. But this duck taught me that information is power, and I'm going to take that approach.

"And why should I do that?" I say. "Won't I just be screwed over again? I'm lucky I'm alive."

"Yeah, about that," she says. "Zambrano's sorry. And I want to win my bet with him."

I laugh at her. "What, did he tell you to say that? Shouldn't he make his own apologies? Does he also have you break up with people for him?" That actually happened to me once in eighth grade. Alyssa Matthews, I'm calling you out. You should've had the courage to say it to me in person. "And I really don't care who wins your bet—you getting to read some books or him getting into Merlin's Vault doesn't matter to me." Of course, after I say that, I do find myself wondering what the heck is in Merlin's Vault. And what sort of secret books Zambrano has. But I'm sure as hell not going to admit that to this demon duck.

"Oh," she says. "I forgot to mention. He's downstairs. He said he didn't want to see what your face looks like when you're snoring."

"Right," I say. "It's good to start an apology with an insult. Like how you always start a wedding toast with a joke."

She gives her little duck shrug. "He also told me not to tell you that he said that, but he's not the boss of me."

"Whatever," I say. "Just . . . give me a couple minutes to get ready. He's going to have to wait a bit longer."

I use the toilet, run a comb through my messy hair, shave, and brush my teeth. When I get back outside, the demonic duck is sitting primly on top of the still-warm PlayStation that I accidentally left on last night, surveying the small studio apartment as if she owns the place.

"How do I look?" I ask Seraphex.

"I'm incapable of lying," the duck answers. "And also kind of a judgy bitch. Do you really want me to answer that question?"

"Screw you," I say, then throw on a baseball cap and head to the elevators. Seraphex pads along behind me. We get in and start moving down, when the elevator slows to a stop a few floors below me, and I glance down at the duck, who seems unconcerned.

"Just act natural," she says. "Humans have weak minds."

The door opens, and a guy in a sports jersey walking his dog gets on. For a second I'm worried that the dog will attack her, but instead it cowers behind the guy's leg. The guy gives me some side-eye, but I stand next to Seraphex and act like everything's normal, and . . . it works! He just gets off with his dog, shaking his head in confusion, and walks out quickly.

"Did he not see you or something? Was that demonic magic?" I ask as we walk to the lobby.

"No, he just assumed everything was fine because you were acting like everything was fine," the duck says. "The force of conformity is very powerful."

"I guess," I reply, "but it's not every day you see a duck just chilling in an elevator."

"Don't forget," she says, "that our friend there is the kind of guy who's been brainwashed into thinking it's normal to follow his dog around and pick up its poop in little plastic bags twice a day."

We get to the lobby, where Zambrano is reclining in one of the armchairs in the building's small lounge, poking idly at his phone. He sits up when I enter and gestures to the chair next to him.

He's wearing a dapper suit with features that are historically inspired but somehow timeless. It looks fairly out of place in the fluorescent-lit apartment lobby, but I'm not sure where Zambrano would look actually "at home." He always looks good but never quite fits in.

"Hey," I say, taking the seat. "Nice suit."

"Thanks," he says. "I had it custom designed in Milan. There's a little shop just off Via Monte Napoleone that gives you a whole personality interview before they design you something. You want to try them? You could use some sharp clothes—"

"Is that what you came here to say?" I interrupt, cocking my head at him.

"No, it's not," Zambrano says with a sigh. "Look, I'm sorry. You were right. I shouldn't have ditched you. We may not be friends, but we're on the same team. I put you in that situation; I should have helped get you out of it. Even if it caused problems."

"Yeah," I say. "Thanks." I kind of want to push him harder, but that's a decent apology. And I'm here on a mission. Zambrano has given me some of the secrets of his understanding of magic. I'm going to get more.

"Also, that was a pretty badass move you pulled off," he says. "Seraphex told me about your escape plan. Very impressive."

"It was, wasn't it?" I say. I kind of glossed over that in my anger and fear. "We probably got those assholes in a lot of trouble."

"So the bottom line is . . ." Zambrano pauses, as if it's taking effort for him to will himself to say the next part. "You're the only person who can get in and stop Vulkatherak's plan. At least, without starting the kind of magical conflict we haven't seen since the seventies. And I certainly don't have the firepower to take him on alone."

"Okay." I get it. I take a deep breath. I know I've already made the decision, but it's still hard to say it out loud. "I'm in. As long as you'll keep teaching me the workings of magic. Let's do it."

"Intern?" Zambrano says, pulling that cursed hat out of somewhere and holding it out to me. I'd be offended, but he's grinning like he knows it's a joke.

I laugh and shake my head. "I think I'll take the custom shop in Milan for my wardrobe, if it's all the same to you."

"Why not?" he says. "Tell you what, come by the warehouse tomorrow afternoon and before we work on the plan to stop Vulkatherak, we can go get you measured for something that will be a little less . . . unremarkable."

"He's saying you look like a peasant," Seraphex pipes up. "He'd be embarrassed to go out with you."

I glance down at myself. I want to argue with them, but I'm wearing a pair of old jeans and a T-shirt from one of my friends' failed tech start-ups.

"I didn't need a translation," I say. "But thanks. As much fun as this little fashion critique session has been, I'm gonna go back up and get some more sleep. See you both tomorrow." I stand up, swiping the intern hat from Zambrano's chair as I pass by.

I hate that hat, but it's the only enchanted item I own. I'm keeping it.

"The spell reactivates as soon as you put it on!" Zambrano yells as I turn the corner to the elevators. On the way up, I hold the hat as far away from my head as I can, and back upstairs I stuff it into the very bottom of my backpack.

CHAPTER 15

The next day, I trek back across the city to the warehouse. True to his word, Zambrano has a teleportrait ready, and he and Seraphex whisk me off to Milan. A few minutes later, we've arrived at a building just a few blocks past a dizzyingly busy and fashionable street, full of attractive Italians and global tourists who definitely don't think my T-shirt, which is from a Dungeons and Dragons podcast that I used to be really into, is at all fashionable. I agree, but it was the only one that wasn't wrinkly as hell.

As we go up the rickety elevator, I am kind of regretting going along with this fashion expedition. But I've never owned a really nice suit, let alone a custom Italian one. And maybe Zambrano and Seraphex will be a little bit nicer to me . . . I think, knowing that I'm lying to myself.

I step out of the elevator into a large room covered in rows and rows of fabric, racks of suits, and a long row of workers at sewing machines, diligently practicing their craft. An older Italian man with puffs of white hair at the sides of his head, a finely tailored suit, and glasses way down the bridge of his nose looks at me with disdain— kind of like his cat just dropped a dead bird on his porch. But before he can say anything, Zambrano steps out behind me, and the man is suddenly all smiles.

"Signore Zambrano!" the man almost shouts, clapping his hands together.

"Flavio!" Zambrano calls out. "Look at you! You haven't changed a bit, have you?"

The man shakes his head sadly. "I'm sorry to disappoint you, Signore Zambrano, but I am not Flavio. I am Luca, Flavio's nephew. As an apprentice, I helped measure you for our fine apparel several times before, if you remember. Don't worry, I never forget a face, or a measurement! Sadly, Flavio has been gone for eight years now."

"Well, you look just as handsome as he did," Zambrano says, seeming to try to cover for his misstep. "And I'm sorry to hear that old Flavio passed away. He was a good man, and he crafted a fine suit."

"Oh, no, no, my uncle is still alive and well," Luca says hastily. "He merely met an American cocktail waitress at a casino in Monaco, stole all the funds from the family business, and ran off to Belize. It was a crushing financial blow to our establishment, one that we very nearly didn't survive. Although from the photos on Instagram, Flavio and Krystal seem to be quite happy."

"That's the Italian equivalent of a 401(k)," Seraphex whispers from the perch she's taken on my shoulder. "Speaking purely in jest, of course."

We stand there for a moment, taking in all the suits and the even more awkward silence. For once, Zambrano seems not to know what to say. The sewing machines along the wall continue humming along as the workers there studiously ignore us.

"But you still make suits here, it seems?" Zambrano says at last.

"We do indeed, signore!" Luca answers. "Right this way!"

As we walk to a dressing room at the far end of the floor, Zambrano and Luca jabber away in Italian, both making gestures that indicate they're talking about various cuts of suits.

"How does he speak all these languages?" I ask Seraphex quietly as we walk. "Is he that smart? Or is it from magic? Or is it just because he's so damn old?"

"Honestly, it's a little of each," Seraphex says. "He really can be frustratingly clever at times. But also deliciously foolish at others. You humans never cease to amaze and amuse."

In the dressing room, Luca begins peppering me with questions as he takes my various measurements, moving my body around like I'm a rag doll. He also frequently seems to be staring at my face, as if trying to place me or figure me out.

"What is your personal style?" he asks.

"Um . . . nice? Cool? Attractive?" I stammer.

"Do you have a fashion icon that you admire?"

"Uh . . . James Bond?"

"What purpose or occasion are you buying this suit for?"

"Er . . . looking nice? At a thing? You know, a formal kind of thing."

Zambrano shakes his head and rolls his eyes. "This is going to take forever. The intern will take a fully canvassed, three-piece in Super 150s worsted wool with a Prince of Wales check—charcoal and light gray. The jacket will be Neapolitan cut, four-inch peak lapels, Milanese buttonhole, double vents, and a flower loop. Flat-fronted trousers, medium-rise, side adjusters, fifteen-inch leg opening, two-inch cuffs. Single-breasted waistcoat, six-button, shawl collar, and a watch pocket. For the shirt, sea island cotton, spread collar, French cuffs, mother-of-pearl buttons, and contrast stitching. For the tie, seven-fold grenadine silk. No pocket square—those are so try-hard these days. And I'll take the same as I got last time but a shade darker."

"Very good, signore," Luca says. "We still have your measurements and preferences on file, of course."

"We'll need them this evening," he says and offers the tailor a wad of cash.

Luca looks down over the top of his glasses, his eyes suddenly gleaming. "This will do nicely, signore," he says, taking the money. Almost too quick for the eye to follow, I see that he splits it and puts most of it in his right pants pocket, but a smaller stack ends up in a hidden pocket inside his vest as well.

He steps out onto the main floor and starts yelling in Italian, and several of the workers scurry to pause their projects and grab new fabric. Luca himself steps in, efficiently organizing his team to get started.

Before we leave, Zambrano hands something small to Luca, and they jabber in Italian for a minute, with Zambrano gesturing at his neck and some of the neckties on one of the racks.

We break for a walk, picking up dress shoes to match the suits and a very lazy Italian dinner. Zambrano takes out an illusion prism and sets it around Seraphex so that people ignore her, and she ends up eating just as much fusilli as we do. A few hours later, we're back at the shop, and both Zambrano and I are trying on freshly finished suits.

I'm full to the brim with pasta, but somehow the suit still falls perfectly on my body. I have to be honest—it feels amazing. I step out of the dressing room and look in the mirror, and I look . . . well, kind of ridiculous.

"I look like an elf. Or a waiter. Or a valet at a fancy hotel who's still in high school," I say, shaking my head.

"You've got to stand up straight!" Zambrano says, poking me in the back. "Don't let the suit own you, kid. You own the suit! We've got to get you to put on some weight. Did you not drink any of those smoothies that you made with all the boosters?"

I try to puff myself up, standing tall and throwing my shoulders back.

"Trying too hard," Seraphex says. "You look like a toy soldier."

I glare at the duck. "Why are we the only ones who get new clothes? Maybe you need a little suit? A duck-sized ball gown? A tuxedo? No, no," I say, grinning as I finally get a jab back at my verbal assailants. "A *ducks*-edo? With a cute little bow tie and maybe some ruffles in the front?"

Luca ignores me. Zambrano chuckles.

"That wasn't funny," Seraphex says primly. "And I can't lie, so you know I'm serious."

Feeling slightly better, I turn back to the mirror, pulling and tugging to get the suit to fit right. I try to stand tall and confident but also relaxed and not trying too hard. I actually feel like I find a happy medium.

And you know what? I look kind of okay.

Luca comes in, beaming. "Excellent, signori!" he says. He steps up to me and makes a few more final tugs on the suit. Satisfied, he walks us out, again chatting with Zambrano in Italian and gesturing with his hands in ways that really do evoke lapels, trouser cuts, and other fashion choices that I have no concept of.

Finally, when we're standing at the elevator waiting for it to arrive, Luca takes a long look at me and nods.

"Ah, your face, Signore Intern!" Luca says. He steps forward, peering up at me. "That nose, those lips. One of your friends, wasn't she, Signore Zambrano? Who came with a large group of you many years ago, when I was a young man. Are you her son, or her nephew?"

"Whose son or nephew?" I ask.

"Those features were so lovely on her; she was so very beautiful," he says with the enthusiasm for feminine beauty that only European men can get away with. It's a shame that it doesn't come together quite so nicely on . . ." he adds, gesturing to me in a way that is really quite rude. "But the suit helps," he adds and pats me on the shoulder. "You look very much improved."

I'd really love to pummel him, but I don't want to mess up my brand-new custom suit.

Zambrano glares at Luca. "All my friends are dead. And have been for decades before he was born."

"So sorry, signore," Luca says, backing away. "My apologies. Enjoy the suits."

We step into the elevator, and a moment later we're back on the street.

CHAPTER 16

Once we're out on the street, Zambrano starts walking quickly. I follow along, confusion bubbling inside me.

"What was that?" I demand.

"I don't know," Zambrano says, increasing his pace and heading for an alley. "You look like one of my old sorcerer friends, I guess. From decades ago. I wouldn't put too much stock into what an old man says he saw forty or fifty years ago."

"He seemed pretty sure. And I was adopted through an agency; I don't know who my birth parents are."

We reach the alley, and Zambrano turns to look at me. He stares for a moment, examining my face like I'm a prize poodle that he's judging at a dog show.

"Huh," he says at last. "Yeah, I see it."

"See what?" I demand.

"You look a bit like Zuzanna, the great sorcerer of Poland. She was a real live wire, that one. Men couldn't resist her. Women couldn't resist trying to stab her. But she died in the 1980s. And she didn't have any children that I know of. Sorcery makes that hard—human reproductive bits are very sensitive and don't like so much magic going around. Not having children is one of the curses we sorcerers are forced to suffer. We do get to abuse our magical powers to give ourselves great teeth and hair though," he adds with a pearly-white grin.

"So, I look like a great sorcerer who died back when mullets were cool, and she didn't have any kids."

"You could be her great-grandnephew or something, I guess. But it doesn't make sense; her being a great sorcerer and you being the least magically sensitive person who has ever or will ever be born. Maybe you just have one of 'those faces.'"

"What if," I say, puffing myself up, "I'm the long-lost chosen one, here to save the world from the demons?"

"Perhaps," Zambrano muses, "you are the Long-Lost Chosen Intern, here to fulfill his destiny by fetching my coffee. Which, by the way, I don't think you've actually done a single time, have you? And to think, I gave you that nice hat and everything!"

"If only there were a human resources department to report him to," Seraphex says from the ground at our feet.

"How did Zuzanna die?" I ask.

Zambrano sighs and looks at the ground, suddenly somber. "She was the last to go, of the Sorcerers of the Circle. She made it easy on me, thankfully. We had seen all the rest go mad, one by one. She recognized the signs of it in herself. She knew how hard it had been for me, battling each of the others as they lost their minds. So when she started to slip too far, she disappeared into the Polish mountains and took her own life."

"Oh," I say. "I'm sorry. I guess that's pretty noble." I feel a weird moment of pride for a woman who might or might not have been my ancestor.

"Do you know anything about Bryce looking like Zuzanna?" he demands, jabbing a finger at Seraphex.

"This speculation is all very interesting," Seraphex answers, "but we're going to be late for our appointment."

"Oh, right, good point," Zambrano says, pulling a teleportrait from the bag holding the clothes he came in.

I glance down at it and notice that it's not the portrait to return us to the warehouse.

"Wait, where are we going?"

"You don't think I got you this incredibly expensive suit on short notice so that you could look good at your college friend's wedding or your Jewish cousin's bar mitzvah, do you?"

I glare at him. "Let me guess, we're going on a dangerous mission that can only be accomplished with my special 'chosen one' talents."

"You *are* learning something from this internship!" Zambrano says. "And since we agreed we're going to do everything as teammates, I'll even tell you the plan first. We're going to the world-famous Nusantara Auction House in Jakarta. I'm going to sell you to a wealthy and eccentric artifact collector to add to his collection of rarities."

"You're going to *what*?"

"Well, technically, I'm going to rent you." Zambrano seems overly proud to be making this distinction.

"You should be flattered," Seraphex says. "You're worth quite a lot, as it turns out! I'll be honest, I was surprised too."

"It'll be fine. Don't worry!" Zambrano adds. "We're going to double-cross him after the sale."

As a loud group of Italian school kids walks by the alley and throws glances at the three of us, I just stare at Zambrano, doing my best to contain my rage.

"He'll freeze you in a slow-time display case in his magically secured secret menagerie that no outsider has ever seen the inside of. This necktie"—he taps the silk tie wrapped around my neck—"has a camera hidden in it. It will send a picture of the interior of the menagerie to me. I will make a teleportrait, pop in, and grab you and the artifact that we need to distract Vulkatherak. This collector won't let anyone with a camera into his menagerie, and he certainly wouldn't let me go in with a paintbrush and canvas."

"So . . . yet more crime?" I ask.

"Admittedly, there's very little I do that's not technically a crime somewhere," Zambrano says. "So many silly little governments, so many pesky rules."

"This guy is a minor seawater demon, who is willing to purchase you and freeze you in time for twenty years as a museum exhibit," Seraphex notes. "And he's done far worse to other exhibits in his menagerie. I don't really mind it, but does that spin your little moral compass a bit, Bryce?"

"Plus, he plays the same song on repeat in his menagerie. That's definite psychopath behavior," Zambrano adds.

"Okay, fair enough," I admit. "But what if something goes wrong? Like, the Wi-Fi connection doesn't work? Or he, I don't know, takes my tie off?"

"I checked both those things. They're pretty unlikely. But sure, if it all goes to hell, I'll pony up some even more valuable artifacts and buy you back. Fair enough?"

"You won't come blasting in, destroying everything to rescue me?"

Zambrano shrugs. "As a last resort, sure. But let's make sure it doesn't come to that, okay?"

I'm furious, of course. But I agreed to try to stick this out. I promised Agent Crane I'd work with Zambrano.

"What, don't you want to help save the world?" Zambrano asks far too happily. "Aren't you the Chosen Intern? The one to save the world?"

I sigh. "I know I'm not some sort of chosen one. I'm just some guy who's bad at magic. But I don't think it's really about being the chosen one. It's about being the one who chooses to do something."

"Spectacular!" Zambrano says with a wide grin. He grabs the back of my neck, Seraphex hops onto my foot, and we're off on—well, we're off on another stupidly dangerous adventure.

Or, hey, maybe this one will go great.

CHAPTER 17

Moments later, we're walking through the streets of Jakarta in what appears to be a particularly rich district. We pass towering hotels and swanky restaurants, eventually reaching a neighborhood full of the kind of showy mansions someone buys specifically to prove that they've made a lot of money. As we walk up the gigantic steps out front, I can see why we needed the suits. Everyone else arriving is wearing formal dress—tailored suits, designer dresses, and the kind of watches that never need to be used to check the time, because when you're wealthy enough, you can show up whenever you feel like it.

"Stay quiet," Zambrano says. "And just follow my lead."

I nod and follow him through the large double doors. What was I going to do, go rogue and start negotiating for artifacts on my own? Somehow, I don't think this place accepts Samba Smoothies loyalty reward points as payment for its artifacts.

The attendees are drawn from all over the world, and I hear several languages that I recognize and several that I don't. No one really seems to take exception to the duck sitting on my right shoulder, though they do seem to notice that she's there. The staff and the auctioneer look likely to be Indonesian, not that I would really be able to tell. Some of the attendees have unique complexions or facial structures—ones that I don't think I've ever seen on humans before. Could they be from some kind of body modifications, demons, or something else entirely?

I try to play it cool, quietly taking the seat that one of the ushers leads us to. As we sit down, my pulse is racing. I've never been around so many magical people and other creatures before, and I don't even know enough to know what sort of danger we might be in.

The room fills up, and I notice that everyone is noticing Zambrano but no one is approaching him. A few even take a look at him, confer with their friends, and turn right out around and walk out. The rest are taking deep breaths, and I can almost hear them trying to calm themselves down. They remind me of employees in a meeting with an explosive and abusive boss, just hoping that the boss doesn't see something to get upset about and chew them out.

They're afraid of him. Is he really that dangerous? Well, maybe. And even if he's not, I suppose many of these folks probably know the history, that a sorcerer can go mad at any time. But that also means that he could technically act sane at any time as well. I try to pin my hopes on that.

The auctioneer starts the proceedings, and the first few items are a confusing torrent of terms and shouting that I don't understand. The whole thing seems a bit more free-form than how someplace like Christie's or Sotheby's works—or at least how they're shown in movies and TV.

About ten minutes into it, I start to figure it out and be able to follow along. The auctioneer brings up an item and the item's sellers, then the bidders, shout out items or services they want to offer in exchange for it. Things like magical weapons, enchantments, spell instructions, body modifications, security consultations, and rare materials and ingredients. The seller gets to decide which bid they feel is currently the top choice, and other bidders can attempt to one-up them. Sometimes it devolves into open bargaining, but everyone is fairly polite. I wonder if that's part of the reason for the formal dress, to encourage acting respectably. I bet a lot of these people are terrible monsters, some of them literally, but in this environment they at least don't yell at one another.

"Why don't they just use money?" I whisper as one of the sellers trades an antique enchanted sword used by the ancient Sultan Saladin for a year of free security mage coverage for Thailand's Grand Palace and prime minister's residence.

"The most powerful wizards and demons can manipulate humans into giving them as much money as they need," Zambrano whispers. "So we don't deal in dollars or euros or yuan. It would destabilize the global economy if we started competing over that sort of thing. Sort of a gentleman's agreement not to mess with the currencies too much—it's been tried before. The Wall Street crash of '29, the Asian financial crisis . . . Sometimes it's done for greed, sometimes for altruism. But it never ends well. You have to let humans muddle around with their own systems."

"You know, you're human too," I note. "Did you forget that?"

Zambrano frowns at me. "That's a rather rude thing to remind someone of, Bryce."

I shrug. "Well, that's fair. I suppose none of us asked to be this way."

Next up, the auctioneer brings out a small bar of gleaming reddish metal as well as its seller, a small Nigerian man with a wispy moustache.

"One-point-eight kilograms of arcanely aligned bronze," the auctioneer says. "The strongest metal known on Earth, forged by the great Sorcerer Olujimi himself!"

I notice both the auctioneer and the seller give a nervous glance to Zambrano, who shakes his head sadly.

"Every year they tear more of the Circle's legacy apart," Zambrano grumbles.

"Don't lose track of the mission," Seraphex urges quietly.

"Fine," Zambrano answers with a sigh.

It seems like a Brazilian mining company is going to take it, and the auctioneer is counting off to end the bidding, but then a young Asian American woman raises her hand and calls out, "On behalf of Mr. Lukas Volker, I bid one Caldera Cannon."

Zambrano gives a low whistle, and I notice the rest of the crowd starts murmuring among themselves. But no one else tries to top the offer.

"Where did an Austrian billionaire get a hold of a full-size Caldera Cannon?" Zambrano wonders out loud. "The last known one was destroyed during the Boxer Rebellion. Though I still have one of the small prototypes."

"They're demonic cannons that shoot pure lava," Seraphex explains in response to my questioning look.

"Volker, that's the Mars spaceship guy, right?" I ask.

"Yeah. He'll probably use the enchanted bronze for the shielding of some key component. At least old Olujimi's work is going to contribute to something interesting. He'd approve of this," Zambrano says with satisfaction.

Apparently, the word of Lukas Volker is as good as payment here, so the young woman takes possession of the bronze bar and immediately walks down the center aisle and out of the room.

"Reputation is a key currency in the magical community," Seraphex explains. "Everyone here has a long reputation for honoring their debts. Though this Volker fellow is new, he may have bought his way in with a few gifts to the right people."

"I certainly wouldn't call them honorable though," Zambrano notes.

A couple more items are sold, with bidding going at dizzying speed, and then Zambrano jabs me in the ribs with rather unnecessary force. As if I could have relaxed or fallen asleep with magical artifacts being bartered at lightning speed around me.

The auctioneer brings out the next seller, who looks like nothing so much as seaweed stuffed into a suit. He's got two snakes where his eyes should be, and it looks like eels and seaweed coiled together for legs and arms. It's, frankly, repulsive.

"This is Slickwardinaeous," the auctioneer announces.

"Can we just call him Slickwad?" I ask.

"I like it," Seraphex says. "And those eels are definitely slick with gross phlegmy stuff."

From the door at the left side of the stage, two of the auctioneer's assistants use a large dolly to roll out the item Slickwad is selling. It's a massive piece of metal, polished to a shine and gleaming in the bright lights of the auction house. The crowd seems to murmur in appreciation.

"This, dear patrons," the auctioneer says, "is a gorgeous work fashioned from porcelain and plated in ninety-nine percent pure platinum. It is one of only two remaining Bohemian Commodes, built and enchanted for the Habsburg royal family in the eighteenth century."

The two assistants turn the dolly to face the crowd.

"You're going to sell me for a toilet?" I hiss. "I realize this is for a double cross, but still . . . a freaking toilet?"

"Not just any toilet," Zambrano taunts in a whisper, "a platinum-plated toilet that is magically enchanted to zap all the nastiness out of your bum after you're done doing your business. It's like a bidet, but without leaving you wet or blowing air up your behind. You just stand up, and you're *clean*. Archduchess Maria Theresa used to let me use it after we—"

I elbow him back just as hard as he hit me before. "How much of this plan is about stealing the artifact to distract the Duke, and how much is about you getting this stupid silver toilet?"

Zambrano shrugs. "Sometimes a plan can accomplish multiple important goals, each of which is equally vital."

"He's been talking about the Bohemian Commode for a long time," Seraphex interjects.

I glare at her.

"But stealing the artifact from Slickwad is also important," she says. "We do genuinely need it to execute the plan."

I have to admit, the not-being-able-to-tell-a-lie thing is actually kind of handy. It's nice to be able to believe someone around here. And I can see how it's kind of a strategic advantage to be able to be believed. Leave it to a demon to turn something that's supposed to be a limitation into a strength.

"Hey, when I was born we didn't have toilets, just a board at the edge of a cliff. And forget about toilet paper! I deserve this."

"Are you sure he will even accept the offer?" Seraphex asks.

Zambrano shrugs. "I saw him accept a similar one twenty years ago—a pair of chimpanzees that were magically trained as British fine dining waiters. It's a shame, I really enjoyed them; they worked at my favorite restaurant in East London."

The bidding starts but doesn't seem as intense as for some of the other objects. Bidders may have already offered their best goods, or maybe, just maybe, a magic toilet just isn't all that important in the modern era of indoor plumbing and Japanese toilets that sing little songs for you.

A Chinese businessman offers a rare dog magically enhanced with gills that let it breathe underwater, and a German woman tops that with an original "living grimoire" of spells that was apparently used at Waterloo in the defeat of Napoleon.

"Old Bonaparte didn't know a single spell, but he still fooled a dozen court wizards and conquered most of the continent," Seraphex notes.

"I always figured he had some kind of a deal with one of your kind," Zambrano says, eyeing Seraphex suspiciously. "So I took a decade away from European nonsense to explore South America."

"Maybe he did, maybe he didn't," Seraphex says primly. "If I know, I'm not telling. The Demonic Code requires that I not lie, but it doesn't force me to tell you anything."

Someone offers a spatula that can flip objects up to the weight of a car. Which I think is pretty cool, but Slickwad shakes his gross seaweed head.

"Declined," he says. "The living grimoire is better for my collection of curiosities."

He goes on to decline a straw that purifies anything that passes through it. Finally, Zambrano stands up.

"Twenty years of display rights to a boy whose mystic potential is statistically negligible. On an arcanometer, he registers as a 0.01 or lower," Zambrano says, his voice booming through the auction house.

"And you have the rights to this . . . unique specimen?" Slickwad asks, the seaweed on his face sliding around itself in excitement. "He looks quite delicious."

"Yes, he's right here. He signed a binding contract. Bad run of luck at the tables in Monaco; has to make good on his debts somehow. You know how it is."

Where the heck did he come up with that? It sounds outlandish to me, but glancing around, I notice with alarm that the rest of the bidders seem to be nodding along as if they do indeed *know how it is*. These people are creepy.

Slickwad thinks about it for a moment, then shakes his head.

"Interesting," Slickwad says. It's unclear how the voice is generated from the hole in the seaweed that makes up his mouth, but I'm pretty sure it's gross and I don't want to know. "Declined, as much as the boy with no mystic potential looks like a tasty little morsel. The grimoire is still a bit more valuable. It has historical significance."

"What?" I whisper. A minute ago, I was pissed that twenty years of my life was going to be sold for a toilet. Now, somehow, I'm insulted that the guy didn't take the offer.

"Very well," Zambrano says. "I counter-offer thirty years on display!"

The auctioneer stares at me. "Does the sorcerer have the legal right to offer that?" he asks.

I swallow. Zambrano didn't warn me that this wouldn't be a negotiation but more like improv. He certainly didn't give me any lines for this part of it!

"You question me?" Zambrano objects, but the auctioneer keeps looking at me patiently.

"Yep, it's in the contract," I say. I try to speak with the same loud authority that Zambrano does, but it somehow comes out like a little croak. "Thirty years is the maximum, however," I add. If he can improv, why can't I? "Earlier in the same game, he lost his Enchanted Snail Slime Face Rejuvenating Serum, so you'll have to forgive him if he's a bit cranky today."

I can see that all the people in the audience here are getting a little nervous, and I kind of like that.

"Don't worry," I continue. "He probably won't snap—not right at this moment, anyway. Shall we get me off to that magically secure menagerie now?"

"Enough of that, Intern," Zambrano says gruffly, but there's a twinkle of amusement in his eye. Everyone nearby is shifting uncomfortably, but none of them actually makes a move to get away. "Can anyone top that?"

The auctioneer confirms that Slickwad accepts Zambrano's bid and then waits a moment and counts down to the sale. No one offers anything else, he bangs his gavel, and the sale is concluded. I wonder if my banter cleverly scared anyone off from entering a competing bid, or if I was just being a dick. I can't say I care too much either way.

Have I been spending too much time with Zambrano? Well, certainly. But has it potentially impacted my decision-making and empathy skills? . . . maybe!

Zambrano takes me by the shoulder and leads me up to the stage. One of the auction house staff mages seems to be taking some readings with a small glass contraption with water and flecks of something in it, sort of like a compass with no needle. I now recognize it as an arcanometer, a more mechanized version of the basin of water that Zambrano used to initially measure my mystic potential.

The mage nods in appreciation, and Slickwad's seaweed twists in pleasure.

As we get close, I start to smell what can best be described as Slickwad's rancid aura. It's like old dead fish and rotten sushi, which I know is technically also old dead fish, but the smell is really bad so the doubled description feels justified.

"I'm going to enjoy having this fresh young oddity in my collection," the seawater demon says, his snake eyes curving toward me in a leering way. My stomach turns, and I'm suddenly worried about how far and how quickly things may go off plan.

I can see Zambrano's face wrinkle, and he sort of pushes me in the general direction of Slickwad and turns and heads back for his seat.

The auction house employees hustle me off into a back room, and as I glance behind me, I see the auctioneer breathing a sigh of relief offstage before turning to lead the next seller out onto the stage.

Backstage, there's some paperwork that I sign without really looking at it, then one of the auction house security guards steps up and frisks me, and suddenly the reality of what's about to happen starts to set in.

I stand stock-still, hoping they don't find the camera. The guy is *very* thorough. I'm pretty sure I don't have any real rights in this place, which is good for the guard, because otherwise I would definitely have a sexual harassment case. Even teenagers experimenting with heavy petting wouldn't be able to figure out how to get that intimate through clothes.

But the guard steps back, gives a grunt of affirmation, and they lead me down in an elevator to a loading dock. Slickwad tags along, his stink filling up the tiny little elevator.

"This will make a fine addition to my collection," he burbles to the guard, ignoring me entirely. "A luscious young man with no magic potential at all. How fascinating."

I'm both creeped out and also kind of annoyed that no one else in the world seems to be as excited to have me around as this mass of disgusting seaweed and eels.

"Yes indeed, a very fine addition," the security guard says, displaying admirable professionalism.

"Humans with unique traits are so very rare," Slickwad continues. "Different sizes, different colors, different bad opinions about music."

"Music, sir?" the guard asks.

"Yes! Humans spend so much time inventing new songs, when Johann Pachelbel wrote the only piece of music worth listening to in 1680. Why reinvent what is already perfected?"

"Ah, yes. The 'Canon in D Major' is indeed a masterpiece, sir," the guard says with a bored air that says it isn't the first time he's heard a rant of this type.

On the loading dock, two guys in coveralls are wheeling out a large glass case. They motion me into it, and I shrug and step in. I didn't realize that this was going to happen so quickly, but here we are.

I want to yell something mean to contradict Slickwad as the door closes, but I can't think of what to say in time. To be honest, Pachelbel's Canon is kind of a banger.

The door to the glass case shuts, and I'm relieved to find that the assault of the smell has diminished a fair amount. Though if there's no ventilation in this slow-time display case, I suppose I may be stuck with it.

For a moment, I watch as Slickwad examines the lock on the case. Then he turns to walk away, and with every step he accelerates. The workers in coveralls move around me like they're on fast forward, then one of them approaches with a dolly, and the whole world turns into a blur. People moving around me are impossible to make out as they flit around at high speed, but I am able to briefly see things when I'm placed in a still location. First there's the inside of a truck, then an airplane hangar, then the bumpy and blurry airplane cargo hold, then another truck, and finally, a large red-painted parlor filled with other cases. It has grand sweeping columns, and there's a thick red and gold carpet on the floor.

Near me, I can see one case with fish in it, several with other humans that look to come from varying historical periods over the last hundred years, various artifacts, and two chimpanzees in tuxedos.

I notice that while the people in the room are blurs as they move through, I can actually see the subjects in the other cases are moving in real time. We must all be slowed down by the same factor. I can see the other humans turning to look at me with curiosity.

I wonder if, given decades spent here, I might end up making friends or enemies with some of them. Luckily, that doesn't happen. I'm only awkwardly watching everyone else checking out the new guy for a couple seconds, when the blurring outside suddenly comes to a halt, and the glass door to my case pops open.

I instinctively step out.

Everything is on fire. Alarms are blaring. The two chimpanzees in tuxedos are lying unconscious on the floor in front of me, soaking wet. And Seraphex is standing at my feet with what looks like a small cannon strapped to her little duck back and something that looks like little duck saddlebags. It's pretty adorable.

"So, that didn't go exactly the way we had planned," she says.

In the background, I can hear the distorted strains of Pachelbel's "Canon in D Major" playing on repeat through broken speakers.

CHAPTER 18

"Did you have a nice nap?" Seraphex asks.

"It seems like it's been ten seconds! What the hell happened?" I ask, staring around at the chaos. Fire alarms are going off, and the carpet under my feet is soggy. I take a step, and it squelches under my feet.

"The sprinklers went off," Seraphex says. "And the waiter chimps must have been knocked unconscious by the smoke and hypoxia. That's lack of oxygen. Or carbon monoxide poisoning, or technically it could even be hydrogen cyanide . . ."

"No, no, what *happened*?" I demand. "Why are you here? Where is Zambrano?" Looking around, I can see that the sprinklers have mostly suppressed the fire, but there are still little bits of flames in the corners. I instinctively pull out my phone, but it doesn't have any service.

"Don't worry, the chimps will be fine," Seraphex says with a wink, "thanks for asking. No time for the full story—take the cannon off my back," she says. "Zambrano made my promise to give it to you as soon as you were free. I must keep to my agreement."

I kneel on the soggy carpet and unstrap the cannon from her back.

"What is this?" I ask, handling it with care.

"It's a miniature prototype Caldera Cannon. After the auction, Zambrano pulled it out of the basement where he's been storing it for years."

"We have a basement?" I say, trying to hold the cannon as gently as I can. There's no clear trigger or lever or anything on it, so I have no way to know what will set it off and make it shoot lava every-where. It is pleasantly warm to the touch, which is low-key terrifying.

"Yeah, he asked me not to tell you about it. But I didn't actually agree to that, so I can. That's where the really good stuff is, like the books that I get to read if I win the bet about you. Grab that keycard from the ground, and let's go!" She turns and starts toward the door, flapping her wings a bit as she rushes.

I look down and fish the keycard out of the soggy carpet and follow along after her as she waddles toward the door. We pass through a long hallway and come to another, even grander room than the one I was in.

"This is the main menagerie, where Slickwad's actually valuable and interesting items are collected," Seraphex says.

"I'm not one of the valuable ones?" I blurt out.

"Oh, yeah, you were in the sideshow room," Seraphex says. "For oddities and freaks. This room is where the real valuable stuff is. Remember, he traded an old toilet for you. Not exactly the most valuable magical artifact around."

"What? I'm not even one of the valuable—" I start, but then cut myself off. What's the point of complaining? It seems that no matter how bad it gets, there's always a new level of insult and humiliation for the magical world to inflict on me.

Seraphex flaps her wings and leaps up onto my shoulder.

"Okay, now open up that case with the egg inside it and grab it," Seraphex instructs. "That was the original goal of this whole boondoggle."

I quickly comply, popping open the cage and swiping the egg, which is made of a rough black rocky shell and pleasantly warm to the touch. Is it a dragon egg? Damn, I really hope it's a dragon egg. That would be so cool.

"Okay, now use that key card on the rest of the cases," Seraphex instructs. "That will start the process of them returning to normal time and opening up."

"Classic prison break?" I guess as I start methodically pressing the key against every case in the main hall. "Easier to escape with everyone else making a run for it too?"

"Yes," Seraphex says, "and also if the others get out as well, no one will be able to trace back that it was us who did massive property damage and blasted half a block of Istanbul with lava in order to free you. But don't worry! Zambrano is breaking into the guardhouse to delete all the security footage. That's why he's not here."

"Security footage wasn't exactly the main worry on my mind right now, but okay."

There are all sorts of creatures in this hall, everything from normal-looking humans and animals to people with feathers, what looks like a fairy with tiny wings, and a narwhal in a case filled with water. We agree to skip the narwhal since there's no way it can survive in the open air.

"Great, now we just go down the corridor to the left here and back out the hole I came in. It should be cooled down enough for us to walk through now."

I glance back before leaving the hall and see that the doors to the cases are starting to pop open and confused figures are stepping out. Two of them immediately start yelling at each other. Do they know each other?

I jog down the corridor and turn the corner. There's a large hole that's been blasted in the side of this building, and there's volcanic rock covering what's left of the floor. In many areas, the floor is open to the basement level, having been burned through by the falling lava. Beyond the hole in the wall, I can see a street with various wreckage and some trees and bushes on fire.

I take a moment to plan how to make it over the obstacle course of joists and rock. I pause, trying to figure out how to do it while carrying a duck and a lava cannon. I gingerly step out onto the first bit of solidified rock, which is still warm underneath my shoe.

"It's like that kids' game," Seraphex notes from my shoulder. "The Floor Is Lava. But the lava is cooled down, and you can step on it because the other lava put holes in the floor. Didn't you play that game like every other kid? So you should be good at this!"

"Sure, it's like that, but the lava is the part I'm supposed to step on. So it's reversed. Or the inverse. Converse? Or something. Anyway, I would always just grab my mom's rolling chair and a ski pole and just wheel myself around. The game never made sense to me."

I take another step forward, then another, and I feel like I'm starting to get the hang of it.

"How did you get in after you opened this hole up?" I ask.

"I'm a bird, foolish intern. At least in this horrible form that I've been forced into," Seraphex says. "I flew. It wasn't easy with that mini cannon on my back though. Luckily, my demon nature makes me quite a bit stronger than your average duck."

"Oh, right," I say. I sometimes forget that she can fly since it seems like mostly she just lounges around and criticizes us. But she did strap on artillery and come charging in to save me from being stuck in a case for thirty years, so I have to give her some credit.

"Hold on!" Seraphex hisses in my ear. I freeze.

"What?"

"Get back," she whispers, "someone's coming."

I take several steps backward, getting us off the lava and back around the corner. I peer back around it and see that there are blue lights flashing, reflecting off the shiny surface of some of the newly cooled lava. Voices are yelling in a language I don't know.

"Let me guess, tons of police are out there?" I ask. "Can we do just one mission that doesn't involve multiple felonies?"

"Maybe next time our plan will involve just asking nicely for disreputable people to give us their powerful artifacts just because they're nice," Seraphex says. "Feel free to suggest it to Zambrano. In any event, we'll have to go out another way. Keep going down the corridor."

I move down the corridor, and Seraphex directs me through the maze of back passages. This place is a major operation with kitchens, maids' rooms, a library, and more. These passages are far away from the lava, so at least nothing here is on fire.

"What's the plan to get out?" I ask. "The back door? Go out the sewers? Is sneaking through air ducts a real thing?"

"We need to get outside so that Zambrano can make a teleportrait to come and grab us without anyone seeing us. This place is probably crawling with police and covered with a thousand cameras. It turns out that this building blocks both electronic and magical communication," she says. "If we can get outside, I've got an illusion prism that should hide us long enough for Zambrano to paint a quick teleportrait."

I glance around, thinking about the possible ways that we could get out. "Pretty much any door will be covered by cops," I reason.

"And even if we make our own hole with this lava cannon gizmo, I won't be able to walk through it until it's cooled down. And the fire has subsided. If it doesn't burn the whole place down. Unless you can . . . ?"

"I'm several times stronger than an average duck, but I definitely can't carry you through the air," Seraphex says.

"Okay, okay," I answer. "So then we need to get outside and wait somewhere stable for a while. How about the roof?"

Seraphex bobs her head. "That should work!"

"I don't suppose you have, like, detailed schematics of the building or something?" I ask, hopefully.

The duck shrugs. "Nope. We could . . . look for stairs?"

"I don't have a better plan," I say, starting to jog through the corridors. "Let's hope we can get lucky."

The place turns out to be huge, a maze of halls and corridors. And I really am quite shocked when we do, in fact, get lucky. We're able to find large open stairs to the second floor and head through a museum room of old documents to a small stairwell to the third floor, then down through a large commercial kitchen to a large storage room with a staircase on one wall that leads up to a roof door with sunlight coming in through a small window. It's marked with a sign that says FIRE DOOR—ALARM WILL SOUND IF OPENED in English and what looks like Turkish. But I'm pretty sure the ship has sailed on worrying about setting off alarms.

There's only one problem—the two chimps in tuxedos have woken up and are hanging out on the stairs right in front of the door to the roof.

"How friendly are they, like, on a scale from one to eat my face off?" I whisper.

The chimps are pounding at the door, probably because they're able to see that small square of sunlight coming through the tiny window. Unfortunately, they don't seem to have figured out how to turn the door handle. I guess they weren't trained for that. They're in full-on feral mode, bashing the door and slapping the walls with their hands.

"I'd estimate . . . eight and a half?" Seraphex says.

"Yeah," I say. "How do we get them to leave?"

The duck casts a meaningful look at the cannon in my hand.

I take a deep breath. "I don't think I can do that. Those poor guys don't deserve an end like that after being imprisoned here for years."

"Those poor 'animals' would smash your bones into a fine powder if given the chance right now."

"Only because they're spooked! Because you set the whole building on fire with a lava cannon!"

"Are you really going to sacrifice your life for a couple waiter apes?" Seraphex asks.

I think for a second. There has to be another option. "You're invincible! Maybe you can distract them? Draw them away?"

Seraphex glares at me but gives her little duck shrug. "Very well, but you owe me," she says.

She half flies, half hops up the stairs, but the apes ignore her. As she gets closer, she flaps her wings and squawks at them. At first they don't seem to notice. Then one of the apes turns, grabs her, and flings her into the air, off the stairs.

Screeching, she tumbles for a moment before righting herself and using her wings to bring herself down in a swoop, landing next to me. Several feathers float down the air beside her.

"I did not enjoy that experience," the demon queen says, ruffling her feathers and shaking herself off.

"We just need something that gets them back into a more comfortable space," I say, biting my lip in thought. "Something to turn their panic off."

"Being buried under a layer of molten rock would turn their panic off," Seraphex suggests. "Metaphorically, you could think of it as a nice warm electric weighted blanket. If you wanted to think of it that way."

"Sorry, I'm okay with all the crime, but I have to draw the line at murder," I say. "Come on, I have an idea."

I backtrack to the kitchen that we just passed through. It's a standard commercial-grade kitchen and has a lot of things I recognize from Samba Smoothies and quite a few that I don't recognize because they're used for making real food, not whatever it was that we sold in the Jersey City Galleria food court.

"What are you looking for?" Seraphex asks, flapping and hopping along behind me.

"If there's a big kitchen, there's probably a dining room right near it," I say as I check the various doors exiting the kitchen. And after a quick search, I'm able to find the dining room.

Between the dining room and the kitchen, I'm able to fill a milk crate with a tablecloth, utensils, plates, glasses, and some scraps of food. I head back into the storage room, where the tuxedo apes have calmed down and are now pounding against the door in a more rhythmic fashion. I can see dents starting to appear in it even though it's a reinforced metal fire door.

Grabbing a couple of boxes, I toss the tablecloth down and lay out the plates, glasses, and cutlery. I never really learned the proper way to set a table no matter how many times my mom tried to teach me. But I don't worry too much about that; having the setting be a little off might even be a feature.

I retreat to the opposite side of the room, then turn to Seraphex. "We need to attract their attention. Can you do sounds as well as voices?"

"Why yes, I certainly can," Seraphex says, having watched my rushed efforts with a bemused smile on her face. "I think this is a huge waste of time, but I have to admit that I admire the attempt. What do you need me to do?"

"I don't know, a bell? Glasses clinking?"

Seraphex hops over to the improvised dining table and makes a series of different sounds. First bells, then glasses, but the chimps just seem to ignore the noises and continue trying to tear the door off its hinges.

"What else?" she asks.

"Um . . . Zambrano said they were trained in London. What about something in an English accent?"

Seraphex straightens up and adopts a snooty pose.

"Waiters! You are summoned to service," she says with a powerful baritone in a flawless upper-crust English accent. At the sound of the voice, both chimps suddenly freeze. "There's an exigent demand at table one; do make haste."

They look around the room in a panic, then one sees the improvised dining table. The two leap down the stairs, swinging off the railing and suddenly standing ramrod straight, moving slowly and steadily. They begin fixing my messy attempt at table setting, moving with grace and care, exactly the opposite of moments ago.

Part of me is mesmerized by them, but I suppress my interest and quietly step toward the stairs. They completely ignore me and Seraphex as we creep up the stairs, turn the doorknob, and sneak out onto the roof.

Outside, we can hear the sirens and shouting of both emergency services and the crowd that's gathered to watch. Luckily, the roof has a low wall around it, so I close the door behind us and run in a crouch, eventually dropping to my hands and knees to reach the farthest corner from the stairwell door. Once there, I hunker down against the wall, catching my breath.

"The illusion prism in my bag is set to hide any living creatures within six feet," Seraphex explains, hopping up to me and turning to let me open the saddlebags.

I open them up and pull the prism out, not mentioning at all how adorable they look.

I place the prism down on the ground in front of us, where it glimmers in the sunlight.

"So we're hidden now?" I ask.

"Try it out," she says, gesturing away from the prism with a wing.

I crawl away, and sure enough once I'm a few feet away, the prism and duck both disappear as if removed by a photo editing app. I crawl back, collapsing against the wall in relief.

I pull out my phone, which is buzzing because a bunch of notifications have all come in at once now that we're outside.

"So we just wait here now?" I ask.

"Yes," Seraphex says. "You should be able to check in with Zambrano on your phone now. We knew that the menagerie was shielded against magic, but they must have added cell phone jamming in the last month or two. Silly Zambrano, not double-checking."

I double-check that the tiny camera in my necktie has a clear view of the rooftop. Looking down, I can see that this incredibly expensive custom suit is already pretty badly damaged by our adventures so far.

I pull out my phone and text Zambrano. And no, he doesn't reply with anything nice like *Hey Bryce, I'm so sorry I almost got you trapped in a magical time box in a crazy collector's house and nearly got you killed in the rescue attempt.* All his text says is *See your camera now, painting a teleportrait. Don't move.*

I hold my breath as a group of firefighters and police officers come up onto the roof. But they glance around for less than a minute, don't see anything amiss, and return back down into the building.

After a few more minutes, Seraphex hops up onto my lap.

"That was good thinking in there," she says. "You got us out of another tricky situation."

"Thanks," I answer. "I wish it hadn't been necessary, but at least we got this," I say, hefting the warm black egg that I stole from the slow-time case. "Please tell me it's a dragon egg?"

"No, nothing like that," she says. "Just a phoenix. The last known one. They're considered the ultimate delicacy for volcano demons. If I know Vulkatherak, the moment he gets reports of a live phoenix anywhere in the world, he'll head there immediately. They're only alive for a day before they burn up and return to their egg form."

I sigh. "I feel like there are several major objections I could have to that plan, but I suppose we've already done worse things."

The duck shrugs. "Oh, the phoenix will have a head start. I wouldn't worry about it; they're very clever."

"Fair enough," I say, trying to convince myself that it's a reasonable plan.

"Anyway, what I was trying to say was . . . I think you've done very well since you became Zambrano's intern. Your birth mother would be proud."

I freeze, and something inside me seizes up. "My what?" I hiss. "What do you know?"

She hops off and starts preening and ruffling her feathers, ignoring me.

"Sera, what do you know about my birth mother?" I demand.

She turns back, giving me a smug grin.

"I know quite a bit, as it turns out," she says. "I know some details about your history that are . . . quite fascinating. Things that Zambrano doesn't know either, before you run off and ask him. But I won't tell you now. I'll only tell you once we've foiled Vulkatherak's current plan."

"What?!" I want to yell at her, but I have to do my best to whisper my outrage. Below us, I can hear chaos as the police and fire teams try to capture and contain all the various creatures and people who've escaped from the menagerie. It's hard to make out the details, and we can't see anything, but there are screams, roars, and the occasional honking of cars as something escapes into the traffic.

She gives her little duck shrug. "No point bothering me about it now. I'm not able to tell you, even if I changed my mind and wanted to. I've committed to a plan, and the Demonic Code requires me to do my best to follow through on what I said."

"You are a such a . . ." I struggle to find words to express my exasperation.

"A demon?" she asks with a sparkle in her eyes.

"I thought we were friends," I say.

"I'm sorry it hurts your feelings," she answers, "but I am a demon queen who's been trapped in a very inconvenient form, and I have to look out for myself. I can't be committed to being your friend. But . . . I will try to make nice things happen for you. If doing so can be made to fit into my plan. And I have at least one idea for how to do that."

I sigh, shaking my head at the infuriating bird. "Aren't you hoping that I die? So you can win your silly bet and get to read Zambrano's special books? And so you don't have to give up your precious passphrase to Merlin's Vault?"

"To be completely honest," Seraphex says, which I note is an unnecessary thing to start with, "those books would be fascinating to read. But I'm rooting for you. I hope I lose the bet. I don't mind if Zambrano gets into Merlin's Vault."

"Is this your little demon way of saying that . . . you actually like me?" I say.

"And what if it is?" she asks, tossing her head with a regal air.

Before I can reply, there's a whooshing sound and a gust of wind, and Zambrano appears almost on top of us. He's holding a tele-portrait in each hand, one up close to his face and one at his side.

"Still got the touch!" he whispers. "And perfectly just inside the illusion radius too. Damn, I'm good. Let's go!"

Seraphex hops back on my shoulder, and Zambrano grabs my neck and switches which teleportrait he's holding up to his face. A moment later, we're torn from the rooftop, and the inside of the warehouse appears around us.

"Good work, everyone," Zambrano says, grabbing the onyx egg from where I've been cradling it. "You got Bryce out, got the egg, and released a ton of the other exhibits, so no one will know it was us that triggered the whole jailbreak."

"Wasn't this supposed to be a quiet little raid?" I ask. "Wasn't that the whole point of selling your intern for a toilet? Which is going to stick with me for a while, by the way."

"Renting my intern!" Zambrano objects, but he's grinning with a self-satisfaction that I can't really bear to smash. "That's true, but I've learned not to get too upset when you have to go to Plan B."

"Plan B was to trade back for him," Seraphex notes. "Blowing a hole in the wall with lava was Plan C."

"Slickwad didn't want my collection of original Great Sorcerers of History action figures from the 1980s. How could I possibly have predicted that?"

"Um . . . any chance those are, like, still available?" I ask. I always wanted those when I was a kid, but they were discontinued decades ago, and buying even one in an online auction would have been, like, a whole year's allowance.

"I'll let you look at them, but no touching!" Zambrano answers, disgust apparent in his voice. "There's no amount of washing that will make your fingers clean enough. I've seen the greasy junk that you order every morning. But not right now. I've got to go drop this egg. Now that it's out of the slow time, it's going to hatch within an hour or two."

He puts the freshly painted teleportrait of the roof of the menagerie on the wall and grabs one with a bleak snowscape labeled SASKATCHEWAN.

"Be ready for the next mission tomorrow!" he says, and his lips purse for a moment, then he disappears in a little gust of wind.

I turn to Seraphex, but she's already waddling her way off back into the library, ignoring me.

I sigh. Another night alone. I guess I might as well go order some greasy food.

CHAPTER 19

When I arrive downstairs the next morning, Zambrano is examining what appears to be a bluish frog floating in a giant glass bulb. The frog is moving slowly through the air as if it's been trapped in slow motion midway through a hop.

"Great, you're here!" Zambrano says with an unusually cheerful air. He presses his hand on the glass, mutters something, and the frog's movement stops and freezes almost completely. "Check this out!"

Stepping closer, I notice the metal box that I stole from Vulkatherak's minions on the boat in Peru sitting on the bench next to the glass bulb. It's bent apart and has clearly been pried open, and it's now empty.

"What is it?" I say, curious despite myself. "Is that what we were after in Peru?"

"Exactly!" Zambrano says. "And it is a glorious specimen, in perfect condition. It's an Amazonian azure frog, a very rare find. Vulkatherak's minions would have gotten quite a high price for this on the black market."

"Wow," I say. "What does it do?" I ask, looking more closely. It has swirling blue and white marks on it in an almost hypnotic pattern.

"It has a powerful intoxicating toxin, which it transfers when it makes contact with a tongue, rendering anyone experiencing it essentially comatose," he explains.

"It's . . . a magical poisonous frog that gets you high when you lick it? That's what I almost died for? A drug frog?"

"No, no, it's far more important than that," Zambrano says. "It's a crucial part of our plan to stop Vulkatherak! Because this frog doesn't just knock out people, it can knock out most any sentient being."

"Rockhide demons, in this case," Seraphex says, appearing from behind a bookshelf. "The ones guarding Vulkatherak's penthouse in Chicago."

"Ah, okay," I say. "A little weird, but I dig it."

"You'll like it a lot better than having two rockhide demons mashing your skull," Seraphex says.

After that, we head upstairs to a large room with a giant conference table, and Zambrano lays out maps and blueprints of Vulkatherak's Chicago penthouse. We run through the plan a few times and make some modifications. I'm surprised that Zambrano even accepts a few of my suggestions, though he does so curtly, without anything even approaching a compliment.

Soon we've got a pretty decent plan. Okay, we've got a plan that makes sense but seems quite dangerous.

I spend the next few days researching and studying. Seraphex hangs out for most of it, giving me pointers about rockhide demons, magical artifacts, and more. At one point, she shows me a crystal ball that can show images of many beings, including the various demons I might run into. She shows me the rockhide demon guards, flying hellions, and the arcane conduit, which is a pair of magical staffs, each a powerful rod of shining twisted metal.

"Can you show me Vulkatherak himself?" I ask when I arrive in the laboratory on the third day. "I'm not supposed to run into him, but I still want to see who it is we're working against."

Of course, the crystal ball doesn't respond to my non-magical touch, and Seraphex's duckbill isn't able to activate it either, so we have to call over Zambrano.

Bored, he comes over from his workbench and makes a few gestures and instructs the crystal ball to activate.

"Duke Vulkatherak," Seraphex says, and an image of Vulkatherak appears in the crystal ball. He's humanoid but made of pure rock with tiny rivulets of molten lava appearing to flow from cracks in his skin, especially from his biceps, hips, and face.

"Ugly fellow, right?" Zambrano says.

"Yeah," I agree. "Is that lava flowing from . . . his nose?"

Zambrano smiles, looking closer. "It does look like it. Maybe he's allergic to the granite on Earth?" he says with a chuckle.

"Yeah, it's like a little volcano coming out of his nose . . . a volcanose," I say.

"Oh, he's not going to like that," Seraphex says, practically beaming.

Zambrano shakes his head in amusement as he returns to a table at the far side of the warehouse where he's working his way through a tall stack of books. Seraphex narrates as the crystal ball shows me what Vulkatherak's demon underlings look like.

"Why are you helping me?" I ask her. "Why are you helping us—humanity, I mean. Shouldn't you be on the demonic side?"

"Oh, you're such a silly human, thinking demons must all be on the same 'side,'" she says, primly rearranging her wings. "And there are two reasons. One, it beats staring out the window. I can't go anywhere, and I'm certainly not going to lower myself to your level. I've heard about your 'social media,' and it sounds worse than the demonic realms. Two, I'm not going to let Vulkatherak succeed where I failed. That melodramatic twit. I've got more style in my left pinky claw than he has in his whole body."

"You don't—" I start.

"I don't have claws anymore, I know," she says. "And that big brute doesn't have any style whatsoever. The metaphor is apt, kid."

I guess that's just, like, her opinion, so it's subjective enough to not count as a lie.

The next day, I'm woken up by a birch butler who pokes my head and gestures for me to follow him. "Doesn't anybody just open the door and yell at me to wake up anymore?" I grumble. But I get dressed and follow the butler down to the ground floor, where Zambrano is sitting in front of an easel. He has a paintbrush in his right hand, a tablet in his left hand, an extra brush behind his ear, and a scowl on his face. He's staring at an image on the tablet, muttering under his breath. Seraphex is sitting on a nearby table with two of the birch butlers grooming her with what looks like pipe cleaners.

"I hate doing this from such a crappy image," Zambrano grumbles, putting the finishing touches on a cityscape.

Leaning in, I can see that the painting matches the image on the tablet, and I can also see why he's so frustrated.

"Is that . . ."

"Yes, it's Google's cached version of an old real estate listing," Zambrano says, peering in at the low-resolution image. "But it's only six months old, so if I just get the view from the window and the wall, this should work regardless of whether they've added some furniture. As long as they didn't repaint the wall."

"And that teleportrait will transport us to where the lookout is?" I ask, impressed despite myself. The first step of our plan is to take out the lookout watching the building from a block away, so that we can break in without being noticed.

"Exactly," Zambrano says. "The lookout sits in a folding chair just to the left of this. We'll catch him by surprise—they don't know that I can make a teleportrait from a photograph."

"Hold on," I say, and Zambrano stops and looks up at me. "All these," I continue, gesturing at the wall of paintings, "are landscapes, not portraits. There's not a single person in any of them. Doesn't a portrait have to have a person in it?"

"Ugh, you are so *literal*," Zambrano gripes. "Do you really think I'm going to let little things like the official definitions of words get in the way of a good pun? I don't let the laws of physics stop me from transporting hundreds of miles in the blink of an eye—why would I let a silly thing like a dictionary stop me?"

"He's very fond of that particular bit of wordplay," Seraphex notes wryly.

"Okay, okay," I say, and lean in to look at the cleverly but inaccurately named teleportrait.

Zambrano's painting is a nicely stylized version of a very bland real estate listing photo, though he's zoomed in a bit to get just the wall and big windows. It still looks sterile, boring, and very brightly lit. It's a bad photo, and whoever rented out this apartment must have decided to cheap out on a real estate agent or photographer and decided to just do it themselves.

"That'll have to do," Zambrano says, throwing up his hands and dislodging the paintbrush from his ear and knocking it to the floor. The birch butler who led me down immediately scurries to pick it up and put it back on the counter.

I eye the birch butler, biting my lip in thought.

"Those birch butlers. They're not . . . sentient, are they? They're not oppressed or something?"

"Just full of annoying questions today, aren't we?" Zambrano says. "But no, I don't have sentient birch butlers. Not anymore."

"Not . . . anymore?"

"Oh, I replaced them with these ones. Not much real intelligence, no identities, no emotions, no pain or pleasure. Just little tools."

"So, you created an intelligent race of creatures, then realized the moral quandary that forcing them to serve created, and so you *destroyed them*?"

"No, no, no, what kind of monster do you take me for? I just stopped making them that way. They're still out there, somewhere," Zambrano says with a wave of his hand. "You should have seen their little faces when I told them to go out and do whatever they wanted to do. They had *no* idea what to do with that," he says, chuckling to himself.

"So you just cut them loose? Sent them away?" I ask. "Don't you care about their feelings?"

"Why should I care about their feelings? I don't feel their feelings. I only feel my feelings. Besides, I listened to my conscience and let them go. I didn't want to be in a whole 'whoops, I accidentally created a class of magically oppressed sentient creatures,' situation. That's just gross! I'm the good guy here!"

I don't know how to feel about that, but I guess there's nothing I can do about it right now. Zambrano is at least trying to be on the side of good, so I guess I have to appreciate that?

"Okay, whatever. I'm ready, let's do this," I say. This time I'm properly prepared for an infiltration, dressed all in black with black sneakers, all same-day delivery from the tablet upstairs that apparently lets me order anything. I'm probably getting too used to that, but there has to be some compensation for this madness, right? The sneakers were expensive, but they feel great and look badass. Now I can risk my life *and* have solid arch support at the same time.

I've also got the metal box from Peru and a few other supplies in my backpack, and I'm holding a collapsed cardboard box tucked under my arm. I don't feel so good about that part. I asked if we could use a wooden or metal box, but Zambrano said the spell we used in Japan only works on paper, which cardboard is technically close enough to. I argued that wood is sort of paper too, but that wouldn't fly, in a literal sense. Next time, maybe we can do some breaking and entering on a one-story building?

A few minutes later, we're ready to roll. Zambrano is wearing ugly sunglasses, old jeans, a Chicago Bears hoodie, and a Chicago Cubs baseball hat. I guess he might fit in Chicago if he gets spotted, but the jeans are skinny and the sweatshirt is perfectly fitted to his form, somehow outlining his pecs and waist perfectly. If you squint, you can almost see his six-pack. Which feels like exactly the opposite of the point of a hoodie, which is that you can kind of disappear into it. Still, it's an attempt.

"I want to go to there," Zambrano says as he grabs my neck and Seraphex jumps onto my shoulder, and I roll my eyes. This guy is way too proud of his dated jokes.

A moment later, the same apartment building twists into real life around us, and we're looking out the window across the Chicago skyline.

"Eye of Jupiter!" Zambrano says as he spins to his left, using the same supergravity spell that he used when I first surprised him in his bathtub. It seems like a lifetime ago. As Zambrano explained in our planning session, it's a harder spell to start and stop because gravity is unwieldy, but it affects the whole area and doesn't need to be targeted too precisely.

I turn as well, eager to see this spell in action from a non-bone-crushing perspective. And the spell works perfectly, slamming the black metal folding chair and a small telescope and tripod against the apartment wall. The chair hits so hard that the drywall around it cracks under the pressure.

But it's just the chair. There's supposed to be a lookout sitting there.

That's not how this is supposed to go.

I turn farther, taking in the rest of the room. The lookout is on the other side of the room, his mouth open and a footlong meatball sub sandwich in his hands. He's a little white guy with a thin wispy beard and deep-set eyes that look like knots in an old oak tree.

"What the hell?" he yells in a gravelly voice, recovering from his shock sooner than I do. He grabs at his belt, pulling up a small hand axe.

"Hey!" I yell at him. It's not the most articulate thing, but I can see him rearing back to throw the axe, and that's literally the only word that pops into my head. As he raises the axe, it starts to glow with a flickering bluish light as if some extra magical power is activating.

Next to me, Zambrano is waving his arms, trying to shut down the gas giant gravity spell.

"You're done for now," Wispy Beard Guy says as he takes a step forward, pointing at me with his left hand while his right pulls back and hurls the axe right at me. As it spins across the room, all I can see is the blue light gleaming off it. It seems to move slightly slower than I would expect, but maybe that's just the natural distortion of time that comes from sudden adrenaline. I take the opportunity to dodge to my left, and Seraphex falls off my shoulder with an angry squawk.

Instead of missing me, the axe seems to glow brighter and curve through the air, redirecting its flight to come straight after me.

"*Deja de moverte!*" Zambrano shouts, jabbing his splayed fingers in my direction.

My breath is caught in my chest as the axe spins straight at me, and then stops in the air, seized and held by magical force.

"*Pergi tidur!*" Zambrano shouts, his teeth bared and his face snarling. He makes a snuffing gesture with his hands, and a bolt of white energy shoots out, striking the man. The guy drops to the ground in a pile of limbs. For a second I think he might be dead, but then he starts snoring.

I'm plastered against the window with the glowing blue axe only a half a foot from sinking into my chest. I shuffle to the side and step back from the suspended weapon.

And then it's all over. The axe is frozen, the lookout is sleeping, and Zambrano, Seraphex, and I are standing in the lookout's unfurnished apartment.

"If that had been a gun, I'd be dead," I say, staring at the axe, which is still hanging in the air. I pause for a moment, taking in the level of danger that this plan is going to put me in. "How can I trust that you're going to get me through this?"

"I just saved you, didn't I?" Zambrano says, though it doesn't seem to me that he's saying it with a lot of confidence. "That guy sits in that chair twelve hours a day. It's literally his job! How could we have known he would pick this exact moment to take a sandwich break?"

I glance at the man lying in a twist on the floor, snoring loudly. It looks uncomfortable. Definitely going to leave a nasty crick in his neck. He's going to need a massage or a chiropractor or something when he wakes up. Maybe just a neck transplant. He also landed right where he dropped his sandwich, so he's gonna need a new shirt as well.

"Okay, sure," I admit. "But what if you're not there next time? What if you run off to do something else and leave me in there?"

"Look," Zambrano says. "Okay, I'm a person. I made a mistake. I said I wouldn't do it again. I'm fine!" he protests. A bit too much, I think.

"You're fine?" I ask.

"At least, I'm not some emotionless monster!"

I glance over at Seraphex and raise an eyebrow. "True or false?"

"Mixed." She clucks sadly and cocks her head at Zambrano. "Are you going to make me tell him?"

"Okay, okay," Zambrano says. "Magic, creating powerful spells . . . it takes something out of you. It dulls some of the things that make you human. Your emotions and sympathy are caught up in connecting with the magic, and you lose little bits of connection with other people."

"Is that why all the other sorcerers lost it?" I reason.

"Yeah," he says, a note of genuine sadness in his voice.

We stand there in silence for a moment, looking out the big windows onto the brightly lit cityscape. Well, relative silence. The lookout is still snoring up a storm, sawing logs like a lumberjack who sweetens his coffee with packets of cocaine.

"And will you lose it too?" I ask.

"Eventually? Probably," he says. He sighs, making a small motion with his hand, which lets the axe floating in the air drop to the floor. "I try my best, but I'm a little like them. I just . . . I don't care. About individual people. I'm probably a danger. I would kill myself if I thought it would help. But if I'm gone, then Demon Duke Vulkatherak and others like him would crash through the defenses of this world, and it would be the end of humans, at least free ones."

"Don't worry, I'd take care of the world," Seraphex says brightly.

"Oh? And how would you do that?" Zambrano asks with a raised eyebrow.

". . . by clawing my way over the heaped bodies of my rivals to seize power for myself and rule over the ruins of a battle-scarred Earth?" Even Seraphex seems a bit embarrassed at her answer.

"That's what I thought. Do you see what I'm dealing with here?" Zambrano says, turning to me.

"Yeah, I get it," I say sullenly.

I reach down and pick up the axe. I've played enough computer and roleplaying games to know not to pass up an opportunity to grab some loot after a battle. I think for a minute about rifling through his pockets, but that seems mean. In the end, he is just a guy trying to do his job, even if he happens to work for a demonic crime boss. "So . . . how do I use this thing?" I ask.

"The guy pointed at you as he threw it, right?" Zambrano asks, his forehead wrinkling in thought. "So, most likely, you just point your finger at a person and throw it, and it will take care of the rest. It's probably intended for long-range use. If he pointed very carefully, he could have thrown it at someone down the street or on one of the buildings out there. Mind you, it can probably only be thrown at something person-shaped that you point at. The magic isn't smart enough to recognize anything else as a target."

"Okay, I think I get it," I say, hefting the axe. I want to say I can feel some sort of latent power in it, making it weightier. But it just feels like a piece of wood and metal.

"Pull out that spyglass," Zambrano says, and I unsling my backpack and rummage through to find the spyglass. I put it up to my eyes and look across to the tower.

From here, we can't see inside the penthouse at the top of the Willis Tower, but through the spyglass I can see that every pane of glass in the top floor is glowing red.

"Those are the protective spells on the windows," Zambrano explains. "Powerful defensive demonic magic. That's why I can't go in there. And also why you'll have to sneak in through the roof."

I jump as a sound starts coming from the sleeping guy. After a second, I realize it's "Every Breath You Take" by The Police in the tinny tones of a cell phone speaker. A bit on the nose for a lookout's ringtone, but you gotta respect the classics.

No one else seems to be doing anything, so I step to the guy, root around for a second, and pull a phone out of his pocket.

"Mei Vulk Exec Assistant" the caller ID says. I almost feel bad about ruining this guy's day. If not longer. I hope Volcanose isn't the type to harshly punish security . . . I really can't go there. Gotta stay on mission here. If heroes worried about that sort of thing, nothing would ever get done.

Oh, crap. Am I a hero now? Okay, I also can't think about that. Mission, mission, mission. But of course, by this point the phone has stopped ringing.

And then the phone starts ringing again, the same executive assistant calling.

"What do we do?" I ask.

"Ignore it?" Zambrano says. "That's what I do on my phone all the time. Or, we could wake him up?"

"No," I say. "This could blow the whole plan. Seraphex, can you . . . ?"

She hops up. "Sure, I think I caught enough of his voice," she says. "Let's play."

"Isaac, where the hell were you? You're supposed to report in every hour on the hour! Everything okay?" a voice that is presumably "Mei Vulk Exec Assistant" says.

"Sorry," Seraphex says in a perfect imitation of Isaac's gravelly voice. "What happened was . . . this sandwich fell and got all over everything. There's a big mess everywhere."

I look over at the guy sprawled in his meatball sub scraps, then remember that Seraphex can perfectly imitate the guy's voice, but she's not able to lie using it. Ruh-roh.

"Everything okay over there?" the executive assistant asks.

"I'm feeling great," Seraphex answers in Isaac the lookout's voice.

"I mean with the Willis Tower, idiot!" Mei says, more playful than harsh. "You're such a weirdo. We're getting close to the portal opening; someone could make a move on us any day now."

"Looking at it right now," Seraphex says, hopping up to the windowpane and eyeing the tower. "Everything on the tower looks perfectly normal from over here."

"Okay, great," Mei says. "Now, don't leave that mess for the next shift like you did last week. You'll clean it up, right?" The tone of her voice is the perfect mix of friendly but totally firm on getting what she wants. I can see how she'd be a good executive assistant.

"I'll . . . make sure it's cleaned up by the end of the shift."

"Okay, good," Mei says. "Talk to you in an hour."

"Understood," Seraphex says.

I press the end call button before the security supervisor can decide to ask any more hard questions.

"Well done, Sera," I say.

"Of course! I've been playing this demonic truth-telling game for a very, very, long time," Seraphex says flippantly.

"How old are you exactly?" I blurt out.

"Didn't you learn never to ask an older lady her age? Rude human!" she says with a teasing air. "I'm 3,498 years old, but I still have the ass of a hot young thing." She glances back at her posterior. "It just . . . happens to be covered in tail feathers right now. Gorgeous plumage, I would say."

I can't imagine what an appropriate reply to that would be, so I just nod, shrug, and smile.

Zambrano, meanwhile, is standing over by the snoring lookout, eyeing the meatballs on the floor. He gently pushes the lookout with his boot.

"Damn it," Zambrano gripes. "Really, Seraphex?"

"What's wrong?" I ask. "She did a great job!"

"She committed to getting the floor cleaned up."

"What? So?" I say. "Screw that, let's go get the job done."

Sitting on the windowsill, Seraphex is grinning. "It doesn't work like that. I was forced to make a promise to our friend Mei, the executive assistant, which I could only do if I felt confident I could fulfill it. And now I have to make every effort to get it done. Which means I'm going to make sure that this room is clean, one way or another—and I am very persuasive."

"She is," Zambrano says. "She'll figure out a way to honor her commitment, no matter what the cost."

"You can make a demonic pact that easily?" I ask. "No need for blood sacrifice or candles or elaborate swearing rituals?"

"No, we don't actually need any of that. We just like it for the style," she answers haughtily.

"And so now it's up to us to honor your promise," I surmise.

"I'd just do the cleanup myself," the demon duck says with a shrug. "But, you know, no hands." She doesn't sound particularly upset about her inability to be of any assistance.

"Okay, so can we use a cleaning spell or something?" I ask, turning to Zambrano.

"General purpose cleaning spells are a lot trickier than you think," Zambrano says. "How does the spell know what's a mess and what's your floor? Or a person's body? And anyway, we have the birch butlers at home, and I prefer to focus my attention on keeping up to speed on useful spells that can eviscerate my enemies, sneak us into places, or keep my perfectly glowing skin."

I have to admit, he is right about his perfect skin. The bastard.

"Okay, so what, then?"

Zambrano shrugs. "Maybe there's a mop for you in the bathroom? Worth a shot."

I groan and head for the bathroom. Maybe I'm not as big of a hero as I was hoping. I suppose I did sign up to be an intern, so I have only myself to blame.

CHAPTER 20

Ten minutes later, the meatballs are all in the trash, and I'm mopping the last of the marinara sauce off the floor.

"What did you mean, keeping up to speed on spells?" I ask Zambrano, who helped a bit moving the guy out of the mess but has since pretty much just sat back and watched as I do all the work. I figure if he won't help, he can at least spill about some of the things I want to know about magic.

"It's like a dancer or a musician memorizing their performances," Zambrano explains as I mop the floor. "There are some pieces that you know so well, they're rattling around in your skull and you'll take them to your grave. But for most of them, you have to keep in practice if you want to use them reliably. The words are fairly straightforward for most spells, but the motions need to be very precise. Word patterns are much more distinct, much easier than hand motions to be recognized."

"Easier to be recognized?" I ask, confused. "Recognized by who?" I can tell that there's something key here, even though he said it in a very offhand manner.

"I'll explain later," Zambrano says. "Clean enough, Seraphex?" he asks, and she nods and hops down from the windowsill. "Great, let's get moving."

We take a moment to scope out the Willis Tower through the telescope, then head out and call the elevator to take us to the ground floor.

"Stay right behind me," Zambrano says, pulling two illusion prisms out of his hoodie pockets and handing me one.

I hold it and look down to see my hands as semitransparent. Seraphex flaps up and perches on my shoulder.

"Don't worry, you'll be invisible to everyone else," Zambrano says.

I look up at him, but he's completely invisible.

"Oh, right," he says. "Hold still."

"Um, okay," I answer. At least he didn't ask me to open my mouth and close my eyes.

"I hate to use a frog spell, but it's the only one for the situation," Zambrano's voice says as I feel a finger touch my forehead.

"*Avec mon puissant pouvoir, voyons ce qui ne peut pas être vu,*" he says, and I can suddenly see him as semitransparent as well. "Ugh, French magic always makes me feel dirty."

"What's wrong with French spells?" I ask. "Is it, like, blood magic or something?"

"There's no such thing as 'blood magic' per se," he says. "Not the way they portray it in movies and such. Human blood is just a nice distinct material, good for recognizability and easily available. So the physical pattern is unique. Human blood poured into rivulets in a star shape—that's easy for magic to recognize."

I don't understand what he's saying about magic, and I desperately want to follow up on that disturbing little magic factoid, but it seems more important to figure out what he's done to me. "So what's wrong with French magic? Why is the spell phrase so long? Does it burn away bits of my soul or something?"

"Oh, nothing like that. French spells just always use full phrases, simply because French wizards are pretentious hacks who think they're better than everyone else. Pompous jackasses, all of them."

"Don't worry, Bryce," Seraphex says from my shoulder. "He hasn't done anything dangerous to you. He just . . . well, he doesn't like French people. Except for that certain one, of course . . ."

"French wizards! And for good reason!"

"He could never quite get the accent right," Seraphex says with satisfaction.

"Whatever," Zambrano says, stepping into the elevator that's just arrived. "If it's good enough for magic to recognize, it should be good enough. Just stay close to me."

The elevator takes us down, and of course stops along the way. An older couple gets in, and Zambrano and I are forced to push ourselves against the walls in the corners of the elevator to avoid them running into us.

Outside, we dodge past pedestrians, and I try to stay behind the translucent form of Zambrano without running into anyone on the sidewalk. It's a busy day, and we end up hopping on and off the sidewalk, skipping away from alternating pedestrians and bicycles. I clutch my illusion prism tight in my right hand and the cardboard box in my left.

I didn't realize until I was walking around invisible like this just how many little accommodations people make to others, and how we assume all the time that no one would actually run into us. Someone blazing by on an electric delivery bike is suddenly a mortal threat.

But before long we're at the Willis Tower, which is a multitiered 108-story monstrosity. We walk around to the only side of the building that runs to the very top uninterrupted, and I take a deep breath as I look up at over a hundred stories of glass windows. This is truly wild and quite terrifying.

I set out the cardboard box, and Zambrano uses a Sharpie to draw mystic runes on it. I recognize now that they seem derived from the Cyrillic alphabet, since this is a Russian spell.

"Will this definitely work?" I ask. "All the way up there?" It's a whole lot farther up this skyscraper than we went at Professor Okamoto's modestly sized apartment building in Japan.

"It's okay, don't worry. If you fall out of the box, I'll catch you," Zambrano says with a shrug. "No big deal."

"You won't say that it will definitely work, huh?" I gingerly step into the box. "And can you really catch me if I fall? You have a spell for that?"

Seraphex hops off my shoulder, flapping her wings twice to ease down and land next to Zambrano. She's having none of this, and she's nearly indestructible!

Zambrano shrugs. "Stopping a person moving very quickly toward the ground is one of those basic spells that I just need to have ready. You'd be surprised how often that situation comes up!"

I look at the flimsy cardboard box that I'm standing in. "No. No, I don't think I would be surprised at all, as a matter of fact."

"Fair enough. I guess the intern is learning something after all, isn't he?" Zambrano says. "Anyway, here you go."

He holds out a small black pebble, which is painted with swirling white glyphs.

I take the stone, hefting it.

"It feels super light." I turn it over in my hand. "Is this going to work?"

"You really think I'd give you a dud enchanted item?" Zambrano shrugs. "It's normal weight when you're touching it, but ten thousand times that when it's not touching something that's alive."

I reach down and drop it lightly on the sidewalk, then scoop it up in surprise when a bunch of cracks start appearing in the concrete.

"Okay, okay," I admit. "Seems like it works."

"The city of Chicago's going to have to pay to fix that damage," Zambrano says, shaking his head. "And you just casually wreck their property. So irresponsible."

"Who cares about a little sidewalk?" I shoot back. "We're here to save the whole city from . . . ugh, you asshole. That's not the same," I finish lamely, seeing him grinning at me.

I step in the box, gripping the stone tightly. I put a wireless earbud in my left ear, and Zambrano calls me, quickly checking that the connection works. It doesn't escape me that prepping for our mission this morning was the first time that Zambrano actually gave me his contact info. Freakin' weirdo.

"*Voskhodyashchaya bumaga,*" Zambrano says in a flawless Russian accent, making a floating hand motion. "Good luck, kid," he adds as the box starts to rise through the air.

As it ascends, the box moves at the slight angle that Zambrano set it on. I crouch down inside it, trying to ignore the swirling wind. The box shakes slightly with the wind, but seems to stay exactly on course, close to the building.

"And we really don't know what exactly I'm looking for?"

"That's what the spyglass is for," Zambrano says, repeating a conversation we've already had. "Look at it through the spyglass, and it will glow as bright as the sun. So, actually, don't look directly at it for more than a second. You'll burn your retina, and the spell to repair that is a giant pain in the ass."

"It will be something demonic," Seraphex says. "So it will glow red."

"Anything else you want to add?" I ask her. "As the actual demon on our team, who knows many secrets of demonkind?"

"It will glow red because it's demonic," Seraphex repeats.

"She knows something that she's not telling us," I say, rolling my eyes.

"She always knows something that she's not telling us," Zambrano says, and I can picture the long-suffering shrug that goes with it.

"I will tell you that if the arcane conduit isn't taken away from Duke Vulkatherak," Seraphex says carefully, "he will use it and many, many of your precious humans will die as a result."

"You're one sketchy goddamn duck, Sera," I say. Looking up, I see the top of the building getting close. "I'm almost there. One shot at this." The cardboard box is enchanted to go upward. Without Zambrano here to stop it, it's just going to continue up into the atmosphere until the magic wears off, at which point it will get caught in the wind and fall to who-knows-where.

"It's okay, if you miss the roof just jump down; I'll catch you in the air, no problem," Zambrano says in a tone that makes me suspicious that he might enjoy that outcome.

"One shot at this," I repeat.

I did a little research before we came here. If I fall from the top of the tower and Zambrano doesn't catch me, it would take about twelve seconds for me to reach the ground. I would be hitting terminal velocity right at the same time I hit the pavement. Now, the phrase "terminal velocity" has nothing to do with how deadly that speed is. It just means that the speed hits a maximum due to air resistance. The fact that terminal velocity would happen to be simultaneous with a terminal deceleration at the sidewalk and a terminal moment of my bones being intact is merely, shall we say, a happy coincidence.

I stand up, holding my breath as the top gets closer. The box isn't moving that fast, just a floor every few seconds.

I put one foot up on the lip of the box and leap just as the box passes the top of the roof of the Willis Tower. But I misjudge the distance—or the timing, or the force, or the inertia, or . . . I don't know, something. I'm not a physicist. Anyway, I go careening forward, stumbling along the low wall at the edge of the roof, then fall forward.

I fall to one knee, drop one arm to the concrete . . . and land in a perfect superhero pose. You know, that half kneeling, one-hand-down pose that superheroes always land in? The one that's completely impractical in terms of not getting injured while landing but looks amazing on a poster?

"Oh, I am so badass," I say. I can't help myself.

"For stepping off an elevator?" Zambrano asks from the headphone in my ear.

I groan. "You can't see me up here, can you?" I sigh. There's no way I could ever do that again. My one moment of glory, and not even the weird sorcerer and suspicious duck witnessed it. "Never mind, I'm headed over to the entry point now."

Shaking my head, I make my way across the roof to the maintenance hatch that leads down into the penthouse.

CHAPTER 21

The hatch is unremarkable, just a steel door set in the ground with a padlock on it. I pull out the spyglass and check it out. The padlock glows brightly, but the metal itself doesn't. That matches what Zambrano told me I'd find. The padlock is enchanted and will set off an alarm if it's opened with either a spell or traditional lock picking. The hatch itself is a simple piece of metal, so if we bust open it without unlocking the padlock, we'll be all set.

Of course, blasting the hatch with a spell, explosives, or a sledgehammer each would attract unwanted attention as well. The kind of attention that crushes you with its giant rocky fists.

So I kneel and hold the little pebble. Hefting it, I feel that it's almost weightless.

"I'm at the hatch," I whisper. "Trying the heavy pebble."

I place it on the hatch and then, gingerly, remove my fingers. At first, it just seems to make a small dent in the metal. But then I hear a low groaning and can see the metal starting to warp, bending under the strain of so much weight in such a small place.

As the metal bends, the pebble suddenly starts to slide down the hatch, and I desperately reach out and grab it just before it falls through the crack created between the hatch and its frame. The moment it makes contact with my grasping fingers, the metal stops bending and the pebble easily comes up into my hands.

"Once the metal bends, the pebble starts rolling!" I whisper.

"Well, be more careful!" Zambrano says through the earpiece. "If the pebble falls, it should be stopped by the concrete floor, but this whole mission is screwed."

"And I have to jump off the roof to get away?"

"Yup," Zambrano says.

I grit my teeth. The next time, I carefully put the pebble down and create a cocoon around it with my hands so that if it starts moving, it will hit my skin and stop being so heavy. That way, step by step, I work my way around the hatch, slowly using the power of weight to bend and warp it.

The sounds of metal grinding feel loud to me, along with my heart beating a mile a minute, but the wind up here is loud. It's certainly a whole lot quieter than trying to bust it open in one go. The power of gravity works slowly but implacably.

In only a few minutes, the hatch is bent back far enough that I'll be able to slip through it. Glancing over, I can see that the padlock is still perfectly in place, untouched. I pick up the pebble, gripping it tightly in the sweaty palm of my left hand. I'll need to hold on to this until I can get it back to Zambrano to deactivate. If it stops touching me, it could break anything it hits and get buried somewhere in the building's bones.

But we planned for this. I pull a piece of tape out of my backpack and carefully press the pebble into the flesh of my arm and wrap duct tape around it twice. It's not super comfortable, but it works.

I scramble my way down into the hatch, carefully maneuvering my backpack through it, then my body. On the way through I cut a scratch along my rib cage, the twisted metal not quite as open as I had thought it looked.

It's not bleeding too badly, so I dab it clean with my T-shirt, which is now cut and ruined anyway. The steel hatch doesn't look too rusty, and I'm not too worried since I'm up to date on my tetanus shots. I mean, I think I am? Probably, right? Who actually knows that sort of thing off the top of their head?

The room below the hatch is a maintenance storage locker filled with what looks like maybe parts for air conditioners. That's what my mind fills in, anyway, it's just a bunch of unidentified mechanical gear to me—I'm not so good at that sort of thing. Remember, I'm a failed magic student who only recently quit working at a Samba Smoothies.

Now I'm in the building, on the top floor. But I'm not actually in the penthouse suite. I take off my shoes and walk across the concrete floor in my socks. I'm pretty sure the no-shoes look is spoiling my cool secret agent fashion, but this is way quieter, and that will make a big difference. I listen at the door to the maintenance storage room, and finally, not hearing anyone outside, open the door and walk into the hallway.

The vibe change from the dusty maintenance room to the hallway is a total departure. This is an opulent building, with dark wood paneling, marble floors, and the kind of classy lighting where you can't see where it's coming from, but everything looks just super expensive.

But I'm not really focused on the decor. I'm mostly absorbed with how, around a couple corners of the layout that I've memorized, there are two rockhide demons waiting. At the other end of this hallway there's a big floor-to-ceiling window, which has a view of the city and Lake Michigan. I go down and peer out for a moment, able to see the street corner where Zambrano and Seraphex are waiting.

But my goal is in the other direction. I proceed quickly down the hall, past the elevators and stairs, then past my security closet, and around the corner. It's after business hours so no one is really supposed to be up here, but that's far from a guarantee. Finally, I reach the last corner before the door the two demons are guarding.

"That wasn't half bad last night," a rumbly voice says.

"Sure, mate, but don't think you get to start expecting that to happen all the time," a voice says. "I'm not your girlfriend. Tunker don't work like that."

The plan was simple. Release the frog, let it hop around the corner, the demons will see it, grab it, lick it, and I'm in. It sounds like the lyrics to a naughty song thirteen-year-old me would think is hilarious, but it's a decent plan. It's simple enough, and Zambrano said that rockhide demons can't resist the lure of the Amazonian azure frog—it makes them super high, and they simply won't be able to stop themselves when they see it.

Which is all great, except for one thing: I open the box, and the frog hops out and promptly turns around and starts going in the wrong direction.

"That is really not helpful," I whisper at the frog.

I spend the next thirty seconds trying to block the frog from going the opposite direction from the demons without actually touching or hurting it. Every time it hops forward, I stick out a hand or foot, all the while desperately trying not to make any noise or get close enough to the corner that someone standing at the end of the hallway there would see. Okay, not someone, two giant demons with skin made of rocks.

It's like the worst, least sexy game of Twister ever.

As much as I block it, I can't get the stupid frog to go the right way. Finally, it seems to get bored of tormenting me and just sits there in the middle of the hallway, slowly inflating and deflating the sacs under its chin.

"Come on, little frog dude," I whisper. "Go that way! Get licked!"

"What's wrong?" I hear Zambrano's voice in my ear. "Are you in yet?"

I retreat down the hallway, keeping my eyes on the frog to make sure it doesn't disappear.

"The frog won't go the right way!" I say under my breath. "It keeps trying to hop away from the demons."

"You need to get it to go the right way!" Zambrano says. "Just convince it!"

"With what? I didn't bring any frog treats!" I answer, exasperated.

What would those even be? What do frogs eat? Something underwater, I guess. The same things fish eat? But what do fish eat? Some kind of special flakes that come in a can . . . This isn't getting me anywhere.

"If you can't get it to go to them," Seraphex's voice in my headphone asks, "can you convince the demons to come to the frog?"

I look around. "I could make a noise of some sort, like shout or hit the wall or something . . ."

"That would let them know there's an intruder. That's no good," Zambrano says.

I pause for a moment, thinking through the options. I need to get the demons to come and investigate the frog while not realizing that anyone else is here.

"Do these frogs make any kind of loud noises?" I ask. "Louder than just hopping or whatever."

"Yes, the Amazonian azure frog has a distinctive mating call," Zambrano says. "It's kind of whiny and annoying."

"Sera, do you know what it sounds like?" I ask.

"Oh, oh, I see where this is going," Seraphex says. "Yes, I know it. It's gross-sounding and far beneath my superlative vocal talents to do it, but I will—"

"Okay, make the frog's mating call in ten seconds," I say, cutting her off. "Zambrano, you stay perfectly quiet!" I say. I know, that sounds like a really unlikely thing to happen. But he actually does stay perfectly quiet.

I tap the speakerphone button on my phone, crank the volume, retreat around the farther back corner, and hold the phone back around pointed toward the frog.

They weren't lying. The mating call is a warbling pitchy whine, and I hate it. But I immediately hear two pairs of heavy footsteps tromping down the hall. I pull the phone back, turn the speaker off, and huddle behind my corner as the footsteps round the one opposite me.

CHAPTER 22

The stomping footsteps come to a halt.

"Oi! Bronk, mate! Look, tasty blue frog!" one of them rumbles. The voice is the guttural rumble, but the accent is . . . distinctly British. And not the fancy English accent that makes everyone swoon in Christmas movies where a clumsy but pretty American falls for a prince. No, it's working-class British, like you'd get from the plumber or truck driver.

"Why's you here, li'l froggy? Tunker, love, he looks lost!" Bronk the rockhide demon answers, interrupting my nervous brain's complete departure from the current situation and the imminent danger that I'm in.

"You think Mr. Vulkie lost the froggy?" Tunker asks.

There's a sudden lurching movement that gives the hallway a shake and makes me jump in surprise. Luckily, the noise of the rockhide demon more than covers it.

"Gotcha!" Bronk says. Don't s'pose anyone knows you're here, do they?"

"Don't do it! Mr. Vulkie might get mad at us!" Tunker complains. "Are you sure we should?"

But there's a loud slurping sound, indicating that Bronk determined that Tunker's seemingly legitimate concerns were without merit.

"Pretty rainbow!" Bronk says. Then there's a thud that really shakes the floor.

"One down," I mouth silently.

But Tunker seemed to be a bit more cautious. How can I take the remaining demon out? I heft the magic axe that I stuck through my belt, but somehow I don't quite see it taking out a demon with skin made of rocks. Could I trick her into the elevator shaft? Push her through a window? My brain is racing with ideas, but I have no clue how to accomplish any of them.

I hear Tunker take a step forward. I'm screwed. I brace myself to make a dash for it if the demon gets any closer.

"I guess you've already been licked once, so too late to worry about what the boss will think!" Tunker rumbles cheerfully. "The damage is done, now let's do some damage, little blue Popsicle!"

There's another disgustingly loud slurp.

And a thump as Tunker's body hits the floor.

I wait for thirty long seconds, listening for any sounds of wakefulness. But the two rockhide demons are both snoring, a raucous symphony of snorts and wheezes that would put a whole family reunion cabin full of sleeping uncles to shame.

I step around the corner, taking in their massive rocky bodies. They are huge, over seven feet tall, with imposing craggy rock where skin would be. They're roughly humanoid and have hands, feet, a mouth, and eyes, but that's about where the similarities to humans stop.

For some reason, what pops into my head is that it's a good thing there are rules against magic or nonhuman players in sports. In an NFL game these guys would turn the opposing team into pancakes on the first play.

"Why do they have English accents?" I whisper into the phone as I step over the giant sleeping forms.

"Everyone has an accent, silly," Seraphex explains. "The sorcerer Rodney Wint first trained rockhide demons in north London in the early 1900s as security for an illegal 'staff of ice bolt' manufacturing and smuggling operation. They all learned it there, then brought it with them when I sent them back to the demon realms."

"Hell of a chap, Rodney," Zambrano says. "If it weren't for his knowledge of demon lore, I never would have learned how to make your transmogrification into waterfowl permanent."

"Hell of a chap, indeed. Shame that in the end, you had to—" Seraphex says cheerily, then cuts herself off. I can easily imagine the look she must have gotten from Zambrano. I would have shut up too.

I glance around, but the poor frog is nowhere to be seen. I like to think that it escaped and hopped off to a better life somewhere, but I suspect my optimism is badly misplaced. Not wanting the frog to have been cruelly licked in vain, I proceed to the doors.

I try to put the sleeping rock monsters behind me and out of my mind as I look at the looming metal double doors. There's a large pattern engraved on them—a circle with a square inside of it and a wavy line across that.

"Is the alarm pattern there?" Zambrano asks in my ear.

"Yeah, it's just like you said it would be." All that we had was a blurry photograph of it in the background of a janitor's selfie that somehow ended up tagged on the internet, but this matched what the sorcerer showed me in our planning session. It's a magical sigil, turning the doors into a very weak magical artifact. This one is simple enough—the lines of the design cross the point where the double doors join together. If that line breaks, it sends out a magical pulse, which at this hour will be interpreted as an alarm. And then a security mage probably teleports in and turns my bones to jelly.

I unsling my backpack and pull out the sophisticated tools I'm supposed to use to navigate this latest obstacle.

"Well, here goes," I say with the level of confidence that I usually have for Zambrano's plans—modest at best.

"Look, if you could use magic, I could have made a spell for you to open it," he says. "But you don't have a soul . . ."

"So in the current plan, I'm using chewing gum and string to disarm the trap?" I mutter, as I put a little bit of silver putty on both sides of each place where the sigil pattern crosses the line between the two doors.

"No, no, it's metallic-laced adhesive and hyper-flexible steel wire," Zambrano scolds. "Sophisticated! Clever! Shiny!"

"Sure," I say as I carefully take lengths of what feels like metallic dental floss and put each end of it in the bits of putty, connecting across each point where the lines will be broken when the doors are pulled apart. "Sera, is this really a workable solution?"

"The magic theory checks out," she says. "The wires will connect the lines of the sigil even when the doors are open, keeping the pattern intact."

"And that *works?*"

"You're about to find out," Zambrano says. Which, honestly, doesn't feel super supportive.

"The pattern was weak to begin with when it was enchanted," Seraphex says. "Hard for magic to recognize the pattern anyway, because there's a break in the doors. So it's more flexible than one that's just carved into something solid."

I stare at the door, which looks pretty silly with silver putty and metal string hanging from it, like those goth pants covered in zippers and chains that serve absolutely no useful purpose. I mean, I'm not here to judge; it's not like fashion is required to always be functional. Give the goth kids a break—wearing all that black and chrome gear during hot summers in New York takes real dedication.

And then comes the moment of truth. I reach forward, turn the doorknob, and pull the door open. I wait for several long seconds, tensed to make a run for it. But there's no flash of blinding light, no security magician appearing to blast me apart.

Finally, I start to breathe easier. Is this actually going to work?

Now, I can't just walk through the door. There's a spiderweb of metal floss in the way. No, I have to awkwardly hold the door open, lie down on the floor, and shimmy my way under the metal and through the door on my back, inch by inch. Looking up at the junk above me, I reflect that this feels like the worst attempt to cheat at a limbo contest ever.

But I'm through, and I gingerly let the door close and stand up.

Inside is even more opulent than the outside, like they sort of mashed together the aesthetics of *The Great Gatsby* and *Mad Men* with no regard for them coming from very different decades. So, not tasteful. Just . . . expensive.

I'd love to stick around and be a judgy bitch about the decor, but I've got a job to do and life not to lose. I pull out the spyglass and do a quick scan of the room, and there are a few glowing things around the room, but nothing that's shining bright like what Zambrano told me to look for.

"The arcane conduit looks like two long staffs," Zambrano says though we've gone over this all before. "They might be together, and they might be apart."

"I don't see anything obvious," I say. "I'll start ransacking the place." We didn't have an exact location for the artifact, but we did know that if I could see it, it would light up through the spyglass like nothing else due to the strength of the enchantment.

I look through the spyglass, but it doesn't reveal anything glowing.

"I'm not seeing any magic in the spyglass," I say. "I'll take a look through the desk."

I step toward the big mahogany desk in the corner, expecting Zambrano or Seraphex to say something snarky and unhelpful, but there's just silence. I pull open each drawer, looking at the contents through the spyglass and waiting to hear from them.

Finally, I pull the phone out of my pocket and glance at it. Nothing. The call has been dropped, and the little icon in the top right says no service.

Shit. There must be some kind of shielding or jamming in here.

That makes me even more nervous. If something bad happens in here, I'm totally on my own.

I hunt through the desk, cabinets full of small rectangles of stone that remind me of protein bars, a bar cart that seems to hold a bunch of different bottles hand-labeled "mineral water" and rock salts rather than booze, and I look behind the paintings on the walls. No safes or anything there. Desperately, I pull back the carpets, hoping maybe there's a trap door or something under one.

My pulse is pounding, and my mouth feels dry. Part of me wants to swig some of that mineral water, but I'm not confident that whatever a lava demon imbibes will be safe for humans to drink.

I keep hunting, glad that I'm wearing gloves because I'm touching everything.

Glancing out the big windows, I can see that the late summer sun is setting outside. How long have I been here? How much time do I have left before someone notices that something is amiss or one of the guards wakes up from their frog-induced stupor? I go to the bookshelf and scan through the books. The books are all real, no hidden compartments in them, and I can see from the thin gap behind the shelf that it's just a wooden shelf, not a secret door.

Seraphex told me that there wouldn't be a bathroom, because apparently demons don't need to pee. Or to poop, for that matter. Fun facts that we're learning this week, right? Which sucks, because I have been at this for a long time, and I am starting to really need to empty the old bladder. Also, it would be really satisfying to piss in this demon duke's fancy lair, but I really do need to go.

"I've got to think this through," I say, even though I know the phone is dead and no one can hear me. Talking to myself is just fine. I'm not crazy, I'm just nervous. "I need to find something bright. How do I do that? Astronomers can find planets that barely reflect light and see stars behind black holes . . . Okay, maybe that could do it."

I pull out the spyglass again and start rescanning the office, this time looking not for a bright light, but hints of one. A reflection, a few rays, anything. As the light outside gets dimmer, it's getting easier to see.

After a long minute and a half of scanning, I draw a sharp breath. There's something there, in the fancy oak wall paneling. Okay, I'll be honest, I have no idea what actual tree it's made of, it's just shiny and has nice molding and looks like it costs an arm and a leg. And that's not what matters. What matters is that around one panel, there's bluish light seeping through the cracks. I put the spyglass back in my bag and advance.

I feel around the panels, wondering if I'm going to have to bash it down. I certainly don't have time to find a secret trigger release hidden somewhere in this room.

But when I press on the panel, it just slides open with a quiet *whoosh*.

Behind it is a tiny office, bare and plain compared to the opulence of Volcanose's main office.

But there's no secret artifact here. Instead, there's a young woman sitting in an office chair, wearing headphones and bopping her head to the music, staring at three big computer screens blazing at maximum brightness, covered in emails and spreadsheets. As I open the door, I can see that she's clicking and organizing them at a pace that I can only compare to pro gamers whose fingers move faster than the eye can see.

She spins on the chair, pulling the headphones off and yelping in surprise. I jump back in shock as well—and I also notice that she looks vaguely familiar. I can't immediately recall it, but I know her face. Where have I seen her before?

CHAPTER 23

What are you doing here?" she shrieks at me. "Bronk! Tunker! Get in here!"

Behind her I can see a door to a bathroom, which I glance at wistfully. And that gives me an idea. "I'm with maintenance," I lie. "There's, um, a water problem in the bathrooms. Plumbing's all backed up." That's a good lie, right? There's always some sort of water problem in a big building.

She looks at me, shaking her head in disappointment. "Okay, buddy, look, I'm not falling for that," she says. "You're not in uniform and you're not carrying any tools whatsoever. And also, you're not wearing shoes!"

I bristle. I really don't like to be called "buddy." Feels super condescending.

"In a few seconds," she continues, "two giant rockhide demons are going to come in here. And you're going to have to explain why you're trespassing." Any hint of fear is gone as she eyes me. "What are you after? Stealing valuables? Corporate espionage? Do you want Mr. Volker's autograph? Oh, no. Are you one of those idiots who thinks they can get a seat on the mission to Mars? I don't care what your tragic backstory is, there are no civilians going on the spaceship."

And then I realize where I know her face from. She was the woman at the auction house, bidding on behalf of Lukas Volker, buying magically enchanted bronze. I make two quick connections. The easy one is that this is the same voice of Vulkatherak's executive assistant that we heard on the phone earlier this afternoon. The more surprising one is that Vulkatherak is actually Lukas Volker, the reclusive billionaire currently leading the space race to make the first human mission to Mars. Or Lukas Volker is actually Demon Duke Vulkatherak, I guess. Why did Zambrano not mention that little detail?!

"I don't want to get on your spaceship," I shoot back. "I took care of your rockhide demons. And I know that Lukas Volker is Vulkatherak." I know that now, but let's act cool and pretend we knew all along, right? "And now you're going to give me the artifact from the Ilopango Crater. The . . . arcane conduit."

I pull out the magic axe at my belt. I sort of heft it, but I don't actually say anything threatening. Because, let's be honest, I'm not going to launch an axe attack on some young woman working in an office building, no matter who she works for.

She eyes me, sizing me up. "You're not going to attack me, are you?" She stands, glaring at me, and pulls her long black hair into a tight bun in an almost automatic motion, like an experienced sailor expertly tying a knot without even thinking.

I stand still, not knowing what to do. But I don't move to use the axe on her, and she smiles slightly.

"Good choice. I'm Mei Song, Mr. Vulkatherak's personal assistant. I don't think he has any particular personal affection for me, but I am very valuable to him and he does not take well to people messing with his ventures or employees. If you harm me, you're in for a world of hurt. But I guess you already know that, since you know everything, huh, buddy?"

See, the only time people call you buddy is when they're being at least somewhat condescending. Watch out for it, you'll see I'm right.

I shake my head at her. I don't know where the artifact is, and even if I was going to try to use violence here, from the vicious way Mei is looking at me, I think there's a good chance I would just get creamed anyway. So I have to try a different tactic.

Asking nicely.

"Do you realize what Vulkatherak is going to do with that artifact? He's going to trigger a massive earthquake and take control of this whole city and most of the Midwest. Could you help me? Please?"

She holds her right hand up. A ring on her finger glows, and the axe rips out of my hand and flies to hers. She smiles tightly. "I was curious to see whether you would actually try using that thing. I'm glad you made the right choice, for your sake."

"Okay, okay, easy there," I say, stepping back from the little office, glancing at the door. From outside, I still hear the rather loud sounds of snoring, though now they're mixed with what sounds like the rockhide demons mumbling in their sleep. Something like "Pass down another helping of granite." Do rockhide demons eat rocks? Just because they're made of rock? Though I suppose I eat meat and am, in the end, made out of meat. So I guess it tracks.

"You came in here and threatened me with one of our own weapons. Why would I take it easy on you?" Mei says, advancing from her office and brandishing the magic axe.

"I'm trying to save this whole city," I plead. "Millions of people! Are you really going to side with your demonic boss on this?"

"How do I know you're telling the truth?" Mei says, eyeing me like I'm a fish wriggling on her hook that she hasn't decided whether to throw back. "No one here has mentioned anything about blowing up the city."

"You work for a demon!" I protest. "And you would believe him over me?"

"Mr. Vulkatherak is a good boss," Mei shoots back. "I don't buy that he's going to blow up the city that his own North American headquarters is in. This job pays well, has great benefits, paid time off, 401(k). It even pays for these glasses—and they're purely for fashion, not even prescription. Where else is an ancient runes and glyphs major from UC Santa Cruz going to get a job like that? You have to make some compromises. He's a bit evil, sure, but what billionaire CEO isn't these days?"

I shrug. That's . . . a pretty good argument.

"Also, he doesn't make creepy jokes and gross suggestions like my last two bosses," Mei says, waving the axe around in a careless way that is making me quite nervous. "He's not interested in me whatsoever."

"Really? A demonic gangster who behaves like a perfect gentleman to his executive assistant?" I ask, curious despite myself.

"Well, he's just not interested. Demons are usually only attracted to other demons. Most of the time succubi and incubi are the only ones who are interested in humans."

"Oh, so he just sees you as, like, a piece of meat," I say and immediately realize how weird that sounds. "I guess, more specifically, a piece of nonsexual meat," I add. Which doesn't really help. Am I really this awkward, or is it just the adrenaline caused by what seems like my rapidly dwindling chances to survive?

"Sure," she says, shaking her head at me. "Mr. Vulkatherak is the only lava demon in the realm." Her voice drops to a low whisper. "I hear he has sex with hot rocks. Rocks sculpted to look like other lava demons and heated in a furnace. Is it technically masturbation if you're doing it with a statue?"

"I guess that's one of those fun little factoids that you can never unlearn and is just stuck in your head forever?"

She shrugs. "I'm just glad I haven't actually seen it in person. But I hear that it's truly . . . majestic."

To be honest, I'm kind of curious what it actually looks like. That's got to be fascinating, right? And it can't be worse than the prank stuff your asshole friends trick you into seeing on the internet when you're fourteen. But, obviously, I don't say that.

"What's that on your arm? she asks. "Did you get hurt?"

I glance at the pebble duct-taped to my arm.

"Uh, yeah," I lie, probably not that convincingly. "Look, I get it," I continue, trying another tactic. "I get that you don't want to lose your job. But what if you could just . . . give me the artifact? And then go back into your office and none of this ever happened?"

She glares at me. "How likely do you think I am to get away with that? Mr. Vulkatherak doesn't allow cameras in here, but he has all sorts of other ways of figuring things out. Who knows what spells the security magicians could cast? Besides, the artifact isn't even *here* in the first place. That's why you didn't find it when you ransacked this place." She glances around at the office, which is a total mess. "Which, you know, I will be the one to have to clean, right?"

"Look, I know it's a risk," I plead. "But Volcanose is going to blow up the whole city. Do you think there's even a small chance that I'm right?"

"Hold on. What did you call him?"

"Um, Volcanose," I say. "Because, you know . . ." I gesture at my nose, making little downward motions to call to mind the lava flowing like a tiny river across the demon duke's face.

"Oh, damn, that's good," she says, suddenly softening a bit. "He would *hate* that nickname. What's your name?"

"I'm Bryce," I say without thinking, immediately wishing that I'd lied.

"Okay, Bryce," she says. "Why do you think Mr. Vulkatherak is going to do what you say he's going to do?"

"Well, number one," I explain, "he told us himself through some sort of mirror communication a few weeks back. Two, Zambrano believes that Vulkatherak will do it. Three, my contact at the MSA believes he will."

"Oh," Mei says, hefting the axe as she thinks. "Zambrano sent you. That makes sense. The only problem is . . . the arcane conduit from the Ilopango Crater isn't here. You've been lured into a trap."

"A trap?" I ask, though I understood her perfectly well. Great, Zambrano has screwed me over once again.

"Yeah. There's a whole squad of security magicians hiding throughout the building. As soon as Zambrano is detected entering the tower, they're going to jump him," she explains. "I imagine that Mr. Vulkatherak didn't lie, since he can't. That's another thing that makes him a great boss, by the way. I'm sure that he does intend to seize control of the Midwest eventually. But he's not using the conduit here. He's sending it to Mars. You know, on the spaceship. The one that you still definitely can't go on."

"Mars?" I ask, shaking my head. My head is starting to spin from all of this.

"Oh," she says, seeming confused. "Mars is where demons come from. Doesn't everyone know that?"

"No, everyone does not!" I practically screech.

"Oh," she says. "I guess I learned that working here. You pick up a thing or two, you know? So if you want to stop whatever's happening with the conduit, one of the two halves is being loaded on the *Vulcan III* right now. The other half is somewhere in Yellowstone. I'm not sure where exactly Mr. Vulkatherak hid it."

"I—thank you," I stammer. It's not the artifact that I had hoped to get, but she has been more helpful than I expected.

"Look, I'm not going to put my livelihood at risk," Mei says. "But if you stop whatever plan he's hatching, then all the better, right? I get to keep my job, and no earthquakes. Everybody wins!"

"Well, you're still the lackey of a demon duke," I note sourly.

"And I bet you eat meat," she counters. "We all have our moral compromises."

My mouth opens and closes involuntarily. "You're a *vegetarian?*"

"Vegan, actually," she says. "A plant-based diet is healthy, humane, and good for the environment."

"What the—"

"No time to lecture me about how I'm not getting enough vitamins and protein, buddy—you'd better get out of here," she interrupts. "I'll give you a couple minutes' head start and then pretend I opened the door and found this *absolute disaster* that you left me to clean up. And I get plenty of protein, *thank you for your concern.*"

She's still on about me making a mess of her office and I didn't say anything about her diet, but there's no time to argue those points.

"Okay, see you later," I say awkwardly, backing out of the room.

"Good luck!" she says cheerfully. "I'll be rooting for you!"

I turn and open the door, remembering to do it slowly and carefully, and slide under the metal wires on my back. As I push like a human mop along the floor, I can see her watching me, smiling wryly and shaking her head.

Soon, I'm out of the door. I carefully step over Tunker, take two steps toward freedom . . . and trip over Bronk's arm, falling in a heap as the big rockhide demon snorts himself awake.

Shitballs.

CHAPTER 24

Bronk sits straight up as I scurry backward, sliding on my back once again.

"Funky froggy dreams gone!" he mutters. And then he stares at me, and I can see cloudiness fading from his eyes in real time. "Intruder, here? Tunker? Tunker! Wake up! Intruder! Mr. Vulkie won't be happy with us!"

"It's okay," I start, "I'm just here for mainten—"

"No, bad intruder tricked us with tasty froggy licks!" Bronk says, struggling to stand up with all the grace of a thousand-pound toddler.

I scurry out of the way as Tunker, also now awake, grasps at me with a giant rock hand. For a second I'm awkwardly crab-walking past them, then I'm able to scramble to my feet and sprint down the hallway away from the two rockhide demons.

As I turn the corner, I hear Tunker's sleepy voice. "You go bash him, I call Mr. Vulkie. Like Executive Assistant Lady told us."

Glancing back, I see that Bronk and Tunker are both struggling to stand up, shaking unsteadily. And then I'm running away, pulling my phone out of my pocket and trying to turn it on and call Zambrano at the same time. Of course it doesn't work, and I need to slow to a trot for a moment to unlock it, open the app, and pull him up.

"Where have you been?!" Zambrano's voice shouts in the earbud, which is still gamely holding onto its place in my ear. I'm proud of that little guy. "Did you get the conduit?" he demands. Straight to the point, no concern for my well-being. Doesn't shock me, but it does annoy me.

"It's not here, and there's no time to explain," I say. "The rock-hide demons are awake and chasing me."

I come to a sliding stop in front of the elevators and door to the staircase, both lit by the last rays of the setting sun coming through the 108th-story window at the end of the hall.

"You woke them up?!" Zambrano says, a note of accusation in his voice.

"No time to explain!" I say. "Should I try the stairs or the elevator?" I could easily be trapped in the elevator, but it's over a hundred stories down. The basic plan had been to take the elevator down and walk out of the building. Security stops people going in, not out, so it should have been easy.

"Run down the stairs!" Zambrano says. "And try to walk through the lobby before they can stop you, maybe?"

Seraphex's voice comes on as well. "I can see security magicians coming out into the lobby," she says. "Security has been alerted."

"Shit," Zambrano says. "Maybe . . . you can hide? Back in the security closet? Go to the roof?"

I hear heavy footsteps around the corner. It seems that Bronk has managed to get his bearings and is on his way to crush me into a Bryce-flavored pancake.

"Won't they just find me?" I ask, desperate.

"Yes, eventually," Zambrano answers. "But it will give me a chance to figure something out. I'm going to get you out of there."

It feels nice to hear him say that, but less nice that Bronk has turned the corner and is now standing in front of the door that Zambrano wants me to flee through. I back up, glancing at the door to the stairs. There's no time to wait for the elevator. That's my only option now.

And then I look farther back, at the big window where lights are starting to glitter all across the city and along the edges of Lake Michigan.

Bronk advances menacingly.

"Give up or get squished," he says pleasantly. "Mr. Vulkie will want to talk to Mr. Froggy Man!"

"I'm coming out through the window," I say into the phone. "Use that spell you mentioned to catch me!"

Bronk starts building up speed, and I turn and run headlong toward the end of the hallway.

"Um, okay," Zambrano says, clearly distracted. "Don't drift out of the cylinder!"

I take that as a clear endorsement of my plan, lower my shoulder, and fling myself at the glass of the window.

But instead of it smashing and sending me flying into space, I just sort of bounce off the window and land in a heap. It hurts. A lot. My shoulder is going to need a doctor, or a chiropractor, or maybe a cybernetic replacement. I don't know, it just hurts like hell.

But there's no time to cry about it. I guess it makes sense that the glass in these giant buildings is tough enough to withstand high winds and hurricanes and other accidents, and it certainly has the strength to stop a skinny guy running into it.

I leap to my feet, seeing that Bronk is moving forward a bit more slowly now, as if confused.

"Mr. Froggy Man wants to squish himself before I can do it?" he says, confused. "That's no fun!"

"I tried, but I can't!" I say. "It's okay, I give up."

He stops and nods happily. "Good! Mr. Vulkie will be happy with that. He can squish you himself."

Before I can even think about it, I start to rip the duct-taped pebble off my arm.

"What's that little rock?" he asks, tilting his head.

"It's a very valuable demon rock," I say, pulling it out of the duct tape while careful to keep my fingers touching it at all times. "Would you like it?"

Bronk reaches out his hand, holding it open to receive the rock.

For a moment I think about trying to use the rock to hurt Bronk, but I don't know exactly how the magic works. If it touched him, would it stay heavy or become light like it is when touching me? I don't know.

And even if I could take Bronk out, security and another rock-hide demon are certainly on their way. No, that won't work.

I fling the rock backward over my shoulder and hear the satisfying sound of the entire window shattering. I'm sure that if I take the time to look, there would be no way to force myself to make the leap. So I step backward and jump myself out into the swirling winds without even looking.

For a moment, it feels like I'm floating, and I can see Bronk standing there, his rocky hands grasping at the air where I stood only a second earlier.

And then my stomach lurches and I'm accelerating fast, cold air whistling past me. I'm staring up at the first stars appearing in the sky, but I still can sense that the ground is coming at me fast. According to my research, I should have about twelve seconds until I'm a messy splatter on the sidewalk.

But suddenly I slow down, and the rushing air slows to buffet me gently. I freeze for a second as my stomach churns and a burst of dizziness hits and subsides. The air around me seems almost electric and has a sort of bluish glow to it.

Cautiously, I'm able to push against the air, squirming until I'm facing downward.

Below, I can see more clearly what's going on. I'm in the center of a large cylinder of glowing force, extending up from a point on the ground until it surrounds me. I'm still falling, but much, much more slowly now. I can feel the air resistance buoying me up, and it looks like I'm dropping at about a story a second. Which at nearly one hundred stories means it's going to be over a minute until I reach the ground.

Down below, I can see a section of sidewalk cracked wide open like a small meteor crater where the pebble must have landed. And standing next to it is Zambrano, still in his Chicagoan gear, though the hat has fallen off and is lying on the ground next to him, revealing his perfectly coiffed hair.

It's kind of fun floating down like this, but I am already getting the uneasy feeling that I'm starting to drift a bit to the side. Glimmering in the night, I can see the border of the tall cylinder that holds me. Zambrano said to stay inside it, so my immediate assumption is that, if I get to the edge of it, whatever effect is lowering gravity is going to fail. Which means rockhide demon squish will be replaced by cement pavement splat. Not okay!

"Zambrano!" I say, but I grab my ears and realize that in all the running and jumping and falling, both of my earbuds are now gone.

For a split second I try to remember if the AppleCare package that I bought covers devices lost to rockhide demon attacks during magical heists, but I really don't have time to get into that right now.

I try to wave down at him, but I can see that he's not looking up at me at all. Instead, he's facing off against a small group of figures charging out of the lobby door of the Willis Tower. Two of them pull out guns, but Zambrano makes a motion and twin bolts of lightning shoot from his hands, striking the two figures, and they both fall over. I guess you don't bring a knife to a gunfight, but you also don't bring a gun to a sorcerer battle.

The other figures are gesturing with their arms, bathed in magical light. Zambrano spreads his fingers and the air below is filled with fire, lightning, and various types of glowing force. Each magic user seems to be protected by a sphere of light, which sends out gouts of sparks each time an attack hits it.

As I watch, Zambrano's hands are almost a blur, and he's holding his own against five wizards, lighting up the sky brighter than any fireworks show I've ever seen. I have to admit, I'm kind of touched. He knows I don't have the artifact, but he's still here facing off directly against a much larger enemy force, exactly what he's been trying to avoid.

On the other hand, I'm still about sixty stories up and drifting closer and closer to the edge of the cylinder of low gravity. He didn't mention this whole bit earlier when he promised that he could catch me. Not cool, dude.

CHAPTER 25

First, I try to swim through the air as I float down. I think I heard something about astronauts doing this in the space station. But air is super thin, and any headway I can make is overpowered by the persistent draft which is causing me to drift to my left. The magic in the cylinder seems to dampen the effects of the wind, but there's still this slight draft.

Desperate, I grasp at the air even though I'm twenty feet from the side of the building and there's literally nothing that I can grab on to. I'm guessing that normally the person casting the spell would have the ability to control the descent, adjusting the magic so that I stay in the safe zone at the center of the cylinder. I even try pulling off my shirt and using it as a sort of a sail, but it's just not enough.

I shout down to Zambrano, but he's sending lancing blasts of pure darkness at a giant glowing golden lion with one hand while his other hand is outstretched and a barrier of raging flames is holding back two mages flinging ice bolts at him.

He's clearly not going to be able to help, so once again I'm on my own. What the heck am I supposed to do to push myself back into the center with nothing to push off against and no way to control the magic? I puzzle for a second, and then realize that this is less of a magic problem and more of a physics problem. More of a space problem.

How do rockets adjust their velocity in flight, even in thin air or the vacuum of space? Simple, they use physics. To move one direction, they push something the other direction. Reaction mass. In the science fiction books and shows, they always use bursts of air from their oxygen tank to push them when everything else runs out. I don't have an air hose to use as a rocket engine . . . but I look down at the shirt in my hand.

I ball up my shirt and fling it as hard as I can in the direction that I'm drifting. It seems to help a tiny bit, so I follow with my hat, my phone, and my bag, though I hold on to the spyglass. Putting the spyglass under my arm, I awkwardly pull off my pants and throw them too. It's too bad I left my sneakers behind. The thrown clothes help a bit, and I'm able to get a lot of force behind throwing the phone, which makes a noticeable difference. Wearing nothing but my boxers makes it so it's suddenly freezing up here, but I've slowed down my drifting quite a bit.

I hold on to the spyglass, hating the idea of throwing it away. But as I get closer and closer to the edge again, I grit my teeth and fling it.

Unfortunately, I've fallen a few more stories and am getting close to the bottom but also once again closing in on the edge of the cylinder. In desperation, I pull off my boxers and fling them, but the flimsy little things barely make a noticeable impact.

I'm still fifteen stories or so up, but I'm so close to the edge now that I could stick my hand out and touch it if I wanted to.

What's left? I'm literally completely naked. No clothes, no jewelry, nothing. What can I use for reaction mass? I'm all out!

Well, I realize, there's one thing left.

Squirming my way into the proper position, I put my hand down on my junk and aim. It takes a moment to get started, give me a break. This is a high-pressure situation. I'm lucky I'm able to start at all, but it helps that I've needed to go for a while now.

I unleash a stream of pee, squeezing as hard as I can to send it out at high velocity as I fall through the dusky air. Bit by bit, I can see it holding my position and even pushing me back a tiny bit. Fortunately, I'm pissing with the wind, not into it. So pretty much all of it disappears off into the air rather than coming back to hit me. That's a huge relief, but even more of a relief is that I'm drifting back toward the center of the glowing cylinder and closer and closer to the ground. Which is good because I don't think I know how to shit in a precise direction.

Finally, I land on the ground and stumble a few steps outside of the cylinder, tripping and falling over as I exit it and regular gravity takes hold. I hit the ground hard, feeling the bruises and scrapes appearing on my right side as I grind into the concrete. I lie there, naked and empty on the Chicago sidewalk. Staring up, I can see the grand rise of the Willis tower and a few twinkling stars.

"Hey! Get up!" Seraphex says, hopping up next to me from who-knows-where.

Groaning, I scramble to my feet, feeling my private bits swishing in the wind. As I shake myself off, I see that several of the security magicians are lying sprawled around the street, and the others are retreating, harried, by what looks like black bats that seem to be able to dive right through their shields. I guess Zambrano figured out a spell to get around their defenses.

"It's okay, we won!" I say, taking in the battle.

Zambrano is standing, arms outstretched, energy crackling around him. Beyond that, I can see that the streets are deserted except for the retreating security magicians. But a number of stories up, there are people hanging out of windows with phones held up to record. Great. Let's hope their phones have older cameras and won't get high-resolution shots of my skinny legs and, well, other things.

"Not quite," Seraphex says. "We've been here too long. He's coming. And he can run faster than you can." She inclines her beak toward the lobby of the building.

I've fallen near the edge of the building, while Zambrano is about a block away. I'm fairly close to the lobby and can see that a piece of the floor has been torn away, revealing some sort of hidden chamber under the building.

"Oh, shiiiit." I can see the figure coming up through a hole in the floor, giant rocky hands gripping the edge of the hole and orange glows coming from the lava eyes and nose. "Zambrano! The lobby!" I yell.

He lets out a string of words that at first I think are a spell, but when nothing happens, I realize he's just swearing in Spanish with particularly creative curses, most of which I've never heard before. And then all the magic around him disappears. He appears to collect himself and take several deep breaths.

"Run to me!" Zambrano shouts as Seraphex takes something between a hop and a short flight to land on my shoulder. I start sprinting, not even daring to glance back to see what's coming after me.

"*Froststråle!*" he screams, performing stiff gestures with his close-fisted arms, then swinging them and casting the rapidly gathering energy at the lobby.

As I run at him, a channel of blue and white icy energy shoots toward the lobby. It's about a foot in diameter, and even fifteen feet away from it I can feel the heat being sapped from the air.

I glance back and see the ray blasting through the windows of the ground floor, icicles mixing with shards of glass in a small explosion. And then the frost hits Volcanose, who has started charging across the lobby in our direction.

I put my head down and run as the air fills with ice, steam, and a deep howl that shakes the street under me. Desperately trying to catch my breath, I reach Zambrano, standing a few feet away as he finishes the motions of the spell.

I look back at the lobby, where the puncture in the glass has spread and there's now an open wall filled with ice, steam, and wreckage. The air is filled with white fog, making it almost hard to see through. And then the spell is over, and the air begins to settle. And I can see through the lobby, the orange glow of Volcanose beginning to advance again.

"That will only slow him down," Zambrano says. "Come on."

He steps over to me and grabs the back of my neck with one hand as he rummages through his pockets for a tiny little teleportrait. "I want to go to there," he says through gritted teeth, and I feel that twisting warmness, which is a relief. And we're back in the warehouse.

Zambrano cocks his head to the side and eyes me skeptically.

"What were you doing in there, just rubbing yourself on all the things in his office?" Zambrano asks.

"No, I—"

"Because if you were, I love it," he finishes before I can protest.

I sigh. I'd like to brag about my clever physics hacks, but I also want to forget the whole thing, especially the pee-related bits.

"The conduit wasn't there," I say instead.

"Do you know where it is?"

"Yeah," I say. "It's . . . on a spaceship. Well, half of it. The other half is in . . . Yellowstone? The national park, I guess?"

"What?!" Zambrano stares at me in confusion. I guess he didn't actually know.

"Lukas Volker, the bioengineered-agriculture billionaire, is actually Volcanose. Who somehow caught up and surpassed all the other rich guys building spaceships."

Zambrano flops down on the stool of his lab bench, clearly exhausted. "He must have been using a glamour or something to create that illusion. And probably used demonic corruption magic to help with bioengineering. And volcanic ore manipulation for the composite materials in the spaceships . . ."

"He's been here long enough that he could have summoned a couple powerful demons to help him," Seraphex says. "And, incidentally, that volcanic ore he manipulates comes out of his behind. He literally craps out space-age supermaterials when he wants to."

"And you knew all this?" Zambrano growls at the duck.

She gives her ducklike shrug. "I have been helping you defeat him. Isn't that enough?"

He ignores her, standing and striding to his bookshelf. "Where's he taking the spaceship? Is he going to put it in orbit or land it on the moon or something?"

"You really don't follow the news, do you?" I ask, shaking my head. "It's been a big story for months. He's taking it on the first colony mission to Mars."

Zambrano freezes. "Mars? Are you sure?"

"Yeah," I say. "I guess that's where demons come from, so he's just taking it home. Does that make it less dangerous, maybe? It'll be millions of miles away. And what's with demons living on Mars, anyway? Really?"

"What, did you think they lived in some alternate plane of existence?" Seraphex shakes her head sadly. "This is the real world, not some fantasy TV show. There's only one universe. Demons used to live underground on Earth, until Merlin and Liao Ling joined forces to exile most of them to Mars. My people have been unfairly trapped there for well over a thousand years!"

"Humanity got tired of having one in twenty babies eaten by demons among other atrocities," Zambrano snaps back. "Give me a minute, okay?"

I take the opportunity to head up to my room, take a quick shower, and put some clothes on. When I get back downstairs, Zambrano has covered a table in tomes opened to various pages but isn't reading any of them. He's just sitting glumly in the chair next to them.

"What's happening?" I ask. "What did you find out?"

Zambrano sighs. "We're screwed, that's what."

"What do you mean?" I demand. "We know what he's up to now!"

Zambrano shakes his head. "Okay, quick lesson in demonology. When they were banished to Mars, the idea was that they would stay there doing their own terrible things to one another and leave us alone. But there were leaks in the system, and every once in a while a demon would make it back to Earth, using a supercharged summoning spell."

"By leaks in the system," Seraphex says primly, "he means that some human sorcerers decided it would be a great idea to summon demons. Like those fools I tricked into summoning me in the early twentieth century. A summoning is currently the only way for a demon to leave the boundaries of the demonic realm and come to Earth."

Zambrano shrugs. "It's true. Humans did this to themselves. But the conduit—that changes everything. Right now, to summon a demon you need years of training, exotic materials, and months of work. And that's just to summon a minor demon, like the rock ones. Our friend Volcanose probably took a decade of work from a team of wizards. Very foolish wizards who were manipulated into thinking they could control him for their own ends—but he immediately broke their bonds and forced them to work for him summoning more demons, one at a time. But now they have the conduit."

"He's a piece of work, all right," Seraphex interjects lightly.

"So what does the conduit do?" I ask, though I'm starting to get a sinking feeling. Okay, the sinking feeling I already had is like the *Titanic* halfway to the bottom of the ocean.

"It is powered by seismic energy, and in a fairly simplistic way it can be used to set off earthquakes or volcanoes. That's what I originally thought Vulkatherak was trying to do. But its primary, original purpose is much more sophisticated."

Zambrano takes a deep breath and begins speaking in a way that reminds me of the professors in the arcane theory program at NYU.

"The two staffs of the arcane conduit are connected to each other and can create a teleportal between them. Similar to my teleportraits but acting over far vaster distances and without needing a sorcerer to perform each teleportation."

I have a million questions, but I've learned that when he gets on a roll explaining something, it's best to just let him go.

"Banishing the demons took two sorcerers because there were two ends to the portal, where each of the staffs are placed. They opened a connection between the artifact and the Ilopango Crater, fed by seismic energy. One of the staffs has to be at a point of seismic power, while the other can be anywhere. Merlin took one half of the conduit through the vastness of space to Mars, while Liao Ling led an alliance of lesser sorcerers and wizards from across the world to drive every demon into the caldera portal." Zambrano speaks almost reverently and is slightly misty eyed—the way my dad is when talking about the great Broadway performers he idolized when he was young, who have been long since forgotten. "The demons were forced through the portal into exile in the demonic caverns on Mars. They've mostly been there since. At the end of the process the volcano exploded, killing Liao Ling and many other sorcerers and wizards as well as destroying several Mayan cities. That was their reward for stepping up to save the world. The Mayans, Merlin, and Liao Ling paid for the rest of us to live without having to fear demons. Mostly."

"Who's Liao Ling? Why haven't I heard of her?"

Zambrano shrugs. "Merlin and Liao Ling were roughly equal in ability, sorcerers of power unmatched before or since. Merlin was the only sorcerer who could travel through space, though his journey to deliver the conduit to Mars was one way, as far as we know. Merlin is still remembered as a figure of legend and mystery because he was tight with the Pendragon monarchs and various other rulers, and he was good at PR. He had a killer beard and was a skilled diplomat.

Liao Ling, on the other hand, was a real firebrand. She ran afoul of the rulers of every country she lived in, and in retaliation they stole the credit for her accomplishments and pretty much erased her from the record. Political leaders back then were a bunch of douchebags with jealousy and control issues."

"So more or less the same as now," Seraphex points out.

"At least some things in history are constant," Zambrano agrees.

"Okay, so if Volcanose gets the conduit, what happens?" I ask, feeling like I already know the answer.

"He will make a direct connection to the Torrid Red Wastes, the demonic caverns on Mars," Zambrano explains, running his hand through his thick white hair. "No summoning required. No rare ingredients, no complicated casting, no danger of the spell going sideways and blowing up in your face or turning you into a goat-person. They just use mystic runes to connect it to seismic energy, perform an opening incantation, and a few minutes later an unstoppable army of demons pours through."

"So we need to prevent him from using it!" Seraphex says with more sincerity than I've come to expect from her.

Zambrano grits his teeth. "They'll be expecting us, but yeah, we need to get to that spaceship and stop it from launching."

I grab a nearby tablet, frowning as I feel that weird missing-appendage effect of not having my phone—I wish I hadn't had to toss it into the air, but that's how these things go. On the tablet, I pull up the news app. The Mars colony spaceship launch is covering three of the top four headlines—the other one is claiming that a "nefarious dark sorcerer" attacked the Willis Tower in Chicago. No time to read that one. I tap the top one, and swallow hard as I see the headline and accompanying video.

I turn the tablet to Zambrano and Seraphex.

"I'm not a dark sorcerer!" Zambrano gripes. "That's not even a real thing."

"Of course not," Seraphex says. "You're just a sorcerer with a long and storied history of doing dark magic. That's completely different."

"Says the demon who tried to destroy the whole world," Zambrano shoots back. "Anyway, my magic is really more 'dark adjacent,' at least most of the time.

"Ugh, no, no, not that one—look at the main article!" I say, pointing at the big video of the spaceship lifting off the launchpad and rocketing into the upper atmosphere.

"It launched while we were in Chicago," I say, looking back at the article. "The launch had been put on hold and then . . ." I do some quick math in my head. "They launched right after the demons caught me in the hallway."

"Volcanose, that weasel!" Zambrano growls, following it with what sounds like curses in a language I don't know.

"It shouldn't be that far away yet," Seraphex says. "It will take months to reach Mars. I'll help you craft a spell to stop it."

Zambrano stares at her in shock. "You'll help me make a new spell? Help me harness demonic magic?"

Seraphex shrugs and preens a bit. "We have a common interest. You want to save humanity. I don't want a demon duke to rule where a queen belongs."

Zambrano nods. "Um, okay then. We just need to do it quickly before the spaceship gets out of range." He seems more surprised by Seraphex's offer than anything else that this crazy day has brought us.

I glance down at the tablet as a new notification pops up in the news app. *Mars colony ship unexpectedly accelerates, crew presumed dead. Magical interference suspected. Is nefarious dark sorcerer involved?* I tap on it and read the first paragraph of the article.

> Observers at NASA, ESA, and other world agencies have confirmed that Lukas Volker's Mars colony ship Vulcan III has suddenly accelerated at a rate of one hundred meters per second per second. Mission control has lost contact with the crew, who would have been subjected to a likely fatal force of ten times Earth's gravity. Magic is the suspected cause, though experts at the Sorcerbonne were not aware of any human magic capable of achieving that level of power. At its current rate, astronomers estimate that the ship could reach the red planet in three to five days.

I look up. Zambrano and Seraphex have already gone deep into technical magic talk about methods, ingredients, and artifacts to craft their spell.

"It will take a couple weeks to gather that much rusalka hair and wyvern scales," Zambrano is saying, "but then we can project enough force over the distance to knock it off course enough to miss Mars's gravity well . . ."

"Um, we have a problem," I say.

"Yes," Seraphex agrees. "We'll need to use the gravitational lensing effect of the moon, so we have to time it precisely and will only get one shot . . ."

"Hello? Zambrano? Sera?" I say more loudly.

"Sure," Zambrano continues, ignoring me, "but we'll need to properly focus it using a heart-trap diamond on this end—"

"It's too late!" I yell, which makes them at last shut up and turn to glare at me.

"Too late? We've got months while the colony ship is in transit," Seraphex scolds me.

I hold the tablet up. "They used demonic magic to speed it up. It'll be there in a few days."

"Well . . . that totally bites," Zambrano says.

"What does it mean?" I ask. "What can we do about it?"

Zambrano takes a minute to read the article and then scrawls some calculations on a pad at the lab bench.

"The reason it takes a long time to get to Mars is physics," he says with gritted teeth. "To go fast, you need fuel. You need to get that fuel into orbit, you need to accelerate your fuel along with you, including all the fuel that you need to slow down at the other end. Mass and energy are intertwined in ways that make everything hard."

"But this is different?" I ask.

Zambrano nods. "Magic has rules that balance it out and limit its energies, but they're not related to mass the way normal physics is. They have more to do with the amount of effort required to create certain effects. There are no hacks for a free lunch—for instance, there's no way to create an infinite loop of energy within the rules of magic. But you can twist the hell out of normal physics with it. You can't use magic to make a spaceship, but you can use magic to supercharge the rocket reactions once you have one." He slams his hand on the table. "So damn clever of him. The magical energy connected to that spaceship has accelerated beyond anything possible with modern technology. It's going a couple million miles per hour, roughly one percent the speed of light. It'll be at Mars in a few days, depending on how much it needs to decelerate before landing."

"And that's it, then? There's nothing we can do to stop it?"

"No, nothing now. We're out of moves. It was a long shot to stop him, anyway. We certainly can't move against Volcanose directly; he's too powerful. Time for Plan B?"

"What's Plan B?" I ask.

"Plan B for Zambrano is always the same," Seraphex says with derision. "Run away, hide in a deep underground bunker for a few years, and hope the whole thing blows over."

"It worked for most of the Second World War," Zambrano says with a shrug.

"You *sat out World War II in an underground bunker?*" I really thought I'd known the worst of Zambrano, but it seems like there's always more to learn.

Zambrano sighs. "Look, kid, even sorcery can't do much against a battalion of panzer tanks or a squadron of Luftwaffe bombers. It wasn't my fight! At least I knew which side were the good guys, okay? Unlike Caravello. I did come out and intervene when she started assisting with their necromancy research."

"Yes, you emerged in 1944 right after the allies liberated Paris," Seraphex notes wryly. "So very brave of you."

I just shake my head. "Whatever, man. But we can't sit this out. We have to stop Volcanose, or the whole world will be overrun with demons."

"No. It's not my responsibility. I tried to help; it didn't work," Zambrano growls. "We're done. It's not my problem."

CHAPTER 26

I plop down in a nearby chair, shaking my head.

"You really want to run away, don't you?" I say. "Like, you actually would?"

"What am I supposed to do against an army of demons?" Zambrano paces, gesturing wildly. I kind of expect magic to shoot from his arms, but he's too controlled for that. "The moment that portal opens, there will be an unstoppable surge of them. Look, I've saved the world a few times, but I don't think I can stop this one. Not in a couple of days, certainly."

"And that's it? Demons rule the Earth?"

"The *wrong* demons," Seraphex mutters under her breath.

Zambrano shrugs. "They'll rule the Earth for a while. They won't wipe out humanity, probably. They're coming here because they want to be in charge of humanity. Nothing lasts forever though. They'll end up fighting, probably weakening each other. You humans are like cockroaches, you'll outlast their rule one way or another."

"*You humans*? You realize that you're one of us, right?"

"Barely, at this point." Zambrano has stopped and is leaning on a table, staring at the wall of teleportraits, smiling wistfully. As if saying goodbye to them. "Look, kid, I've come to be a bit fond of you. I can store you in a slow-time case and bring you out in a few hundred years when it's safe again."

"A few hundred years?!"

"Look, I'm the only living sorcerer," Zambrano says, starting to step around the room and gather items into a satchel that he's pulled from somewhere. "I can't run into every dangerous situation to try to help humanity. I'm the last of my kind. You wouldn't understand."

"Sure," I say. "Is that why you let me sneak into all those places for you? Because you're afraid?"

He ignores me, striding to the library and plucking several ancient-looking tomes from the shelves.

I take a deep breath. I want to yell at him, to berate him, to try to force him to help. But somehow, I don't think that will work. I need to work this the smart way. Get him thinking.

"Okay, okay," I say. "Let's just slow down for a second. Can you explain to me why we can't stop this from happening? Why can't we just shut down the portal from this end?"

"The demon duke has been a step ahead of us all along here. He will certainly be guarding the half of the conduit that's in Yellowstone. For a portal to bring through a whole demon army, it will be drawing its power directly from the seismic energy of the supervolcano there."

"Can we just blast it from a distance? Or call in an air strike or something?" I ask.

"Not at this point, no," Zambrano says, shaking his head. "If we sever the connection violently, it would unleash all that energy. The Yellowstone supervolcano would probably erupt. I haven't done the calculation for how bad that is, but it's *bad*."

"Well, perhaps it would be fine?" Seraphex says. "It might be worth the risk."

"The last time, it killed one of the greatest sorcerers of all time and destroyed several Mayan cities," Zambrano notes dryly.

"No setting off supervolcanoes!" I scold the duck. "There has to be another way to take out Volcanose," I say, turning to Zambrano. "Can't you defeat him with magic? Turn him into a duck or something? You seem to have done that to Sera easily enough."

"Easily?!" Seraphex squawks, and it's the closest I've ever heard her to sounding like a duck.

Zambrano sighs. "That was a very long time ago, in a different world. I didn't do it alone; we had a whole Circle of Sorcerers. Two of them *died*," he says, casting a meaningful look at Seraphex. "The whole plan was Alix LaFontaine's clever spellcraft—I just rallied everyone in the Circle together and was the keystone caster. She would have gotten most of the credit if it hadn't been for . . . what happened later."

Zambrano has stopped and is leaning with one hand on a bookshelf, staring into the distance again. I know better than to ask what happened to Alix LaFontaine—he's already explained to me what happened to most of those sorcerers.

He shakes his head. "What a high goddamn cost," he says, staring daggers at Seraphex. "She ended up being the connecting thread for way too much arcane energy, after Olujimi was hit by the barb of a scorpion demon and collapsed. It was coming for me next and would have ruined the whole spell if Zuzanna didn't have a petrification spell that she could cast one-handed."

On a nearby counter, the demon queen is uncharacteristically silent, not looking up at the last living sorcerer. They both just stare for a while, neither saying anything.

"Okay," I say, breaking the icy silence. "Is it even possible to destroy the conduit if we could somehow get to it?"

Zambrano shakes his head, then a shudder goes through his whole body for an instant. He looks at me, wincing like he's pulled himself back from somewhere else.

"The conduit is an ancient artifact, and Volcanose is an archdemon. They're both virtually indestructible. Believe me, if it could be destroyed, I would have done it long ago. We tried, you know, Alix and I. Even the Circle's power wasn't enough."

I snap my fingers nervously, trying to will some sort of idea into existence.

"So we can't destroy the conduit. And we can't kill Volcanose. At least, you weren't able to when you tried."

"Exactly," Zambrano says. "Hundreds of years ago, when I had other powerful sorcerer allies to help me. Demons can never truly be killed, they always reform. So you have to trap or exile them."

I bite my lip. Maybe, just maybe, there's an option here.

"So that was hundreds of years ago, right?"

"Yeah, exactly," Zambrano says. "Things were different back then. I cared more, for one."

I sigh and plop down on one of the stools at one of the workbenches, leaning back against the bench. I'm sure that normally

Zambrano would yell at me for being dangerously close to knocking over his experiments or whatever, but right now he barely even notices.

Seraphex and I sit there in silence for several minutes as Zambrano goes back to sorting his books into different piles and muttering to himself.

"Things *were* different back then!" I say, jumping back up. "A lot of other things were different too. Like, there were no spaceships. If Volcanose can use them, why can't we? What if the conduit were, say, dropped into the center of the sun? By a supercharged spaceship?"

"Oh, damn you," Zambrano says, slapping the book in his hand on the table. "I hate you. I really do."

"What, because it's a bad idea?" I ask.

"No, no," he says, more quietly. "Because . . . because it might be possible. But where would we get a spaceship?"

"If it's for saving the world, maybe I can convince someone," I offer. "Just maybe. If I can get us a spaceship, will you occupy Volcanose long enough for us to get the conduit out of there and launched into space?"

"You can get a spaceship?" Zambrano asks with a raised eyebrow.

"Um, maybe? I can try," I say. "I have an idea that—"

He leans forward and puts his face in his hands, and I instinctively shut up. It's not that he said anything or made a sound, but humans are incredibly sensitive to vibe shifts. And he has suddenly gone from his usual sarcastic and combative self to something completely different.

Zambrano sits there for long seconds. I look at Seraphex, but she's just staring at him, seeming as surprised as I am.

"Hey, um . . . are you okay?" I ask.

He just twists his head in his hands, shaking a bit.

"I don't want to do this again," he says, and his voice is suddenly raw and cracked. The studied baritone is gone. He sounds hoarse, and . . . old? As if the ancient man, the one who should have been dead and buried centuries ago, is speaking from all those years ago. "All I do is fight the same damn battle over and over again. And I keep losing."

"You're a total bastard," I say, "but you've saved the world before. You won."

"And no matter how many times I win, I still just lose, and lose, and lose," he says, still holding his head in his hands. "Every victory comes with a terrible price. With a friend who loses even more. I can't do it anymore. I don't know, maybe they're the lucky ones. The ones who died noble deaths. The ones who lost their minds. How am I the one who gets to stay sane?"

"Well, sort of sane," Seraphex interjects, but I give her a furious stare and she shuts up.

"They were *better than me*," he continues, his voice still cracking on every word. Despite all the awful things he's done and said to me, I can't help but feel bad for the guy. "I was the loose cannon, the irresponsible one, the antihero who teamed up with the good guys because it seemed fun. I used to have Olujimi and Caravello to keep me in line, you know."

"Do you want to tell me about them?" I ask almost automatically. I want to think it's because I think that's what a good therapist would say, but I have to admit I want to know for myself as well.

CHAPTER 27

Olujimi was the most compassionate of us. The pride of Lagos, he was the one who pushed us to make fewer spells to destroy things and more spells that could create life and encourage growth." Zambrano jerks upright, grabs the illusion prism in one hand and starts gesturing with his hands, somehow choppy and powerful at the same time. The lights around us dim, and a shadowy version of Olujimi appears on the desk. He's a tall Black man in a finely embroidered robe, holding a staff of multiple tree branches twisted together.

"We would talk and drink until late in the night, and no matter how much I made fun of him, the next day I always went out and did the thing he told me to. He taught me to mold and grow living flesh, and what did I do with it after he died? I gave myself a thick head of hair and a jawline you could open a beer bottle on. He had the talent to revolutionize modern biology and medicine, to save millions of lives. And instead, he died fighting. He was the one sorcerer who hated battle magic."

The illusion shifts, and we see a battle with shadowy figures in a circle surrounding a tall demon queen with smaller demons appearing from her flowing capes, each being cut down one by one. Finally, a massive scorpion demon leaps forth and charges at a figure that I recognize by the bright white hair as Zambrano. Next to him, Olujimi steps out of the circle and uses his staff to block the scorpion's pincers. He struggles with it and pushes it back but not before its stinger can lash forward and strike the sorcerer in the arm. Olujimi falls to the ground, and the circle contracts. The scorpion advances on Zambrano but another sorcerer, a blond woman, uses her right hand to shoot a bolt of energy at the scorpion while her left continues casting the spell binding the demon at the center of the circle.

"And Caravello . . . she survived that battle. She and Zuzanna led the remaining members of the Circle in trapping the Dread Leviathan of the Pacific Rim in 1929. Ilyas Rahmani, master of electrical magic, went mad on the spot, and we had to put him down a few weeks later. He had always been a kind and gentle man, but after that battle a furious energy took hold of him." The illusion shows several sorcerers on the deck of an old-fashioned ocean liner with colossal smokestacks, battling a massive creature in a stormy sea. One of the figures unleashes such an intense blast of flames that he collapses on the spot. "But Caravello was always the one who spoke up for honor. For respecting the rights of individuals and standing by our principles. Not playing god with the lives of normal people, even if we had the power to. When I wanted to take revenge on someone for their unbelievable idiocy, she was the one who would sit me down and talk me out of it. And you know what happened to her?"

He suddenly turns and stares at me.

I shake my head. "No, I don't," I say. "Something about World War II?"

"It took many years after the Leviathan. A slow slide into obsession. But she lost it all. Her mind deteriorated, and she forgot about all her high-minded principles. Or maybe she became committed to them in the most extreme and twisted way. She became forgetful, and she was obsessed with death. She started doing horrifying experiments in the name of some greater good. Trying to reanimate the dead. And she would forget, halfway through, what she was doing, leaving them halfway between life and death. Necromancy has been banned since the Renaissance for a reason—no one ever comes back right. I finally caught up with her in Dresden in 1945."

His hands twist and grasp, and the illusion becomes a city on fire, with planes falling from the sky and buildings aflame. Two sorcerers battle it out amid the flames, their own cascades of deadly spells mixing with the flickering destruction of the falling bombs.

"She was the principled moral conscience of the Circle. And after the power she summoned to fight the Leviathan, her mind just slowly came apart. And so I had to put her down. At least that one was in the heat of battle. I had all the adrenaline of a sorcerous duel when it happened. Though it wasn't as merciful as Zuzanna, who had seen all the others fall and realized what was happening and took her own life."

His hands fall, and the illusion disappears. All I can see is his suddenly haggard face. "It wasn't that way with Alix. She was super-charged with demonic magic, and she had always been my equal, anyway. I had to convince her that I was on her side, that I'd forgiven her, that I'd decided to join her in opening the gate for the ultimate evil. I had to lie to her, get close to her, kiss her, put my hand over her heart, and drain the life out of her in an instant. Because if she had even a moment's warning, she would have defeated me and destroyed the world."

There are tears on his face, but he's not crying or sobbing. Just staring at me, haunted by his memories.

"I'm so sorry," I say, knowing that it's not enough.

"So you can see, now, why I don't want to go up against the demon duke directly," he says. "It's not just that I'm afraid of dying. All these years trying to help my friends, I've only just lost everything. Centuries where every victory comes at a terrible price. And who knows, if I use magic that's too powerful, what will I become? I can't do it."

"That's tough," I say. "But it was worth it all, wasn't it?"

"Worth it for everyone who didn't die. Who I wasn't forced to kill or sacrifice. For everyone but the people I cared most about. When it should have been me. Why should I care? Why should I go back into feeling like that, into losing like that? I should just be done. What's the point of even living or trying anymore?"

"If that's how you feel, then why not try one more time? What do you have to lose? We can do it together. I'll help you any way I can. You don't have all those old sorcerers . . . but you do have a kickass intern buddy with magical invisibility superpowers."

He shudders and twitches as if physically shying away from whatever he's thinking.

"No. No. You're not my buddy, okay?" he growls at me. "You're not in the Circle, you're not my friend. You can help, but you're just the intern. If you can survive, that's great. If you end up as demon fodder, that's how it goes."

I can feel my eyes stinging from the sudden rejection. We only met a couple weeks ago, but we've been through a *lot* in that time. I kind of felt like we were starting to have something. Not friendship, exactly, but the kindling of it? Some sort of respect at least.

I look around at the lab, taking in the centuries of artifacts and knowledge collected here. This guy has sacrificed everything to keep the world safe, even if he likes to frame it as selfish. If Zambrano doesn't want to be my friend, that's his business. The fate of the world hangs in the balance. My hurt feelings don't matter.

I promised Agent Crane that I'd do what I could to help. The fate of the whole world hangs in the balance. I take a white-knuckled grip on the edge of the table to steady myself. Zambrano doesn't have to want to be my friend. I can still be his no matter what he says. I take a deep breath and a long moment to collect myself.

"Okay, understood. We've got to do what we've got to do. We can keep it purely business. Just get the job done, foil the Duke's plot. If I don't make it out, I don't make it out. You don't need to worry about it either way."

He sits there silently for what seems like several minutes, then suddenly gives a shrug, and the worry and age on his face melt away.

"Okay, kid, sure," Zambrano says with a seemingly unnatural grin. "If you can get a spaceship. Whatever, let's do it. I don't care. Let's try this hero thing one more time."

I cock my head to the side in surprise. "Really?"

"Once more unto the breach, and all that," he says offhandedly with the air of a fast food worker agreeing to take on an extra overtime shift. "Yeah, let's give it a shot. That underground bunker smells super musty, anyway. If I die, so be it. At least then, everyone will be rid of me. If I go crazy—well, good luck with all that."

"Okay, that's great," I say. "I'll work on the spaceship thing. What else do we need to make this happen?"

Seraphex stands up in a ruffle of feathers. I'd almost forgotten the demon duck is still here, she's been so quiet. "I can help with instructions on how to safely handle the conduit and get it launched into space, and help them increase its speed the same way that

Vulkatherak did so that it can't be caught. And I can show you how to hold your ground against the Duke while we make our way in to where he's hiding the conduit. I know some tricks and weaknesses of his that should help to buy you a few minutes."

"Thank you, you goddamn demon monstrosity," Zambrano says, and it's not with the affection he sometimes seems to have for her. "Bryce, thank you for helping me remember how much I loathe this demon duck."

I expect a barbed retort, but Seraphex just ignores Zambrano's insults, instead launching into a bunch of magical jargon that's way above my head. Within minutes the two of them are deep in discussions of magical lore and technique that is far beyond me and probably beyond any other living human being.

I head upstairs. They have their job to do. And I have mine.

CHAPTER 28

I use what I'm coming to think of as the "infinite money" tablet to order a new phone with curbside pickup from the closest store and walk to pick it up. At least this time I can make Zambrano pay for it, which is nice. I spring for the newest and most expensive model. An hour later I'm back at the warehouse with my brand-new phone fully set up, and I plop down on my bed, thinking everything over.

I stare down at the fresh new screen. Agent Crane told me to just type things into Google to get in touch with her, so I type *Please connect me to Agent Crane. It's urgent* into the search bar and wait. It's a new phone, but I'm signed in to all my old accounts, so I have to hope that they're still tracking me. Which I think is a good bet, because we all know how the government feels about us regular people having privacy. They don't seem to like it, if you haven't been paying attention!

Nothing happens for about ten minutes, so I try another tactic. I hold up my phone.

"Hey, Siri, connect me to Agent Crane. It's an emergency."

Another ten minutes later, I'm looking at the main page of the MSA's website, hunting around for contact info when UNKNOWN NUMBER pops up on my phone. I shrug and answer it.

"Hello?"

"You've reached the Worldwide Home of Waffles on Forest Avenue," a bored voice answers the phone. "Pick up or delivery?"

"Um, sorry, you called me," I say.

"No, sir, you called us," the voice says. "The phone just rang."

"Oh, um, yeah," I say, taking a guess at what might be happening. "Sorry about that, must have dialed the wrong number."

"Okay, whatever," the voice says, and the line goes dead.

Shrugging, I look up this Worldwide Home of Waffles on my phone. It's about a fifteen-minute walk away. It is also, somewhat embarrassingly, the number one place I've been ordering delivery from while I've been at the warehouse.

I stand up and look around my room. What do I take to a possible clandestine meeting with a secretive government agent? I feel like I should be bringing something, but it's too warm for a jacket and I don't really have any weapons. Plus, I doubt Agent Crane would appreciate me coming armed.

Shrugging, I grab my phone and wallet and just walk out the door. A short walk later, I'm strolling into the Worldwide Home of Waffles, a little bit of classic corporate America that does a pretty consistent job of making its namesake food. Which I guess shouldn't be that hard—the waffle iron does most of the work.

Agent Crane is already there with a big plate of waffles sitting in front of her.

"Is all this cloak-and-dagger really necessary?" I ask, sliding into the other side of the booth. "What if I didn't realize that call was meant to be instructions? Couldn't you just, like, text me or something?"

The MSA agent shrugs, taking a bite. "It's probably not necessary," she says after she finishes chewing. "But you never know who's watching, even in other government agencies. And standard procedure is to keep you off-balance a bit. Sorry about that, but it works. You're lucky I was in town. I was sent here as soon as you disappeared from Chicago."

The server comes out and slides a big plate of chicken and waffles onto the table in front of me. I stare at it, not sure what to say.

"You've ordered it three times in the past two weeks," she explains. "Zambrano may be a genius sorcerer, but he's not exactly a digital security expert."

"More keeping me off-balance?" I ask.

"You're getting one of your favorite foods on the government's dime. I feel like 'thank you' would be more appropriate."

I purse my lips for a second. She's not entirely wrong. And my stomach is rumbling like the kettledrums at the end of a big symphony. I realize that I actually haven't really eaten anything all day. I've been preoccupied with the end of human civilization, okay?

"Thank you," I say, grabbing my fork and digging in.

"So . . ." Agent Crane says as I'm eating. "You said there's an emergency? I assume related to this madly accelerating spaceship and the deceased astronauts that our entire nation mourns," she says, not betraying the slightest hint of actually mourning. "Is Zambrano responsible for that, as well as the attack in Chicago?"

"Uh, no," I say. "Zambrano's not responsible for either of those things! Not exactly, anyway." And I explain the situation, trying to paint both myself and Zambrano in the best possible light.

"Well, that's certainly an interesting spin on events," she says, polishing up the last bite of her waffles. "An army of demons invading from Mars in just a few days' time? Through this 'conduit' artifact?"

I nod. "The half that's still here on Earth. Seraphex agreed with that assessment. She's a demon, so she can't lie."

Agent Crane taps her index finger on the table, her features appearing even more hawkish and strained than usual. "The MSA's dealings with demons have led us to conclude that their truths can often be more dangerous than most lies."

"I believe her," I say. "On this, at least."

"Very well," Agent Crane says. "Your story does match with various classified reports that I can't discuss in detail. Supposing that I believe you. What can we do to stop this? An air strike? Cruise missile? What are you asking for?"

"Well . . ." I say. "That won't work. If you hit it with a missile before the conduit is disconnected from the volcano's energy, it will trigger the supervolcano."

"Understood," Agent Crane says, lips tight. "So that's a backup option."

"A what?" I object. "That would be a disaster!"

"It would be," Agent Crane admits. "Massive loss of life, global food shortage, societal disruption. But the MSA's estimate is that a full demonic invasion would be an order of magnitude worse for humanity. We're prepared to make tough decisions."

"Okay, sure, but can we ideally not have either of those happen?"

She smiles. "I find your idealism inspiring. If you're not here looking for an air strike, what are you looking for?"

"I kind of . . . need a spaceship."

She gives me a blank stare. "A spaceship?"

"Yeah. To drop into the sun. We can help with that. Well, Zambrano and Seraphex can help with that; they can give you something to speed the spaceship up. I still don't know much about magic, or how to actually do it," I say. Which, I have to note, really kind of sucks. I've learned a few things, but it's only made me want to understand more. Even if I'll never be able to actually cast a goddamn spell.

I shake my head, focusing on the important thing here. You know, the coming invasion of Earth by an ancient demonic army returning from exile on Mars.

"So," Agent Crane says, glancing at the check and dropping a handful of cash on the table. "We need a spaceship to send an ancient artifact into the sun. In order to prevent literal hell on Earth. And how soon do you need it?"

I stare down at the sad bits of chicken and waffles remaining on my plate. "Thursday?"

"Understood," she says with a nod. She stands up, adjusting her clothes. "You'll find a new messaging app on your phone. You can use it to call or text me. Don't abuse the privilege."

"Wait," I say as she turns to leave. "Can you do it? Get us a spaceship?"

"No guarantees," she says. "But we're the MSA, not the DMV. We can actually do things. Though the director is *not* going to like this. And the paperwork is going to be an unmitigated nightmare. I'll be in touch. Wait at least five minutes before leaving so we're not caught on camera together."

And with that, she heads out the door and disappears into the summer night. I'm left there marveling at both my own boldness and the fact that it just possibly might have actually worked. I dutifully wait five minutes, then make my way back to the warehouse. The whole time, I'm trying not to glance over my shoulder, wondering who is watching me.

I don't think I would want to be an MSA agent, it seems super stressful. Of course, I am currently living a very safe life where I'm about to reveal to a rogue sorcerer that I've been able to get ahold of a spaceship for us from his hated enemy, the government. I've come up with a plan to lie and say that Agent Crane is my aunt, but I'm not feeling super confident in it. I could try to explain it, but I worry that revealing my connection to Agent Crane might put Zambrano in a shoot-fireball-now-ask-questions-later kind of mood.

I want to reach out to Parth and my friends on WizardWatch, but that seems like too big a risk. If the government can monitor my online activity, a billionaire demon might be able to do so as well. Telling them what's going on could reveal our plan, and I can't bring myself to lie to my friends.

I think about calling my parents, but I have no idea what I'd say to them. *Hey, Mom, so I'm going to try to steal an ancient artifact from a demon. Love you, wish me luck!* Or, *Dad, if I don't ever come back, it's because I've been burned into a crisp by a walking, talking volcano.* These are not conversations I am eager to have.

The next morning, I wake up to a notification in the new secure messaging app that appeared on my phone after meeting Agent Crane. I'm not sure whether to think it's cool or scary that the MSA can just do whatever it wants to on my phone. I guess a bit of both.

I open it up and read the message: *Emergency request to use the Eridani spacecraft approved. I stuck my neck out here for you, don't screw me over on this. When you get the artifact outside, signal me and I'll pick you up in a heli-jet to fly it to the Kennedy center for the launch.*

I head down to the lab where Zambrano and Seraphex are leaning over a glass contraption, a sphere with all sorts of holes and internal tubing. Honestly, it looks like the world's most unnecessarily complicated bong.

"Holy shit," Zambrano is saying. "This is actually going to work!" He glances over at me with a gleam in his eye. "This demonic magic is fascinating! Learning how it works almost makes our imminent deaths worth it, wouldn't you say?"

"Uh, sure," I answer. "So the superbong will make the spaceship go fast?"

"Yes," Seraphex says. "Space is big. Once it's launched and up to speed, there will be nothing that Volcanose can do to catch up to it."

"I hate to ask," Zambrano says, "but how are we doing on the spaceship?"

"I've got it," I try to say nonchalantly.

"Okay, great," Zambrano says. "So we're good to go. We have just a few more adjustments to make on the 'superbong,' here, as you called it. Then let's make our final plan of attack and hit them first thing tomorrow."

"We'll, um, need to get the superbong to the Kennedy Space Center. And drop it off so they can have it on the spaceship. My aunt, who works at NASA—" I start with my attempt at a lie, but Zambrano cuts me off, shaking his head.

"What?" I ask. I stand there, waiting for the questions to come. For the other shoe to drop.

Zambrano stares at me. "It's okay. I'm not going to look into the real story of who you've been talking to and how the guy from the smoothie shop can pull a NASA spaceship on short notice."

"You're not?"

He sighs. "In the days of the Circle of Sorcerers, we had a rule. If we desperately needed help and one of our members had a powerful resource to bring to bear, we didn't question how they got access to it. You know, illegal experiments, arcane thievery, meddling with dark powers, consorting with the enemy," he says with a suggestive glance at me.

"Sorcerers are very secretive," Seraphex explains. "If they are worried about being blamed for having powers or artifacts, they won't come forward and offer them to save the world."

"Exactly," Zambrano says. "We can't have anyone holding back their power. So whatever sketchy liaisons you've got, I'm not going to hassle you about it. Even if it makes me pretty damned suspicious."

"And you wonder why the media call you a dark sorcerer," Seraphex says with a self-satisfied wave of her beak.

"Okay, thanks," I say with a gulp, breathing a sigh of relief. Zambrano has turned back to the superbong. "Is that . . . is this feeling that I'm feeling right now you actually showing me respect?"

"No," Zambrano shoots back. "Shut up and come hold this tube in place for me. Seraphex has been very helpful, but she is *never* getting her arms back. Not after what she did to me."

"Why do you keep her around" I ask, "if she took so much from you?"

Zambrano sighs. "The spell that made Seraphex a duck was Alix's last great work. It's been over a hundred years. Nothing much else remains of her. Sera is the only other person who was there, who remembers her. That goddamn demon duck is my last connection to the only person I really gave myself to."

"So she's a memento?"

"Not quite. She's also indestructible and incredibly powerful. She has to be somewhere, and as much as we are enemies, we are also the only two on this planet who really understand each other," Zambrano says. "I could lock her away somewhere safe, but if I let her be relatively free to come and go, she gives me useful information. Her knowledge is vast. Our 'friend' Volcanose is mighty, but Seraphex is on another level. If he achieves his goals, he would rule over the world with an iron fist. But it would still be a world, with humans serving a single repressive authoritarian government. There would still be humans living human lives, with happiness and sadness and all that. If Seraphex had succeeded in her plan all those years ago, this would have turned into a literal hell on Earth."

"Oh, it wouldn't have been *that* bad," Seraphex protests.

We both glare at her.

"Well, not for me, anyway," she says, sulking.

Zambrano rolls his eyes while I consider whether throwing a chair at her would count as animal abuse.

"Also, he keeps me around because he's bad at math," Seraphex says. "And he's too embarrassed to ask for help from anyone else."

"Shut it, you murderous monster," Zambrano growls. "You've just got demonic precision and speed. It saves time."

"I can't lie. He's bad at math," Seraphex says primly. "He struggles to solve even the simplest class of partial differential equations."

We sit in silence for a long moment.

Finally, Zambrano sighs. "You know, I was supposed to have a date tonight, not be stuck here with you two," he says. "That was . . . optimistic of me. I guess I'll have to cancel."

"Do you ever actually bring any of these dates back home with you?" I ask.

He shrugs. "Only if I really like them," he answers. "If I'm actually interested in them."

"And when was the last time that happened?" I ask.

"It's been a while," he grumbles, putting the glass down hard enough to make the ice clink and a tiny bit splash out.

"It was 2007," Seraphex interjects. "And he only came by twice."

"Wow, and how long have you been here, Sera?" I say, suddenly realizing that I don't actually know that.

"Let's just say that I've gotten very used to the molting process every year," she answers. "It's very unpleasant, but I can usually find a local spa to take care of everything for me."

I suppose I should have known better than to get a straight answer out of either of these two.

CHAPTER 29

The next morning, I dress in hiking gear for a stupidly dangerous adventure in one of our country's most famous national parks. I come downstairs to the lab to see Zambrano putting the finishing touches on a teleportrait. This time Zambrano is dressed in all black like he's going to a funeral or like he's Luke Skywalker at the end of *Return of the Jedi*. Probably because he thinks he's going to die. He is so damn dramatic.

"Are you just copying that," I say as I look more closely at the painting and the tablet open next to it, "from Instagram?" The painting has a distinctive mountain range in the background and a big wooden YELLOWSTONE NATIONAL PARK sign in the foreground.

"Yep," Zambrano says. "It's not a very pretty picture and this person's feed is full of bad photography, so I'm fairly sure it hasn't been edited. Sometimes photographers photoshop multiple pictures together to make them pretty, and it ruins the whole teleportrait. So I troll the feeds of tourists who don't know how to take a decent photo."

"Huh," I say. "Would it be possible to just use the sign? Or have, I don't know, something like QR codes spread out in stickers on every city?"

Zambrano smiles. "That's another reason why the egghead magic researchers at the big universities haven't been able to replicate what I do. They're super focused on more and more complicated two- and three-dimensional patterns. They want to make a simple system and then replicate it everywhere. But it's not about that. The teleportrait has to be describing a real, physical place. It's about the *feel* of a specific location. The physical features are an important part of that. But magic isn't a computer program even if it has general rules and predictability. If you give it a hundred QR codes or barcodes or something, it's going to see exactly the same thing that you and I do—a crap ton of black-and-white nonsense that all looks the same! Magic sees the world holistically. Magic cares that there's nowhere else in the universe that *feels* like this location."

"Huh, okay," I say. "Thanks, that kind of makes sense. But why are magic items and artifacts so intricately designed with so many unique and special ingredients?"

"Ah," Zambrano says. "That's to identify that type of thing specifically. For example, every illusion prism of a design operates the same way and can do the same things. If you make small changes to the design that don't specifically tweak what it does—that just makes magic stop recognizing it as enchanted at all. It will work less strongly or not at all."

"So enchantment isn't really the way to think of it then, is it? Like, magic isn't imbued into the object. The object is simply fashioned to be a design that is supposed to be identified by magic?" I say. I notice that he's started speaking the word "magic" more like a name than a force of nature. Like it's a person, or an organization, or something.

"Exactly. Unfortunately, all this arcane and artistic knowledge doesn't help so much in this particular situation. Teleportraits are fairly straightforward to block if you know what you're doing—so Volcanose has put protective magic that disrupts teleportrait use entirely in every area closer than this spot that I'm painting here. The same kind of thing from Slickwad's menagerie. Can't get in, can't get out," Zambrano says, putting a few finishing brushstrokes on the painting. "Now, magic lesson over! Less talk, more bravely dying for a lost cause or whatever we're about to do."

"Um, yeah, okay," I say. "Let's do it."

"I can't believe you talked me into this," he mutters, then shouts across the room, "Seraphex, we're ready to go!"

Seraphex waddles out from behind a bookshelf. She is . . . wearing clothes. She's still a duck, but she is somehow wearing a duck-sized-shaped green army camouflage uniform.

"You're getting dressed up for this?" Zambrano asks.

"Oh, yes indeed," she says. "I actually care about this now, so I'm going to try to help. Playtime is over, let's defeat the demon duke. As a team, and all that."

"Where did you get that, Sera?" I ask. "Who sells duck camouflage?"

Seraphex shrugs. "Have you been to this internet place? They have things that are far, far stranger than this."

"Okay, fair enough," I agree. "It's nice that you finally care. Unlike the previous five times I've been in mortal danger . . ."

"Well, I didn't want to be here in the first place, and certainly not in the shape of a duck. But here we are, and our purposes are aligned. Let's save humanity from Vulkatherak."

Zambrano looks dubious, but he grabs me by the neck, Seraphex flutters up onto my shoulder, and a moment later we're standing in front of the Yellowstone National Park sign.

"I've traced the flow of seismic energy to a geyser field about a mile from here. Vulkatherak has set up his operation underneath the visitors' center."

As we walk, I try to calm my nerves by marveling at what's actually happening here. Sure, I haven't learned to do actual magic myself. But I have learned a hell of a lot about how it works. And I'm on an adventure with the world's last sorcerer and a demon queen to try to save the world from a horde of other demons. They're both irredeemable asshats, and the two of us humans are probably going to die. But still . . . it's pretty cool. Not what I had in mind for myself, but damn impressive.

"Seraphex, you're going to need to go in with Bryce while I hit our friend Volcanose with everything I've got. Now, there can't be any funny business about this."

"Really? That's no fun," Seraphex pouts. She seems mildly disappointed, like he just told her they couldn't stop for ice cream on the way back from picking up the dry cleaning.

Zambrano rolls his eyes. "I need you to promise, no funny business, okay?"

"You really should know better than that," Seraphex shoots back. "That's not specific enough for me to agree to. Unless you want me to just not practice my tight five-minute stand-up set."

"I mean you need to stick to the plan," Zambrano says. "Get the conduit and get it out to the helicopter. No seizing power for yourself or using the conduit or any artifacts. You have to just stick to the plan."

We're walking along a calm road, and it's a buzzy and pleasant summer afternoon. The fir trees are rustling slightly in the breeze, and it just does not seem like a day where an apocalyptic magical showdown is about to take place.

Seraphex seems to think that over. "How often do our plans go smoothly? What if something changes?"

Zambrano sighs. "Okay, okay. Follow the plan, unless"—he looks over at me—"unless Bryce thinks it's necessary to change the plan. And then you can change it how *he* thinks necessary."

"Well that's nice. It means she'll also have to help keep me alive," I add in.

"Not a bad side benefit," Zambrano acknowledges.

Seraphex readjusts her feathers, thinking it over.

"Okay," she says. "That works. I agree to stick to the plan, unless Bryce agrees it needs to be modified. And then I'll follow those modifications."

"Okay, good. Bryce," says Zambrano, patting me on the shoulder in an uncharacteristically paternal way, "be careful. She's a crafty one, even if she can't lie. Sometimes *because* she can't lie. You'd think it's a huge drawback, but somehow she makes it into a superpower."

"Okay, understood," I agree.

We round the corner, and we've reached our destination.

Zambrano stands there for a long moment, staring at the building where Vulkatherak the demon duke is waiting. "I don't want to do this," he says in a small, quiet voice that I've never heard before. "Not again."

I have no idea what to say. Do I have a right to try to force him to do this? To put his life on the line for an ungrateful humanity once again? So I don't say anything. I just lean over and put my arm around his shoulders and give him a squeeze. For a moment, he puts his arm around me and we just stand there together as the beautiful weather seems to be subtly darkening as arcane powers gather ahead of us. It doesn't feel any different, but the light is a bit darker.

I can practically feel Sera rolling her eyes at us, but I really don't care. And then Zambrano stiffens, drops his arm, and straightens up.

"Okay, let's do this goddamn thing. Let's wreck this demonic asshole."

The way ahead is blocked by cones, yellow caution tape, and a VISITORS' CENTER CLOSED FOR RENOVATIONS sign. We can see up to the visitors' center, a massive building with a large glass triangle entryway. There are still plenty of tourists wandering around, so we mostly blend into the crowds hoping to see the geysers. Some people look curiously at the duck following along with us wearing army fatigues, but other than a few kids pointing, no one actually says anything.

Ignoring the signs, we duck under the caution tape and continue on.

"Good luck," I say, but Zambrano just nods. His brow is furrowed, and he's storming forward, stepping slowly but with a force that almost looks like his steps are going to crack the earth open. He hasn't started using magic yet, but from the look of him, he's already started to gather arcane forces around him. He probably feels like he's crackling with power—but I can't sense that sort of thing. So it just looks like he's walking angrily.

"He's getting into the zone. Let's go," Seraphex says from my shoulder. Following the plan, Seraphex and I peel off and circle around to the right side of the visitors' center, approaching through the parking lot and weaving our way quietly between the cars while Zambrano walks up the deserted main road.

We're most of the way around when I see him stop in front of the visitors' center.

"VULKATHERAK!" his voice booms, magically amplified and rolling across the parking lot. "Your time has come! I'm here to end you, you bastard. Let's finish this!"

He's standing in the road leading up to the visitors' center, hands raised, and now I can even see the pulsing and flickering power gathering around him.

I glance around and see that some of the tourists have started running for their cars, while others have pulled out cell phones and are recording. I really wish Zambrano didn't sound so much like a villain, but I guess he just can't help it. His voice and tone really do not make him sound like a good guy. He's psyched himself up to this confrontation by getting angry, and . . . clearly there's a hell of a lot of anger in there to tap.

We hustle around to the other side of the building, dodging fleeing tourists, with Seraphex somehow gripping on to my shoulder with a combination of webbed feet and wings. I'm not sure if she's extra strong for a duck or if ducks are just much more jacked than I give them credit for.

As we pass out of view of Zambrano, I take a final glance and see that Vulkatherak has emerged from the visitors' center, a giant hunk of horned rocks and lava with a twisted grin on his face. Meanwhile, the clear blue sky has darkened with thunderclouds gathering above us all.

"So you saw through my distraction, did you, little sorcerer? Well, that's no matter. The conduit has been activated, and my legions will be here soon. But I don't need their help. You will never be able to stand against my might in pitched battle."

A moment later, the air is filled with spells. An icy hailstorm, gouts of lava, lightning from the sky above, some kind of ghostly green phoenix swooping through the air . . . I can't see which is coming from where, but they're clearly throwing powerful opening salvos at each other. I can see Zambrano backpedaling under the onslaught already. I hope it's because he's trying to draw Volcanose away, not because he's already losing.

"Since demons can't lie, it must be true, right?" I whisper. "Zambrano will lose?"

"Demons have to say what they believe to be true," she says, clucking like a disappointed school teacher. "But Zambrano doesn't have to hold against him forever—just long enough for us to shut down the conduit and get it to the helicopter."

"Won't he just follow us? Teleport ahead and destroy us?" I realize that I should have asked these questions beforehand, but the plan sounded so good when Zambrano laid it out back at the warehouse.

"Teleportation isn't a demonic power except with an artifact like the conduit," Seraphex explains. "And none of his security magicians have that ability. Only sorcerers have learned how to use teleportraits."

I want to ask more, but there's no chance to follow up, as we've arrived at the door on the opposite side of the building.

Through the glass, the inside of the Old Faithful Visitors' Center looks normal, just kiosks with pamphlets, signs to the bathrooms, that sort of thing. According to Zambrano, the real action is all taking place in the basement. In the sudden darkness that's fallen over the area, I see there's a door marked "staff only" that has some sort of flickering light behind it. Beyond that, through the window on the other side, I can see Volcanose's back, cracked rock with molten lava running down it, as he takes slow steps forward, pushing through some sort of blue forcefield.

Zambrano said that the door would magically ward off most sorts of creatures. But demons would be allowed in and out, and I shouldn't be detected. The big bummer is that magical items would set off all sorts of alarms. So we don't get any sort of superpowered weapons.

That just leaves the problem of the locked door. But this is just a tourist attraction, not a high-security building, and the door and the whole facade is made of glass. I should really learn to pick locks if I'm going to be doing all this *Mission: Impossible* infiltration stuff. I'm surprised that it takes me several throws, but a large rock gets the job done just as well as some fancy lock-picking course. I stoop and step through the hole that I've made, with Seraphex hopping behind me. For a second I worry about her cutting herself on the glass, then I remember that she's an invincible demon queen and I'm a squishy, delicate human, and I kind of hope she at least gets some sort of annoying cut, even if it insta-heals or however invincibility works.

Mei Song steps out from behind a rack of postcards, glaring at me.

"What the hell are you doing here?" she hisses. "I already spared your life once! If I do it again, it's going to start looking suspicious." I note that she's still carrying the magic throwing axe on her belt, and her hand is drifting down to it.

"Um, I'm trying to save the world?" I answer.

"That was your excuse last time!" she says. "I helped you. Ugh, you failed to stop him, didn't you?"

"Well, yes," I protest, "but your boss used demonic magic to speed up the spaceship."

"And so now you want me to look the other way while you cause problems that put my job at risk, *again*? Did you know that my vision plan includes *unlimited free glasses*?"

"You're still worried about that?! Look at what's happening!" I gesture at the door, which now has significant glowing rays of light coming through all the cracks, and there's a distinct humming sound coming from the floor below us.

"They're just doing some magic bullshit, like always," Mei says. "And *your* boss just showed up and started a battle that's going to cause tons of damage to a national park."

"He's not my boss," I say automatically. Though, is he? I can see how it would look that way, and technically I am his intern . . . no time to think about that now. I notice that there is a blizzard swirling around the Visitors' center, shot through with orange light. "Can't you see what's going on here? A sorcerer battling a demon outside, an ancient artifact being powered up for the first time in millennia, drawing on a massive natural power source. This is a *classic* apocalypse scenario. Volcanose is going to summon a demon army from Mars, and when they rule the world who knows if there'll even *be* optometrists anymore."

Mei glares at me. Like, as if she kind of knew all that but didn't want to admit it to herself.

"God damn it. Screw this bullshit," she spits out and follows it up with a string of inventively foul profanity that, frankly, I would rather not think about. There are laws protecting donkeys from that sort of abuse.

"So you're going to help us?" Seraphex asks from my shoulder.

"You're right, of course. *Fine.* Okay, how do we save the world or whatever?" Mei says, seeming to take the talking duck perfectly in stride.

"What's guarding the conduit downstairs?" I ask. "We need to shut it down and get it out of here."

Mei purses her lips. "Most of the security magicians aren't in fighting shape after what your boss did to them in Chicago, but there are still two down there, plus the rockhide demons. I can get the mages to come up here, but the demons are under orders not to leave the conduit under any circumstances. I'll distract the mages, you'll need to get past Bronk and Tunker."

"Okay, sure," I say, eyeing the glowing door nervously. "How do I do that?"

"You'll have to figure it out. They're total idiots, and you're . . . well, less of an idiot. You're the big hero with all your 'morals.' You got this."

"Um . . . can I have that axe back?" I ask. "Just, you know, borrow it for a bit."

"Whatever," she says, rolling her eyes and handing the magic throwing axe over. "Now hide," she says and pulls open the door, letting out a flood of reddish light and a buzzing noise. "Hide!" she mouths, waving for us to move.

I crouch behind a big information desk, with Seraphex fluttering down next to me.

"Hey! Fernanda! Piero!" Mei shouts. "Get up here!"

Pressing myself down, I hear the voices of the two security magicians from my Peruvian encounter.

"It seems they have called in reinforcements after what happened in Chicago," Seraphex whispers, but I shush her.

Soon Mei has them upstairs and is spinning an elaborate lie about how Vulkatherak told her that the sorcerer is just a distraction and there's another attack coming from the opposite direction.

I'm surprised at how easily they're conned into doing what Mei says. But I guess when you're the executive assistant to the big boss, people tend to hop to whatever you ask of them, regardless of whether the big boss is a giant demon with lava snot or just the CEO or president or something. I can tell from how politely they answer her that they're completely aware that she controls access to the big guy.

Soon Mei has led the two Peruvian mages outside using the doors that we came in.

"Well, here we go," I say as I stand up and scamper across the room to the door. I really, really, really don't want to go down those stairs. I don't want to die any more than Zambrano does.

But he's out there, risking his life for me. For all of us. I've got to at least try to do my part.

I step down into the hellish red glow underneath the visitors' center.

CHAPTER 30

The stairwell goes down farther than I would have thought, several stories, and when I creep to the bottom, I can see that it opens into a large room with a kind of military or scientific look. Somehow, I doubt that this is what the National Park Service originally designed underneath the visitors' center—it has the look of a recent secret addition. Especially as it's filled with giant metal pylons that are sticking up through the floor as if they go far down. And they are glowing red and vibrating.

The bad news is that these metal pylons are harnessing seismic energy in order to summon an unstoppable demon army to ravage the Earth. But the good news is that they provide both cover and background noise to make it easy for me to sneak into the room. I can see from the bright intensity of the glow on the far side of the room that that's probably where the main action, and the artifact, will be found. The ground shakes, a mini earthquake that I can only assume is a bad sign.

Doing my best impression of a special forces soldier, I ghost from pylon to pylon, sneaking as close to the far side as I dare. Seraphex clings tightly to my shoulder, using a combination of supernature balance and feet digging into my flesh that would be uncomfortable if there weren't so much adrenaline in my system.

I'm careful not to touch the pylons, which are humming and glowing with a power and vibrating in a way that might sound exciting to some of you reading this—but I assure you that it looks far more likely to break all your bones than to help you get to sleep with a smile on your face.

As I get closer, I see two familiar shapes and hear their annoying, rumbling, rocky voices. The ground below me shakes again. I glance down at my phone as it buzzes. There's a message from Agent Crane on my new secure app. *Helicopter and jets in position, get the artifact there and we'll handle the rest,* it says.

There's another mini earthquake, and I lose my balance for a moment. They're starting to come steadily, and I pause for a moment to count it out. Yes, the "seismic energy" powering this thing seems to be shaking and rattling my teeth just about every eight seconds like clockwork. I approach closer and peer around a pylon, finally catching my first glimpse of it: the conduit.

It's a long staff made from shining metal, and it almost looks like three or more staffs have been twisted around one another to make it. They're not arranged in a neat braid but are entwined in a way that's more reminiscent of tangled vines. The staff is lying lengthwise on the ground, held into place by heavy metal clamps. The clamps look like miniature versions of the big metal pylons, also sunk deep into the ground.

A tall rectangle is projected up out of the horizontal staff, producing an interwoven and glowing tapestry of reddish hues. If I stare at the shimmering colors and shapes for a moment, I feel like I can almost see shapes waiting, ranks on ranks of demons. But they're just shadowy translucent outlines—for now. The portal is about six feet wide and almost twenty feet tall . . . I don't want to know what giant demon requires an entrance that large. Even Volcanose, as massive as he is, would only take up half the size of this thing.

I need to shut the staff down and get it out of here, but first, there are two huge rockhide demons standing right there in front of it.

"It's getting' bouncy in here!" Bronk is saying in his weird demonic English accent. He's doing a sort of happy shuffle back and forth, like a kid excited for his mom to finish making his favorite sandwich.

"Soon we'll get to see all our mates again!" Tunker is standing still, staring at the wavering red projection like she's about to see her favorite buddy in the image. And she might well be right about that.

"Even Jugger? I don't like that bloke!" Bronk whines.

"Yeah, even Jugger," Tunker says, her mouth breaking into a twisted, sick grin that makes me suspect that her excitement is more than you'd feel for a normal colleague in demonic business. It's more than a professional relationship, is what I'm saying.

"Huh. Jugger is a bloody dumb git," Bronk says in a sulky tone.

I heft the axe in my hand. I've got some ideas, but taking out one of these demons at a time would be hard enough. Both is a tall, tall order.

I pull back behind the pylon, still careful not to touch it as it vibrates like a video of an industrial clothes washer in spin cycle.

"Sera, do you know all these various demons?" I whisper. "Do you know Jugger?"

"I am a demon queen," she says. "I know all my subjects. Whether they know they are my subjects or not. Bronk isn't wrong—Jugger is dumb, even for a rockhide demon. He does have a very strong jawline though. He's very popular with—"

"Okay, okay, I get it," I say. "Can you do his voice?"

Seraphex looks almost offended. "Of course I can."

"Okay, well, go to the end of the row and use his voice to get them to separate."

"As you wish," Seraphex says, hopping off.

"And make it *flirty*," I hiss after her, and she turns her head back and gives me a glare as she waddles off.

But a few minutes later, a gravelly low voice rings across the large room, echoing over the humming and shaking. "Bronk is a daft weakling compared to Jugger. Jugger is bigger, stronger, and has a jutting granite jawline." I have to admit, it's a low and sultry voice, dripping with the kind of animal sex appeal that a skinny guy like me can only dream of. I've got other good qualities though, right? RIGHT?!

"JUGGER?!" Tunker squeals, though it's somehow a squeal in an octave lower than my voice. "You're 'ere! Did ye get summoned early?!"

"Big dumb ugly git," Bronk grouses.

"Your demonic superior wants you over here, Tunker," the tough guy voice says. "For roughin' up."

"Oh he does, does he?" Tunker says, licking her lips with a stony tongue. "We'll see who's superior to who when I'm done with you, Mr. Jugger," she says and starts sauntering across the room.

"We're s'posed to stay here and guard," Bronk objects, pouting.

I have to smile. Seraphex's ability to get people to do what she wants without actually lying is scarily impressive.

I wait, hiding deep in the shadows until Tunker is positioned perfectly. I point the index finger of my left hand at her, pulling back the magic axe in my right hand. And then I unleash it at the exact right moment, counting carefully to make sure I throw it right after one of the mini earthquakes that hits every eight seconds.

It spins across the room, suddenly lighting things with a bright blue glow. I'm not sure if it's necessary or magic weapons just have to show off that way—but it works perfectly. The axe slams into Tunker, shoving her backward just a couple feet, where she collides with one of the vibrating pylons.

It rattles her for a long second, and I can see stone teeth flying and stone limbs flailing. Finally, she collapses in a heap, fissures running up and down her body. She's broken open, revealing rocky insides, but she's a demon, so according to Seraphex she'll eventually reconstitute herself.

The axe flies out of her body, sailing across the room and embedding deep into the wall.

I sprint to where the axe has landed in the wall, hoping to grab it before Bronk can recover and come after me. And I'm right, the first thing he does is thunder across the room and kneel next to Tunker's body, wailing in anger. And he stays there for about fifteen seconds, gnashing his teeth and howling before he turns on me.

"YOU!" he bellows. "Li'l froggy man!"

Unfortunately, I have completely wasted the time that his distraction bought me. Yank, pull, and pry as I might, the magic axe stubbornly stays deeply embedded in the concrete wall. I grunt with exertion, but I've spent a little too much time asking Zambrano about magic and not nearly enough in the gym. Okay, none in the gym. *I guess I'm going to have to change that,* I think, as a thousand pounds of rocky muscle tromps down the row at me. I'm forced to scamper away, running for it down one of the rows of vibrating pylons. I mean, there's no amount of time at the gym that would make me look like *that*. Or be able to take it in a fight.

I run a few laps around the grid of deadly vibrating pylons, able to outmaneuver Bronk mostly because of my excellent turning radius relative to his container ship level of maneuverability. But soon I'm breathing heavily, and he seems to be thundering after me just as enthusiastically as ever. A couple times, the periodic mini earthquake hits and I almost bash into a pylon, but I'm starting to get the hang of those.

I . . . could also stand to do some cardio if I'm going to be doing this hero thing on a regular basis. It has been a *long* time since my high school decathlon days. I don't know why that's the sort of thought that's in my head right now, but I guess it's my brain's way of coping when I'm about to get pounded into a Bryce pancake by a giant rockhide demon with granite for brains.

Poor aerobic conditioning aside, I do have a plan.

"Looks like your girlfriend is going to be out of commission for a while," I taunt him. "She's . . . cracked under the pressure." That's how you're supposed to taunt villains, right? Dad jokes?

I've pulled myself up at the end of a row in front of pylons, positioning myself precisely. "She's not me girlfriend, mate," Bronk growls. "We've got ourselves a no-strings-attached sort of dealie."

"I don't know," I respond, backing up and counting in my head as he advances. "It seems like you're jealous of this Jugger fellow." My heart is beating like a coked-up heavy metal drummer and every part of my body is screaming *Run*, but I push that down. We're saving the world today, and that's that.

"I ain't jealous o' that bloke, I'm just passionate about—" he's roaring as he lunges forward at me, but I never get to find out what deep emotions ol' rock-for-brains has. Because just then, the mini earthquake hits, and I dodge around Bronk.

He's off-balance and moving forward, and I duck behind him, lower my shoulder and slam into his backside with every ounce of strength my skinny frame can produce. I honestly have no idea if my body blow actually moves him any, but it feels like it does.

He overcorrects and topples forward just enough to hit his hand on the pylon ahead of him.

The vibrations shudder through him, and he convulses, cracks shooting up and down his body. He falls with a massive thud, broken apart with stony sinew and bones showing.

Damn. I'm a *badass*.

I also can barely breathe.

I just need a few seconds to gather myself, then we can get back to saving the world from a demon army. I collapse on the floor, drawing in ragged breaths as my adrenaline surges and my heartbeat pounds in my ears.

That settles it. I do cardio now. Starting on Monday.

Assuming we survive.

CHAPTER 31

Thirty seconds later, I'm able to stand up and start walking toward the conduit. Now that the rockhide demons aren't running around, I can hear the sounds of the battle above. Explosions, the screams of tourists, and a roar that sounds like a dinosaur, maybe?

Seraphex has reappeared and pads along next to me.

"Well, Bryce, my darling," she says. "It's time for you to make a decision."

"Decision?" I ask. "This is the part that Zambrano actually prepared me for! I just undo the release bolts on the sides of the clamps, grab the staff, and run as fast as I can." The running part still seems like a tall order, but I have to imagine I'll get another round of adrenaline and will be able to run it upstairs.

Back at the warehouse, Zambrano had made a whole prop version of the clamps for me to practice on. It's fairly straightforward, and he "claimed" that I wouldn't somehow get fried by arcane seismic energy.

"We don't have much time," Seraphex says. "So I'll cut to the chase. Before we came, Zambrano made me agree not to deviate from the plan unless you agreed."

"Uh, yeah, okay," I say as I examine the clamps. The red wavering portal projected up from the conduit is stronger now, and I feel like I can see blurry ranks of demons on foot and more flying in the air above them.

I've knelt next to one of the ornate metal clamps, ready to pull the release bolt just like I practiced. But then Seraphex says something that makes me freeze.

"Now you've defeated the demon duke's plan. You have control over the gate and can do whatever you want with it. So I can tell you more about your birth mother, just like I promised on the menagerie rooftop."

"Okay, that's awesome, but does it have to be *right now*? Can't we finish this, first?"

"The reason you can't do magic isn't that you're some statistically unlikely genetic abnormality," she continues, ignoring me. "Your magic potential was intentionally locked away. Sealed deep inside you. By your birth mother. She made the change to herself, and so then it was genetically passed on to you."

"WHAT?!" I explode. I want to disbelieve her, but if there's one thing I'm sure of now, it's that she doesn't lie. "Who was she? A wizard? Am I really a descendant of that sorcerer from Poland like that tailor guy thought?"

"Luca the tailor was more right than he knew. You are not just a descendant—your mother was the great mentalist sorcerer Zuzanna herself. Zambrano thought that Zuzanna died, but it was only her magic that died. In 1982, when she was losing her sanity, she went into hiding and used her own mental magic to change her mind and her genetics to remove all her arcane potential. Two decades later she ended up having a child—that's you. And of course her lack of arcane potential was passed on to you. But the change can be reversed."

This is all way too much at once. "Why did she give me up for adoption? Why didn't she tell Zambrano? Where is she? Is she alive?" The questions pour out of me in a jumble.

"I won't tell you anything more about that right now," she says. Which I realize is brilliant, because now that she's committed to it, she's bound by that. Nothing I say can force her to reveal more, at least for now.

"Damn you," I say, gritting my teeth. "This is absurd. Then what *can* you tell me?" I clench my fist and lock my emotions away. It's too much to deal with right now. I never knew my birth mother. I was just always told I was adopted through an agency and that was that. There're definitely some feelings in there, but . . . I can't deal with them now. I have to deal with what I can deal with.

"I can only tell you that your arcane potential can be returned."

"So she locked the magic away, but it can be unlocked? Really?"

"It's true. There's no human alive who could undo the change since Zuzanna no longer has magical abilities. My demonic powers are the only ones I know of that could reverse it. I can unlock your magic for you, Bryce," she says, regally drawing herself to her full duck height.

"You can?" My jaw actually physically drops. And then I get an icy cold feeling on the back of my neck. "And *what* exactly do you want in return?"

"I can fix you. I can reverse what was done to you. But I can only do it if I have my full demonic powers," she says. "You see, Zambrano doesn't know this . . . but if I pass through the conduit portal, my whole form will be reset. I will once again be the resplendent demon queen. And I can unlock you. You will be able to learn magic, from Zambrano or from anyone else. You can finally learn magic the way you always wanted. And you will be *good*. You have the talent for it."

This is what I've been dreaming of. This is what I risked my life for, what I've kept risking my life for, just to be *close* to it.

"Okay, okay," I say, taking deep breaths. "But then what happens? The demons invade? You rule the Earth."

Seraphex smiles. "I will return to my form and come here and restore your powers. And then I'll immediately go back through the portal. And you have my word, I will stay there for twenty years. And I will keep all of the demon legions there for twenty years."

Twenty years. That's a long time. Enough time to learn magic. To live my life. For humans to become more powerful. For all sorts of things to happen. But . . . no matter what I agree to, I know the truth deep inside.

Seraphex is a demon queen. Zambrano said that at her peak, she was an order of magnitude more powerful and evil than Vulkatherak. He said that she tried to bring *literal hell on Earth*.

But in twenty years—surely we could prepare for that? With my new magic skills, I could help Zambrano. We could gather our forces and defeat her again. She had been defeated before, why not again? And I would have magical powers! I could be a mage, or a wizard! With Zambrano's help, who knows? I may even be able to become a sorcerer! And maybe I can even force her to make some more agreements to clarify the twenty years' grace period . . .

I shudder, shaking the feeling out of my whole body. I glare down at Seraphex, staring up at me with her little self-satisfied duck grin.

"So, Bryce Alexander," she says. "Are you ready to learn magic? To fulfill your potential?"

I pause for a long moment and close my eyes. From above, I hear what sounds like lightning strikes.

Yes, it's what I've always wanted. It's what I've been working for, hoping for, dreaming of my whole life.

But I know Seraphex. No matter what I make her agree to, it won't turn out the way I intend. I can't do it. I just can't. I can't set humanity up for an apocalyptic battle and the risk of hell on Earth, even if it's in twenty years, just because I want to be awesome.

I pull the bolt out of the magical clamp. The red flickering portal collapses into the conduit. Gritting my teeth, I jump down to the other side, and pull out the second bolt. The pylons stop vibrating with one final shuddering earthquake. The constant shaking is suddenly gone, leaving me moving unsteadily, like I've just stepped off a ship onto dry land.

I expect her to scream at me in fury, but she just sort of shrugs.

"Okay, well, fair enough," she says. "The plan stays on, then. Let's get the conduit out of here."

I heft the conduit, which is shockingly light for a large metal staff. I can't believe her. The nerve of her, to hold out on me. She knew the truth about me all this time and never even gave a hint! She saved it to use at a moment of rush and weakness, and I almost gave in.

I kick her. She flies across the room in a flurry of feathers and squawks. There's no way I'm letting her stay close to this artifact, not if she can use it to return to demon queen form.

Cursing that damn duck under my breath, I run back past the pylons and the two cracked rockhide demons and charge back up the stairs.

Back on the surface level, things have changed. Every bit of glass in the visitors' center has been blown out, and the pamphlets have been thrown wildly. I run outside, and it looks like a tornado hit.

Several tornadoes. Cars in the parking lot are strewn about, and trees, signs, and fences are cracked and smashed. The sky overhead is a mix of cloudy and smoky, lit by flashes from Volcanose's lava.

I look over to see where Zambrano and Volcanose are still locked in mortal combat—and, oh boy, it does not look good.

Volcanose has somehow grown in size, swelling with demonic power, and lava and sparks are flying off him. He's advancing, smashing a huge fist down on a wavering green glowing shield.

Zambrano is on his knees, teeth gritted, bleeding from his head and several burn wounds on his body. He's waving his hands in a magical manner, but his spellcasting motions seem weak, and the green protective bubble around him seems to be shrinking slightly with each blow that the giant lava demon lands on it.

But it's okay. If I can just get to the helicopter, as soon as we lift off, we can give the signal to Zambrano, and he can teleport out. The conduit and I will be safely soaring through the sky.

I start sprinting toward the designated pickup point, hoping against hope that Agent Crane can see through the haze. And to my surprise, she can! They must have been waiting at a distance, watching through binoculars, because as soon as I start running, the sound of beating rotors fills the air, and the helicopter comes screaming in, heading for the one large patch of parking lot that isn't covered in overturned cars. I can see the open side door, with the distinct form of Agent Crane leaning out of it, waving for me to run faster.

But it's far away, and I'm slow. And I hear a roar of anger and frustration, shaking the entire parking lot. And then there are steps coming from behind me, shaking the earth with each thundering thud. His size dwarfs even the rockhide demons.

I glance behind me and see Volcanose has abandoned the cowering Zambrano and is charging for me. After a few steps, I realize that there's just no way for me to escape just by running. The lava demon is moving too fast.

I'm not going to make it. The demon is going to catch me, fry me, take the conduit, and restart the whole portal process. After all this, it's going to be over. Is it all because I didn't do enough cardio? I hope not, I don't know if even an Olympic sprinter could make this run in time.

So I need to improvise. I've already sacrificed my chance to learn magic, what does it matter beyond that? The helicopter is still easing its way in to land, but I yell and wave my arms, beckoning them to come closer.

And they seem to understand, lifting up and swooping over toward me. I can see the door open with Agent Crane leaning out. She looks like she wants to grab me and pick me up, but there's no time for that. Volcanose is only a few steps away.

I rear back and throw the staff upward, like a javelin.

Volcanose alters course, and instead of crushing me, he leaps into the air, giant glowing orange lava hands reaching for the helicopter. Somehow, despite his size and weight, he's able to vault through the air like an NBA player leaping from the free throw line in a slam-dunk contest.

But Agent Crane leans out as far as she can and grabs the conduit right out of the air. She yells at the pilot, and the helicopter rises and banks away just as the giant lava demon passes by.

Volcanose comes back to the earth with a crash as the helicopter soars into the air, gaining altitude rapidly. I fall to my knees, watching as the chopper disappears into the smoke, accelerating hard.

They're making the right decision, of course, to leave me behind. The helicopter is going to take the conduit to a jet, which will fly it to the waiting spaceship. Within hours, it will be soaring off the earth, being sent to plummet straight into the sun. Any second that they delay, there's a chance that one of the demon duke's agents could disrupt the plan. The MSA doesn't mess around.

But that leaves me here, facing down a royally pissed off lava demon.

The demon duke turns and stalks back toward me. I groan, staring up at him with bleary eyes.

"You have defeated me," Volcanose rumbles. "You have stolen my prize. You are the sorcerer's new apprentice, are you not? My agents have told me of you. You are the boy who makes the juice drinks? The fruit lava?"

"And you're the infamous Volcanose, whose apocalypse was just foiled by a kid who works for minimum wage at Samba Smoothies, huh?" I say. "Though I guess technically I'm a manager in training now. And I'm not Zambrano's apprentice, Volcanose. I'm his *intern*."

"I am not Volcanose," he roars. "I am Vulkatherak, demon duke, lord of the demon hordes! My reign over your world has only been delayed, not stopped, pathetic human."

I glance over to where I saw the demon and sorcerer fighting when I emerged from the basement. Zambrano has disappeared. My shoulders drop a bit, but that's for the best. I'm glad he still had the strength to teleport to safety. He didn't want this fight, but he did it for me anyway. For us. And he'll survive this, to keep on fighting and protecting humanity from Volcanose and others like him.

"At least I get one consolation, Little Juice Man," Volcanose roars. "I get to tear you apart slowly. Bit by juicy bit."

As he reaches his giant hands for me, I can feel the temperature rapidly rising. There's lava coursing across his hands, so I also get a little consolation of my own: I'm pretty sure that I'll fry to death long before he can really torture me.

The hands stretch toward me . . . and then Zambrano appears in between us, flinging an illusion prism at Volcanose. It smashes in the demon's face, releasing a shower of sparks and a small blast of energy, and the demon steps back for a moment, blinking.

"Can you get us out of here?" I yell.

"Teleportraits are still blocked," Zambrano shouts back. "You're going to need to make a run for it."

The giant lava demon roars, veins of pure molten rock bulging angrily out of his head as he steps forward. "Out of my way, meddling sorcerer! Little Juice Man is mine!"

Zambrano swirls his arms, and the temperature around me drops as snowflakes are suddenly twisting through the air.

"*Puissiez-vous être empalé par le glaçon froid de ce sort de blizzard conçu par Alix la sorcière,*" he screams, speaking one of those long French spells that he despises.

But hate French spells as much as he does, it damn well *works*. A massive gout of ice explodes from his hands, far more concentrated than anything I've ever seen before. A snowy blizzard whorls around it, but a single powerful icicle extends from his hands, freezing itself from the water in the air as I shiver in the suddenly ice-cold wind.

"He's not yours, Volcanose," Zambrano shouts as the air swirls around him with the whistling winds of a mighty blizzard. "He's mine. My friend. My goddamn intern!"

The massive icicle in Zambrano's hands grows, vibrating as it expands and sucks water and heat from the air. Volcanose advances but is pushed back by gales of snow and ice. Finally, the icicle explodes forward with incredible speed.

The icicle strikes the demon duke, impaling him and flinging him backward. He flies back about a couple hundred feet, crashing into a pile of wrecked cars, with the giant icicle protruding from his chest like the sword in the stone.

The moment that the spell is complete, Zambrano collapses to the ground in a heap.

Volcanose has gone gray with steam and smoke rising off him in plumes. His fires are quenched, frozen, as the icicle slowly melts in his chest. He lies still, finally immobilized.

I breathe a sigh of relief, crawling forward to check on Zambrano. He's out cold, bleeding from a ton of wounds including a nasty-looking gash on his head. I rip parts of my shirt off, trying to bind his wounds and apply pressure to stop the bleeding.

But as I'm trying to take care of the sorcerer's wounds, I hear a rumbling and hissing. I glance over at Volcanose's corpse, and my heart feels like it stops. The blazing light is gone, but the embers are still there and are gaining in heat. That deadly orange glow is growing again, and his arms are flailing weakly. And then his burly smoking arms snap down and grab the icicle. It melts away as the lava on his entire body relights, glowing steadily brighter and hotter.

"Zambrano!" I hiss. "Wake up!"

I shake him, but it's no use. His eyes are rolled back in his head, his body just moves around as I shake him.

"Zambrano!" I yell in a panic. "We've got to get out of here!" I see the outline of the teleportrait in his pocket, but even if he could wake up and use it, the magic blocking it would still be in effect.

"Alix?" Zambrano mutters, eyelids fluttering. "Is that you? I'm sorry, *mon coeur*. I'm so sorry. Please forgive me."

"Zambrano! I need you!" I say, but his eyes are unfocused, and he's now just mumbling incoherently.

"I guess this is it, buddy," I say to the unconscious Zambrano as Volcanose stands up, glaring at me. "Thanks for letting me be part of the magic in my . . . special way."

Part of me wants to run, but I just don't feel like I can leave Zambrano here. I stand and hoist him up. Somehow, with all the adrenaline in my body, I'm able to mostly pick him up. At best, I'll be able to get him a few steps, but damn it, I'm going to try anyway.

"Your sorcerer's little spells are no match for my might!" Volcanose roars. "You may have foiled my plan, but we will not be stopped—the tyrant will be released!" I have no idea what that means, but it sounds really bad.

And then there's a screaming sound overhead, the roar of a jet engine.

I look up to see a fighter jet streaking across the sky with two bright lights splitting off from it trailed by plumes of smoke, screaming down toward us.

I duck and cover my ears as the missiles smash into Volcanose, pummeling him into the ground. He disappears into a crater as a plume of smoke erupts above him.

I try to shield Zambrano's body as best I can with my own as a volley of dirt and rocks rains down on me. For about ten seconds, I'm too stunned to move, and my ears are ringing, and my vision is swimming. My shaken brain notes that it really feels just like in war movies when a shell hits the heroes—cinematographers do a good job of simulating this feeling. It's just a sudden blast, then nothing makes sense for a little while.

Finally, the ringing in my ears subsides, but there's still another ringing sound.

My phone is suddenly ringing loudly even though I have had it silenced since before we started this crazy adventure. Seriously, what reasonable person these days ever has a phone set to ring in public? I pull it out and glance down at it.

"Bryce! You would not believe the day I've had." Agent Crane's voice comes out of the speaker. "I called in a few favors with an old friend who happens to be in command at Warren Air Force Base in Cheyenne. I'm probably going to be fired for this, and Colonel Evans is definitely going to be court-martialed. Now that the conduit is disconnected from the seismic energy, air strikes are a go!"

"Thank you." It's all I can think to say.

"Luckily, that demon thing burns almost as hot as a jet engine, very easy to target. They have enough ordinance to come through for another barrage. Keep your head down and don't say your government never did anything for you, huh?"

I've never been a big fourth-of-July-fireworks-patriotism sort of guy, but I can't help but feel something stir inside as the pair of fighter jets streak by a second time, unleashing another wave of missiles. The projectiles scream down onto the battlefield and Volcanose disappears, buried under explosion after explosion. I close my eyes and look away as the light of multiple blasts washes across the area.

"Do I still have to pay taxes?" I ask when the brain-melting sounds have quieted into a moderate ringing in my ears.

"Not really my area," she says. "But yes. You do. Somebody has to pay for all this hardware! Do you know how much each of those AGM-65 Maverick air-to-ground tactical missiles costs?

"Um . . . a lot?" I guess.

"Let's just say you'd need to blend a whole lot of smoothies," she says.

"I'll get right on that," I say, and the phone beeps as the call ends.

Zambrano is coughing and reaching up for me, so I lean down and check on him. He doesn't seem to have any obvious life-threatening injuries, so I figure the risk of moving him is worth it. The first aid advice they give is not to move someone who's hurt, but most of the first aid advice I've heard doesn't include an angry lava demon in a smoldering crater who might take a while to recover . . . and might not.

Pulling Zambrano's arm across my shoulder, I start half dragging and half walking him. Volcanose might be incapacitated by those air strikes, but I'm not counting on it. We need to get out of here.

Zambrano mumbles something incoherent but is able to stumble along a bit, helping move himself ahead. Slowly, over the course of several minutes, he groggily comes to full consciousness.

"Can you teleport us?" I ask.

He looks at the teleportrait, but his eyes cross. "I don't think so," he says, shaking his head. "I have a killer migraine. And I really don't have much magic left."

We stumble down the road for another few minutes, and the smoke and haze above has cleared. I keep glancing behind us, but there are no earth-shattering footfalls, no heat of lava.

"Damn, dude, you smell bad," I say. Helping him walk along, I'm up close to the sorcerer, and there's a really funky smell coming off him.

"Don't you know that smell? That's burning hair. I guess when you're fooling around with magical effects enough, you get kind of used to it." Glancing up, I can see that his normally lustrous mane of white hair is blackened and charred in spots. He hobbles along for a few more minutes, then points to a pickup truck with a park ranger logo that's been abandoned by the side of the road. With him still leaning heavily on me, we make our stumbling way to the truck.

"I can't cast a full teleport spell, but I can do a few little cantrips," he says, touching his finger to the locked door. There's a small yellow flash, and the door unlocks and pops open. He does the same trick on the lock on the steering wheel, and the pickup purrs to life. "You're driving," he adds, leaning heavily on the truck as he hobbles over to the passenger door.

I jump in and throw the truck into gear as soon as Zambrano is buckled in and holding my torn shirt up to the wound on his head. I see a first aid kit under one of the seats, but that'll wait until we get a little farther away from danger.

The roads are fairly deserted, with everyone having fled an hour ago when the magical battle started, and I floor it through the scrubland, not slowing down until we've crossed the border into Montana.

When the adrenaline has faded a bit and we pull up to a stoplight, I reach down to my pocket to check if I've gotten any urgent messages.

I groan. My pocket is empty. My phone is gone. I must have dropped it when I hung up with Agent Crane and went to help Zambrano.

Well, I'm definitely not driving back to look for it. I guess I'm going to be setting up yet another new phone. I should probably buy two or three, just to have them on hand for next time.

CHAPTER 32

As we drive farther, I fill in Zambrano on what happened in the cavern underneath the visitors' center. At the mention of Seraphex's attempted betrayal, he slumps down in the seat.

We continue in the silence, broken only by the occasional turn signal or slight squeak of the truck's brakes.

"It's my fault," Zambrano says. "After everything else, somehow years of having her around made me think she could be trusted. It was nice, having one person around who still understood all the history and everything, even if she was responsible for some of the bad parts of it. Demons can't lie, but . . . they can deceive as much as they want to. They can lead you to the wrong conclusions as long as you come up with them yourself."

"I really thought . . . I kind of thought she liked us. Like, she was becoming my friend," I say.

"Yeah," Zambrano says. "For me, what she'd done was always there in the back of my head. But as decade after decade passed . . . I guess I somehow was there too. Despite everything. But a demon can't ever really be your friend, and still be a demon."

I grip the steering wheel tightly, feeling my jaw tighten as I think more about it. "Was everything she did just to play us? Just to maneuver us into a position to get power again? To offer me the one thing that I want. And now I won't ever get it. And won't find out whatever she knew about my birth mother."

Zambrano just sighs and nods.

"I mean, I don't really care about that. I guess. I never knew my birth mother. Whoever or whatever she was, she's not my mom. And she . . ." I glare ahead at the road, as if the pavement somehow is at fault. "She took the possibility of magic from me. In a way that no human magic can remedy. What kind of mother does that to her son? I think I'm kind of pissed at her, you know?"

I know that what I'm saying isn't really true. It still keeps creeping into my thoughts, wondering about her. Why she did what she did. Is she still out there somewhere? But I can't think about it now. She stole my magical potential and left me. I have two perfectly good, real-life parents in New Jersey. If she had wanted to find me or know me, she would have done so already.

"I would help unlock your magic if I could," Zambrano says. "You've certainly earned that much. That sort of mental manipulation was Zuzanna's strongest suit—I could never compete with her abilities in that realm. If I tried to undo it, I'd only fry your brain."

"Yeah." I grip the steering wheel tightly, using the force to burn off a nervous energy I didn't realize that I had. "Maybe Seraphex or some other powerful demon could help me get it back. But the cost of that trade would be far too high, I'm sure."

Zambrano purses his lips and shakes his head. "Goddamn demons. Heartless. I mean, figuratively. And literally, they don't actually have hearts. Also they just suck."

"Well, I guess I'll never get to learn real magic or be your apprentice," I say.

"You've still got the cool intern hat," Zambrano shoots back with a weak grin. "That's something, right?"

We travel on. I'm not sure whether it's the bandages from the first aid kit, the hamburgers from a roadside diner, or just some time to rest, but before long Zambrano is feeling a little bit recovered and is able to use the teleportrait to take us back to the warehouse.

I spend the next couple days refreshing news and social media for any hints that Volcanose is still around, but beyond coverage of the event itself, there are no details. Zambrano spends the better part of the time sleeping and magically fixing himself, and when he emerges the morning of the third day later, he is looking just as perfectly handsome as before. I'm sitting in the upstairs kitchen, eating an order of chicken and waffles and scrolling through the news again as he walks in, having finished his morning bath. I swear, the man is centuries old and never learned how to take a shower.

He's wearing a bathrobe, and the burns and cuts are gone completely, and he's trimmed his hair short to remove the scorched parts. Despite looking great on the surface, he does still seem to be walking with a bit of a limp and is overall moving slowly. It's giving off a sort of old-man energy, to be honest.

On a whim, I popped on the intern hat, which feels like a nice little bit of grim ironic humor now. The damn hat is the closest I'll get to having real association with magic. But Zambrano either doesn't notice or doesn't mention it.

He limps to the fridge and pulls out one of his gross kale salads. "There are some problems that even sorcery can't fix instantly," he says with a shrug, noticing me eyeing at his trailing leg.

"You mean like your personality?" I ask.

"Fair," he says with a laugh. He sits down heavily, waving a hand lazily as the birch butlers spring into action to bring him a coffee. He helps himself to a piece of fried chicken without asking, but it came from his magical iPad of Infinite Food, so I can't feel too offended. Plus, I ordered enough to leave some leftovers for lunch, so there's plenty.

"Speaking of your personality," I say, voicing a concern that's been nagging at me for the past few hours. "How are you feeling? After using all that magic."

"You mean, am I losing control of my sanity and are you going to need to call in an air strike to take me out before I use my sorcery to turn all of Manhattan into Jell-O?"

"Well . . . yeah, that's pretty much it," I admit. "Sanity check-in?"

He chuckles. "I'm fine. No worse than I was this time last week, anyway. I feel kind of invigorated, to be honest. It feels good to have done something positive."

"That's good. And you know, I hadn't thought of the air strike idea. I'll have to talk to Agent Crane to see if she can set that up. Just in case, you know," I say with a wink.

Zambrano tosses the chicken bone over his shoulder without looking, and it lands perfectly in the trash can.

"I know you're joking," he says, fixing me with a stare, his stupidly green eyes blazing intensely. "But if it comes to something like that, don't hesitate. And don't feel bad. You have my permission to do what you need to do. I trust your judgment."

"I . . . thank you?" I have no idea how to react.

"And don't worry, if you have to do it, I'm going to add you to my will," he says, putting a hand on my shoulder.

"You're adding me to your will?" I ask, shocked. I know we've made a lot of progress in our relationship, but this seems too good to be true.

"Yes, of course!" he says, grinning. "I'm leaving you my sexy underwear collection. I've got it all—silky, mesh, fishnet, everything the modern man needs for bedroom success. You might need to do some squats to fill them out though. Think of it as an aspirational inheritance."

"You asshole," I shoot back. I pull out my phone and pretend to dial it. "Hello? MSA? How quickly can you deliver a couple missiles to Queens?" I say as he laughs and steals another piece of my chicken.

I open up the carton of the brussels sprouts that I ordered to try to pretend I'm eating healthy, and a small piece of curled up paper falls out onto the table.

"I was wondering how that would come," Zambrano muses, grabbing the little card and looking it over.

"What is it? What's that writing?" I ask, leaning in to take a look at the script. It's a bunch of symbols that I don't know, very angular and jagged, like the kind of font heavy metal bands use for their album covers.

"It's written using the futhorc, old Anglo-Saxon runes," he says. "The old system used for writing Old English before the Latin alphabet was introduced. I don't read it, so I'll have to have a friend translate what the exact words mean. But I'm pretty sure I know exactly what it is, and who sent it."

I wait patiently for several seconds, but he is intent on looking at the card and seems to think it's okay to just end the conversation on that cliffhanger. Rude!

"And what is that?" I prompt him.

"It's from Seraphex, wherever she is," he says. "It's the passphrase for Merlin's Vault in the Challenger Deep. I won the bet, remember?"

"Oh. Right," I say.

"Well, don't look so glum about it!" he admonishes me, shaking his head. "You survived long enough to sneak into the Duke's penthouse. And you stole the arcane conduit, the artifact from the Ilopango Crater. The terms of the bet didn't require those two things to happen at the same time. You know," he says, eyeing me thoughtfully, "you continuing to be alive after the mission wasn't part of the bet. I guess that's just sort of a nice little side bonus."

"Yes," I say, rolling my eyes. "I would also describe not dying as a nice little side bonus. Like when you order onion rings and there are also some french fries in there."

"Exactly! We both got that nice little bonus together," he says, perfect white teeth widening into a grin. He leans in, looking at the tablet that I was scrolling through when he came in. "So how are the authorities spinning it this time?" he asks, gesturing at the blurry pictures of the battle on the screen. "Ah, *Dangerous dark sorcerer wreaks havoc in Yellowstone, Air Force called in to stop him*. Really classy of them."

He leans even closer and scrolls a bit farther down.

"Well, at least the spaceship plan worked," he says, pointing to the next article, about a second spaceship accelerating out of control due to magical interference. "Oh, good, and now they're blaming *both* of them on me." He sips his coffee and dips the chicken in maple syrup before taking another bite. "It's fine, I guess. Governments have always been this way."

"Really? Why? They never give you credit?"

He shrugs. "They have to make me a villain. It's been that way ever since Julius Caesar came back from using sorcery to defeat the wizards of Gaul and seized power in Rome. The knife that Brutus stabbed him with had an enchanted sapphire gemstone that prevented Caesar from using magic to heal himself. Governments like heroes, but superheroes are too much for them. Once people start trusting and relying on a superhero, the superhero becomes too powerful. Honestly, whatever, I get it, I certainly shouldn't be put in charge of anything real. And if people actually appreciated some of the things I do, they'd want me to replace the current clowns running things. But let's be honest, I would make a terrible president."

"Well, you're right about that," I admit. "You would . . . not be good at that job."

"I can't solve their problems," he says. "Maybe someone else could, but I can't. I'm like those fighter jets your buddy at the MSA sent in to help us out. When I'm not in use, it's best to just leave me in"—he gestures at the warehouse around us— "the hangar. So, I don't mind getting no respect from all the damn idiots writing their news articles," he says. But he doesn't sound that happy about it.

"Well," I say, "check this out." I open up a different page and hit play on the video. It's a YouTube breakdown of the "Battle of Yellowstone," using blurry footage from tourists' phones to piece together what really happened.

"So the government hasn't released any details of what really happened here," the narrator says in the part that I skip to. "But there are several clear indications here that the large reddish figure is actually a lava demon, a type believed to have disappeared centuries ago. So this 'dark sorcerer' actually is battling one of humanity's ancient foes. Certainly, he did all the collateral damage that they say he did, but maybe that's with a good reason?"

Zambrano shrugs. "So, one kook on the internet figured it out."

I grin. "He's actually an assistant professor at Merlin College. He's asking for people to send in more footage so that he can write a paper on you." In addition to watching the news, I've also been on WizardWatch constantly the past two days, working with Parth to feed them the bits of information that they need to put together what really happened. We had chatted initially and decided that we shouldn't just tell them everything. Instead, we've been dropping hints and clues, giving them the chance to discover more information and piece it all together.

Our careful work is starting to filter out into the broader world. "And check this out," I say, scrolling down below the video. "Four and a half million views, and it just got posted yesterday."

"Huh," Zambrano says, sitting back and taking a long sip of his coffee. "How about that. That's kind of cool."

"You're still not going to try to be president though, right?" I say.

He laughs. "No, that is *way* too much hassle. I think I'm going to take a little time off, assuming no one else tries to torch the planet this month. Vulkatherak will likely lie low for a while, after the beating that we gave him. We've got time to explore some other things."

We sit in silence, eating for a couple minutes, but Zambrano seems to be smiling a bit, which is pretty unusual.

"What do you think happened to Sera?" I ask. It's been kind of weirdly quiet around here since she's been gone. The birch butlers are helpful, but they don't have anything to contribute conversationally. I didn't expect to miss her—and her constant talking down to me— but I have to admit that I kind of do.

"I don't know," Zambrano says. "She's probably off sulking somewhere, or planning some sort of plot. But she'll be back when she needs my help for something. Maybe we can get her to explain more about Zuzanna eventually. I'm not sure how she knew all that—it seems that she's had more contact with the rest of the world than I was aware of. She must have some allies out there who've been working with or for her all these years."

"Yeah, maybe," I say.

I don't know what to do about it. I'm not sure how much I want to know. It just . . . it's such a big thing. I should be so curious about it. I should be desperate to hunt down the records, to quiz my parents, to figure out what the heck happened to me. But right now, it just feels too big. I don't want to think about some parents that aren't *my* parents.

We take a couple more bites of chicken and waffles in the silence that Seraphex would usually fill with some sort of verbal provocation.

"Can I ask you a question?" I say as I finish my last bite of syrup-soaked waffle. "Unrelated to that stuff."

"I'm not telling you about my love life," Zambrano says, glaring at me. "That's private. But, um, I promise I'm not related to you somehow. Intense magic use has long since left me sterile, and"—he gestures vaguely at each of our appearances—"I've used magic to mess with my appearance, sure, but not *that* much."

He's right, of course. We look nothing at all alike. Eyes, face, skin, build, everything.

"Which isn't to say that your mother and I never . . . well, Zuzanna pretty much always got what she wanted. But that was in the late 1800s; it was just a short fling. I was on the rebound, you see . . ."

"I thought you said we *weren't* going to talk about your love life?" I interrupt.

"Oh, right, yes, yes, all very private," he says.

"Okay, great," I say, taking a deep breath. "Let's change the topic to . . . well, literally anything but you boinking my mother two hundred years ago."

"She was very good, if that helps," Zambrano says with a catlike grin.

"Ugh! No. Okay, moving on." I need to change the topic or I'm going to strangle Zambrano, killing the last living sorcerer and Earth's best hope against the demons. So I ask the question that I came down here to find out about in the first place. "I want to know . . . what exactly is magic? Why is there magic and not just physics?"

I can't do magic. I will probably never be able to, not without unleashing a demon queen on the world, at least. But I still want to know. To understand a bit of it.

"Is this why you're wearing the hat?" he says, gesturing at the garish hat on my head. "To trick me into telling you secrets?"

"I suppose so," I say. It's ugly, but part of me has become kind of attached to it. And not in a magical way, thankfully. "Is it working?"

"Sure, why not?" Zambrano says, visibly relaxing. "Well, there's never an ultimate answer as to why, is there? You can ask why gravity exists. And maybe you get some sort of answer about waves or strings or particles or folded matrices or whatever the scientists say these days. But at some point, the 'why' stops and the world just is what it is. Someone might be able to explain it at a deeper level than I can, but ultimately, neither I nor anyone else can really answer 'why' magic is. Or even 'what' magic is. They're not really defined by either of those things. Magic just exists."

"Okay, then *who* is magic?" I ask, finally starting to put it together.

Zambrano smiles. "See, that's the right question. These days, everyone wants magic to be a system. To be rules that can be defined with math and engineering. And that sort of works but not very well. Before everyone was obsessed with math, a lot of wizards would say that magic was like a beautiful lover, to be delicately romanced. That's really not right either. Also, those guys were, ironically, usually quite mediocre lovers."

He pauses, remembering something that makes him chuckle. But I figure it's about his love life, so I don't pry. Not out of politeness but out of desperately not wanting to picture him naked. I've seen enough already as it is.

"Magic is most like a puppy that just wants you to be happy," he continues. "You can create new spells by teaching it to associate certain patterns of motions, sounds, or ingredients with certain effects. That's why spells can be created with words from any particular language. Why rare elements and ingredients make for the most powerful items and artifacts. Why spells grow stronger or weaker over time as they get used more or less. It's a complicated process, but the core idea is no different from teaching a seal to jump out of the water and hit a ball or a dog to fetch your slippers. And you can use a lot of math and science, certainly, but ultimately it's about a relationship that can't quite be quantified."

"Huh," I say, leaning back and taking this in. "So, magic is . . . like a dog?"

"Just be glad it's not like a cat!" Zambrano says. "Can you imagine how impossible it would be to convince it to do anything?"

I think this over as he finishes eating and the birch butlers clear away the scraps from my finished meal.

"So what happens now? What do we do?"

"Hmm," he says, mulling it over. "Ever been to New Zealand?"

"Nope!"

"Oh, we should go," he says. "I need to update my teleportrait for Auckland. And we can check out where they filmed those old *The Lord of the Rings* movies from the early 2000s. You know, the good ones."

"That sounds great! We could use a break, that's for sure."

"Plus, there's a harpy on a mountain there, whose feathers have some really wild magical properties—they're the ingredient I need for the magic to counter the high pressure in the Challenger Deep. The Mariana Trench is not very hospitable; we're going to need some powerful artifacts to help us get down there. I'm certainly not trusting a submarine, that's for sure. Now, unfortunately, the harpy who has what we need can smell me and my magic coming a mile away . . ."

I groan. "Ugh. Okay, I'll get some hiking and climbing gear delivered. And maybe . . . a helmet or something?" I briefly wonder if maybe I should just wear a helmet 24/7, with the possibility of magical escapades ensuing at any moment.

"We can take a few weeks to get our things together and recover from this crazy week," Zambrano says. "I need some time to heal. And a helmet does seem like a solid idea. Do you want me to write 'intern' on the helmet in nice big glowing neon letters?"

I roll my eyes, then shrug. "Why the hell not? I'm sure that won't get in the way of stealthy thievery at all."

"Ugh, fine," Zambrano says. "Okay, we can write it in some nice subtle colors with a tasteful font. Like comic sans. Or that Metallica font."

"Different fonts for each letter, and some sort of protective enchantment?" I counter.

"Done," Zambrano says with an evil grin. "That's downright evil. And they say *I'm* the nefarious dark one."

"'Nefarious' seems like it's giving you an awful lot of credit," I say as I stand up and stretch. A magical enchanted helmet seems like a pretty handy thing to have in my tool kit—I can't say I'm a huge fan of receiving blunt force trauma to the head at this particular point in my life. "Let's do it. When do we head out?"

MAGICAL SECURITY AGENCY

SIGNAL INTELLIGENCE REPORT—TOP SECRET

TO: MSA DIRECTORS AND ABOVE

FROM: SPECIAL AGENT ANGELICA CRANE

The following message exchange was intercepted from our intelligence assets in the sorcerer's current residence. While Mr. Alexander remains cooperative, we assess that he is not fully sharing information with us. Despite his lack of candor and recent success in preventing the volcano demon's use of a dangerous artifact earlier this year, we remain confident that he is deserving of our support and protection.

BRYCE: Thanks for spreading the word about what really happened at Yellowstone. I think it made a big difference for Z, he's so used to being made out as a bad guy in the media.

PARTH: No problem dude.

PARTH: Didn't want to tell you this before because you were having so much trouble with school, but it seems like you're doing pretty well for yourself. I got accepted a while back and I'll be starting next week at the Indian Institute of Magic in Hyderabad. Learning real magic!

BRYCE: That's awesome! Congrats. You totally deserve it.

PARTH: Does Z know anything about the posts that just went up on WizardWatch about the disturbances near Guam?

BRYCE: Oh damn, let me check it out.

BRYCE: Wow.

PARTH: Yeah, it's wild. Really high arcanometer readings coming out of that part of the South Pacific.

BRYCE: Wait, is that where the Mariana Trench / Challenger Deep is?

BRYCE: Just checked, yeah it is.

BRYCE: Uh oh.

BRYCE: Z just got a passphrase that gives him access to something down there.

BRYCE: Actually headed there rn.

PARTH: What?

PARTH: Dude, what does that mean?

PARTH: Bryce, it's been two days, where are you? Are you okay?

PARTH: Now they're saying the arcanometer readings spiked and then stopped. What's happening down there?

Mr. Alexander has not yet replied as of the time of this report. There have been no sightings on the warehouse roof and no food deliveries in the past seventy-two hours. We have initiated a request for the redeployment of a United States naval unit currently stationed at Naval Base Guam. The unit was directed to proceed to the vicinity of the Challenger Deep to provide observational support. As of the current reporting period, Mr. Alexander has not responded to multiple communications seeking confirmation of his current status and location.

ABOUT THE AUTHOR

Gavin Brown is a novelist, video game director, and entrepreneur. His books include *Josh Baxter Levels Up*, *Monster Club: Hunters for Hire*, and installments of the 39 Clues and Spirit Animals series. He also created the hit indie mobile game Blindscape and directed the 39 Clues, Spirit Animals, and Scholastic's Home Base video games. Brown lives in a former ice cream factory in New York City.

Podium

DISCOVER MORE

STORIES
UNBOUND

PodiumEntertainment.com

www.ingramcontent.com/pod-product-compliance
Lightning Source LLC
Jackson TN
JSHW021422280125
77976JS00004B/38